The MAQUINNA LINE
A Family Saga

NORMA MACMILLAN

FOREWORD BY
ALISON ARNGRIM

AFTERWORD BY
CHARLES CAMPBELL

TouchWood
Editions

TouchWood Editions
www.touchwoodeditions.com

Library and Archives Canada Cataloguing in Publication
Macmillan, Norma, 1921–2001
The Maquinna line : a family saga / Norma Macmillan.

ISBN 978-1-926741-03-1

I. Title.

PS8625.M545M36 2010   C813'.6   C2010-900234-2

Editor: Marlyn Horsdal
Cover and interior design: Pete Kohut
Cover images: Jamie Farrant, istockphoto.com

 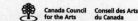
BRITISH COLUMBIA ARTS COUNCIL
Supported by the Province of British Columbia

Canada Council for the Arts   Conseil des Arts du Canada

We gratefully acknowledge the financial support for our publishing activities
from the Government of Canada through the Canada Book Fund, Canada
Council for the Arts, and the province of British Columbia through the
British Columbia Arts Council and the Book Publishing Tax Credit.

Mixed Sources
Cert no. SW-COC-001271
© 1996 FSC
FSC

The interior pages of this book have been printed on 100% post-consumer recycled
paper, processed chlorine free, and printed with vegetable-based inks.

1 2 3 4 5 13 12 11 10

PRINTED IN CANADA

For Thor Arngrim

CONTENTS

ꙮ ꙮ ꙮ

Foreword

"A nihilistic, almost amoral sense of detachment." Not the words one usually expects to use when discussing one's mother. But then, most people's mothers don't write books. If they do, they certainly don't write things like *The Maquinna Line*. However, Norma Macmillan wasn't like most mothers.

Years ago, when she told me she was writing a book, I wasn't surprised. She had always written. I knew that before I was born she had written plays—hilarious, lighthearted, satirical romps that spoofed drawing-room comedies and Cold War sensibilities.

She was most famous, though, for her voice-over career. She created the sweet, childlike voices of Gumby, Casper the Friendly Ghost, Davey of *Davey and Goliath*, Underdog's girlfriend Sweet Polly Purebred and others familiar to millions of baby boomers. In her onscreen roles, in both films and commercials, she was the ditzy neighbour, an older version of the Gracie Allen dumb blonde.

I'm sure everyone thought the same thing I did when we heard she was writing a novel—"Oh what fun!"

But then she began to retreat into the bedroom with her typewriter for hours on end. She became quiet. She wouldn't tell us what the book was about. "It's a family saga," she'd say, among other vague statements. At the time, I took to referring to it as "the Canadian version of *Roots*."

Then there were the trips. My mother would simply announce that she was leaving Los Angeles to go "up island" and take off for the airport. She was gone for days. Sometimes weeks. She phoned and wrote, of course, but her whereabouts were often mysterious. These were not exactly tourist attractions she was visiting. The Strait of Juan de Fuca. Nootka Island.

To stay in a cabin alone with no TV, no visitors, just her and her Olivetti portable typewriter (the brand allegedly favoured by Sylvia Plath and John Updike).

I was occasionally allowed to read small excerpts (and sometimes "borrowed" others). I wasn't sure what to say. In Hollywood in the 1970s and 1980s, there was comedy and drama, and right and wrong were black and white. I grew up playing the flatly evil Nellie Oleson on the deeply moral *Little House on the Prairie*. My mother's book wasn't like any of that. It was not simple, and it was not, to put it mildly, a lighthearted satirical romp as I imagined her plays to be. It was sometimes darkly comic, but often simply dark. To be honest, I found some sections downright disturbing.

It is a story about families—about socially prominent Canadian families and working-class families, about colonists and Aboriginals. It's about how things change over generations, in a bygone era very different from the one I grew up in.

My mother was raised in a socially prominent Vancouver family, in another time, so she was very familiar with their attitudes and customs. And their secrets—the things that were not discussed in "polite company."

I'm not entirely sure that her old family would have appreciated this book. My mother has pulled up the shades on the behaviour and attitudes of another age: attitudes about class and position that affected every facet of their lives, every relationship, and every decision made.

And she lets you judge them however you see fit.

No wonder she had to sneak off to the islands to write this.

—Alison Arngrim, author of *Confessions of a Prairie Bitch: How I Survived Being Nellie Oleson and Learned to Love Being Hated*

Winter Harbour

Zeballos

Comox Valley

Nootka Island

Nanaimo

Arnason Is.

CANADA

Vancouver

Cowichan Valley

Clo-oose

Port Renfrew

Victoria

Vancouver Island

Olympic Peninsula
USA

Vancouver Island, March 1778

Maquinna, the Moachat chieftain, knew first that something had happened.

He stood in the rain on the rocks outside his longhouse at Yuquot, his wet face with its high cheekbones, large nose and full lips beneath the thin black moustache turned westward to the ocean. The surf splashed against the reefs below his bare feet, while the rain blew in drenching gusts, driven by the winds sweeping from the northwest off the ocean. A stream of water poured off the wide brim of his cedar-bark hat, sliding off the sea-otter-skin cape he held around his lean body.

Although nightfall was hours away, he could see nothing except the rain and the grey-black clouds that made sky and ocean into one. Yet Maquinna knew that something was out there—something that had never been there before.

It was natural that he should know before the others, that his instincts should make him aware of the portent of some auspicious event. Had he not known that his people must leave their winter village at Tahsis for their summer home at Yuquot before they usually did because the salmon would come early this year? It was all part of a vast order that he, Maquinna, alone among his people, could understand. Even the shaman did not know that anything was out there, nor did the witch, Ha-Hat-Saik, nor his family, nor his friend Nanaimas. No, only to a truly great chieftain would a sign of this miracle be revealed.

The presence had been there for almost five days, and now the hour for revelation was approaching, and his life on this earth would never be the same again. The miracle was about to take place. He knew that this was so, yet he did not know what that miracle would be. He tried once more to pierce the mist with his sharp eyes, the small round black pupils so distinct against the white, but there was nothing to see but the clouds, the rain, and the surf crashing against the rocks. He turned and went back to his longhouse, where his wife, his sons and his beloved daughter were waiting for him. He had not informed them of the presence, but they were concerned about him. His mood, so his wife told him, was the same as the days before he led the great whale hunt each year. But it was too early for the great whale.

Tomorrow, thought Maquinna. Tomorrow I will know.

As he turned from the shore, he heard the flutter of wings and thought it was a seabird returning to shelter in the eaves of his longhouse.

Then, in the dim light, he saw that it was Raven, the Trickster. Its wings brushed close to the brim of Maquinna's hat, skimming the surface deliberately. Maquinna was angry. "He knows. He's been out there. The rascal knows more than I do!" They had always been rivals, but never had Maquinna envied Raven more than now.

"But tomorrow," said Maquinna, "tomorrow we will be even."

He slept fitfully, alone, as he did each year before the coming of the whale. Just before dawn, he felt the change of the wind and knew that it came directly from the west and soon the storm would be over; the thick clouds would be driven eastward into the mountains, and the skies would clear. He slept again, briefly, and was awakened by the voices of his people. He rose up, throwing off the beaver skins that covered him, certain now that the time had come.

He took time to dress properly. He put on the ceremonial hat of cedar with the rings around the crown indicating how many whales he had slain and his finest long cloak of sea-otter skins. When he was ready, he went out into the morning where the sun shone for the first time since their arrival at Yuquot. His brother, Calicum, came to him first, excited at being the bearer of the news.

"Two great fish," announced Calicum, "have come to us."

Maquinna looked out to sea at the shadows in the parting mist. While he had never seen anything like it before, he knew they were not fish.

🐦 🐦 🐦

James Cook had seen the raven too. The bird had landed on the rail at the bow of the *Resolution* where Captain Cook had been standing, his eyes trying to pierce the clouds. The raven and the captain had looked at each other, and Cook, like Maquinna, envied the bird his knowledge. Cook knew the land was there, not far off the bow, engulfed in the rain and fog. During fragmentary moments when the clouds had parted, he had caught glimpses of dark green above grey rocks and forbidding mountains beyond the shore. He had reason enough to land when the opportunity arose—timber was needed to repair a broken spar, and the supply of fresh water was dangerously low. He sent some of his men in a longboat over to his second ship, the *Discovery*, to tell the master, William Bligh, that they would attempt to land when the weather cleared.

It had not been easy on his men to head into the uncertain reaches of the Pacific in February of 1778. He had not, in fact, intended to make this third voyage at all, but His Majesty King George III's government, and especially His Majesty's Admiralty, wanted their share of the New World. The Spanish had laid claim to much of it already, the French were firmly planted in New France, the Russians were entrenched in the North Pacific and, just two years ago, competition emerged from a new country, the United States of America, no longer a British colony but a nation talking about the west and expansion.

What the British Admiralty wanted most was to discover the long-sought waterway that would unite the two great oceans across the top of the continent, so English ships could trade more easily with China and the East Indies. A forty-thousand-pound reward awaited the discoverer of the passage. The Admiralty's politely worded communique stated that Cook should also extend British claims whenever and wherever possible, but he was not to cause conflict with other European claims, nor infringe on the rights of natives who were "not agreeable to the act of possession."

The two ships had been travelling northward up the coast of Nova Albion, so named by Sir Francis Drake on his voyage of 1579, but they had caught only occasional glimpses of land, of mountains, rocks and dangerous reefs. Nowhere had they seen a possibility of shelter.

Supposedly there was an indentation, perhaps a harbour, or even the mouth of the elusive passage itself, somewhere just north of the forty-eighth parallel. The only indication that such a waterway existed was the tale of an old Greek seaman, known as Juan de Fuca, who had talked about it around Europe, having sworn that he had discovered it in a journey as early as 1592. For years he attempted to raise money for another voyage, convinced that he had seen the entrance to the great passageway that would unite the Pacific and the Atlantic, but he was unsuccessful. Most people believed that it was just another old sailor's story.

Cook had seen no sign of an opening in the rugged coastline so he continued his journey northward, until he became more concerned with obtaining fresh water and timber for a new spar than in searching for what he honestly believed to be a mythical passage. At a point close to the fiftieth parallel he dropped anchor, having caught sight of a harbour that he was sure would provide the necessities of his voyage.

🐦 🐦 🐦

Some fifteen hundred people had gathered along the headland, their excitement mounting, climaxing with the arrival of Chief Maquinna to tell them what to do about the miracle.

Beside Maquinna stood his young daughter, Sa-Sin, the Hummingbird, as she was known. She was his favourite, even above his sons. She was not more than nine years old, tall for her age, beautifully formed, with the high cheekbones and startling eyes of her father but, fortunately, a more delicate nose than his. She also wore a cape of sea-otter fur. She stood very erect, looking calmly out to sea.

Silhouetted against the stark white sky were the largest canoes Maquinna and his people had ever seen, floating on the pale green water. On the vessels, those on shore could see creatures moving, waving, making noises.

Maquinna watched carefully, pondering his strategy, for his people depended on his wisdom and his leadership. Above all, he must assure them that there was nothing to fear—his people must never know fear. For a moment he looked behind him and saw that Raven was perched on top of the longhouse. Their eyes met. The bird put his head a little to one side and made a sound. The old hostility sprang up between them, for the sound was one of unmistakable mockery.

Maquinna decided to dispatch two canoes, carrying his strongest warriors, to examine the phenomenon. As they put into the water, he could see much activity on the two vessels. When the canoes arrived, some of his warriors sang a sacred song, explaining that they were protected by spirits, while the creatures on the vessels called to them, waving their arms.

The warriors soon returned to report to the chief what they had seen at close range, and to seek his advice. "We have seen the two great vessels out there," one reported, "and all over them are fish that have come here as people. One is a dogfish, another is a humpback fish, but they are all fish appearing to us as people."

"They *are* people," Maquinna told them. "Perhaps not all people are like us. Return to them, be friendly and try to find out what it is they want."

Warmth came now from the sun as the last of the clouds were blown inland. Maquinna watched as his men went to sea again. Now they would accept the gifts that the strange people handed over the sides of their vessels.

Then he saw James Cook, and even at this distance he realized at once, in the way that one chief can recognize another by his bearing, that this was the leader. Maquinna's lips curled in a slow smile. Now he knew he was indeed in control of the situation.

In the cedar chest in his house, where he kept his most treasured possessions, were two silver spoons, received in trade almost four years ago from his friend, rival and sometime enemy Wikaninnish, the chief of the Clayoquots to the south. He had told Maquinna a story of floating islands carrying creatures all in black with much hair. Wikaninnish's men had given furs in exchange for many wonderful things made of hard materials, and among them were the silver spoons.

These two vessels must certainly carry treasures that would assure Maquinna's position, so that all the people of the coast, and the interior too, would realize that he, not Wikaninnish, was the greater chieftain. Now he would have access to wealth beyond that of the others, to be used at the great potlatches. With his gains from these curious strangers, he could barter with the other tribes so that none would be as powerful as Maquinna.

🐦 🐦 🐦

When James Cook observed that the natives were friendly, he instructed his men to behave in similar fashion, suggesting that they hand out pilot biscuits as an opening gesture. He noted that the natives took the biscuits readily and examined them but did not understand that they were to be eaten. Instead, they put them into the skin pouches they wore around their necks or waists, presumably to be evaluated later.

Cook saw that the village on shore was large and estimated that more than a thousand natives were gathered on the headland. Immediately south of the village was an opening—a wide body of water divided by what was either an island or a peninsula into two channels. It was there that they must obviously go for shelter and anchorage, as it did not seem possible to make a landing directly on the shore just below the village.

The head warrior in the lead canoe stood up and indicated to the men on the ships that they should go around the headland into the sound. "Nu-tca icim! Nu-tca icim!" they called, gesturing toward the south.

Cook nodded and turned to his first mate, Lieutenant Burney and said, "I wonder if they're trying to tell us that this place is called Nootka." Cook, of course, had other ideas and called the harbour King George's Sound. That night they anchored in the sound by a small, uninhabited island, which Cook designated Bligh Island after the master of the *Discovery*. As for the site where he was first welcomed, he gave it the name Friendly Cove.

Captain Cook and his men remained at Nootka for a month. They repaired the spar and received all the fresh water they required. Cook learned that Chief Maquinna and his people, the Moachats and the Hesquiats, were at the nexus of a vast trade network that reached inland as well as along the coast. They were intensely proud.

Cook, Bligh and some members of the crew, such as the young George Vancouver, observed that this was an established society whose beliefs obviously went back some time. However, many other crew members were less impressed. They disliked the natives' keen interest in anything metal, as they had assumed that the glass beads they had brought would be all they needed. They considered their ceremonies, in which men wore costumes and masks in imitation of animals, revolting. Maquinna himself had danced for them, dressed in a bear costume, an event that Captain Cook viewed with courtesy and respect but the crew thought ludicrous. Cook could hardly help but notice the people's regard for animals, but it went beyond regard—theirs was a reverence he did not understand.

Soon, James Cook would leave Nootka, taking with him notes and drawings, precise astronomical charts for the entrance to Nootka Sound, and fifteen hundred sea-otter skins, as well as beaver, mink, wolverine and weasel skins. These would ensure warm clothing for his men for the duration of the voyage. In exchange he had parted with buttons, belt buckles and anything else made of brass, which the natives particularly coveted. Indeed, Cook had discovered that his men had been guilty of stripping the brass fittings from the interior of the ship to supply their hosts with the brass they wanted.

He would return to his beloved Sandwich Islands, so very different from this cold, wet place.

🦦 🦦 🦦

Maquinna watched the two ships as they slowly made their way against the wind, out of the sound to the open sea, guided by his warriors in their canoes. He leaned on the broadsword that Cook had given him and wore the three-cornered hat with the gold braid that Cook had presented to him at their first meeting. Cook waved to him from the bow of the *Resolution* as it sailed past the promontory of Yuquot, wearing the beaver-skin cloak that Maquinna had taken off his own back and wrapped around Cook's shoulders.

It had gone well. He had seen to that, although he had to admit that Cook was also a man of honour. Cook had restrained the crew from fighting and from abusing the women. Without his leadership, things might have been different, as many of Cook's men did not understand the respect due to the people of the coast.

James Cook had promised to return, but Maquinna knew that he would not. He had felt the aura of death about his friend.

Other visitors would come now, and he, Maquinna, would turn their visits to his advantage, gaining untold treasures with which to maintain his superiority at the potlatch and to pass on to his daughter. In time, all would come to respect him. These new people would learn about him and the wonderful land that he had preserved for himself, his daughter and her descendants. He smiled in triumph, raised his head proudly and walked toward his longhouse and the welcome that his family and friends would give him.

Then he stopped. Peering down on him from the eaves was Raven. They looked at each other, and some of Maquinna's triumph dimmed as he realized that once again his old enemy possessed some knowledge of the future that was different from his. Angered, Maquinna made a gesture with the sword of James Cook.

Raven flew away to the high branch of a nearby spruce and watched as the Lord of the Coast entered the longhouse for the celebration.

CHAPTER ONE

The Garden Party, Victoria, 1910

There had been talk of postponing the annual garden party in aid of the orphans of Victoria because of the death of King Edward VII, but Eleanor St. John Trevor, at whose home, Blenheim Oaks, the event was to take place, argued in its favour.

"We simply *must* carry on," she told the committee in her lovely clipped English accent. "We should think of it as a tribute to our new King and remember that dear Bertie would have wanted it this way. He did so love a good party with all the ladies dressed in their best, so we should think of the party as a tribute to dear Bertie too. I remember how, back home, we all looked forward so much to the Queen's Garden Party. What a thrilling day it was! I shall never forget any of them. The dear Queen, old as she was, would make an appearance, but it was really Bertie who enjoyed himself the most, so I feel we should continue our tradition just as they do at home. All the best people in Victoria *want* to come, and others can come too if they can afford it. And another point is that we really ought to think of the orphans, because in a way the party *is* for them, I suppose, poor things, isn't it?"

So the garden party proceeded because it was understood that Mrs. Trevor would know exactly what the late "dear Bertie" would have wanted.

She had seen it all. Besides, she was related to the Churchills on her mother's side. The upper crust of society in Victoria thought that they were lucky to have her. Eleanor agreed with them but would add graciously that perhaps they were *all* fortunate, especially to be living in such a beautiful new city as Victoria.

Eleanor was thirty-six, a tall, slim, attractive woman, mother of the dark and elusive Victor, sixteen, and the gregarious, eleven-year-old, red-haired Georgie, on whom she doted. If not actually beautiful, Eleanor was outstanding with her brilliant red hair, which she usually wore swept up into a chignon at the top of her long, thin neck and puffed into a pompadour over her forehead. She had prominent green eyes, fringed with orange lashes, beneath two perfectly semicircular orange eyebrows. She took great care to emphasize her striking appearance and colouring, and was happy to be acclaimed the arbiter of Victoria fashion. "Everyone always says I'm so daring to wear pink with my red hair," she would laugh, "but we Churchills are nothing if not daring!"

For many years she had studied the style of Queen Alexandra and copied what she thought would best suit her. Now there was a new Queen, the former Princess May of Teck. Eleanor had seen many photos of her but so far was not impressed. She decided to maintain her own style, based on her own ideas.

She might well have stayed in England and continued the social life into which she had been born. Her father, the Honourable Sir John St. John, was a Member of Parliament, and her mother was a Churchill. Immediately after her coming-out party, she attended a ball at Buckingham Palace and was presented to Queen Victoria and danced with dear Bertie, then the Prince of Wales. "What a charmer he was!" Eleanor would tell the breathless ladies of Victoria during one of her tea parties. "Really quite, quite impossibly wicked—but such a dear!"

Eleanor could have married into one of England's best families, at least the nobility if not into the Royal Family itself, but she fell madly in love not long after she came out into London society. Marrying plain George Trevor from the colonies could appear to be a step down for someone in her high position, but the Trevor family had already made their mark in British Columbia shipping, with a fleet of ships carrying lumber around the world. Young George was visiting English shipyards to purchase more ships when, at a London ball to which he was taken by his hosts, he met Eleanor, and it was love at first sight. Although George had some doubts as to whether his bride could adjust to life in Victoria, he need not have worried. She took to it at once.

"London was becoming so dull," she would say. "Besides, I have the Marlborough love of adventure. Mother always told me I was just like Cousin Winston. What a young scamp he was! We always spent weekends at Blenheim, you know, and he was constantly teasing me. I simply lived in *terror* of him, but people did say that we were more like brother and sister than cousins. I'm only thankful I have the Churchills' red hair and not their temper!"

Such comments as these were manna from heaven to her friends in Victoria, and there were many who thanked God for having sent Eleanor Trevor to brighten up their lives.

By 1910, Eleanor, George, Victor and young Georgie Trevor had lived in their Rockland Avenue home for two years. They had previously resided in fashionable James Bay, next door to the senior Trevors ("George I," Eleanor called her father-in-law, and got away with it because the old man considered her such a "sport"). However, as young "George II" and his wife became more successful and socially prominent, it was deemed advisable for them to have a more sumptuous estate, and so Blenheim Oaks was built, just a few houses away from Government House and from the monumental Craigdarroch Castle. Eleanor felt that no more favourable location, considering their position in Victoria, could exist. Blenheim Oaks was designed by the young Englishman Francis Rattenbury, already famed for having designed the Parliament Buildings and the Empress Hotel.

Next door to the Trevors, in a house slightly smaller than theirs, lived Sir Neville and Lady Wallingford. Their house was designed by Samuel Maclure, of whom Sir Neville was a staunch supporter. "Good clean lines," said Sir Neville. "Not like that crazy Frenchie stuff of that fellow Rats."

"Francis Rattenbury is an Englishman," his wife reminded him, "who has done very well both in the old country and here in Victoria."

"Rubbish. The fellow just claims to be English. Look at our Parliament Buildings—a disgrace. Just like the bloody Taj Mahal and all that other foreign stuff. Like a bunch of Nanking bawdy houses."

Sir Neville was an old China hand. He had served with the British army in Shanghai for many years, and in 1900 he fought in the Boxer Rebellion before retiring to the moderate climate of Victoria. But the weather had no effect on his temperament. His wife always knew when to change the subject, so she mentioned the afternoon's garden party, with which she had no better luck.

"I've no sympathy for it—none at all!" Sir Neville declared. "People have no business having orphans. There's enough bastards in the world already. Anyway, we don't want any damn fool garden party next door to us! We'll have the public coming into the neighbourhood—bunch of damned idiots."

Lady Wallingford knew how to nip this tirade in the bud.

"Well, it was Eleanor Trevor's idea to hold it at her place this year."

One could almost *see* Sir Neville's angry red countenance fading into its natural parchment colour. "Well, I don't understand it, but if that little lady wants to bring those people out here, she must know what she's doing." He shook his head, but his thin lips twisted into something almost resembling a smile.

Sir Neville would do anything for Eleanor Trevor. "Blood will tell," he would say. "She's a Churchill, you know, on her mother's side. Good stock."

Francis Rattenbury, never afraid to mix his styles, had designed the Trevor home with exquisite dormer windows reflecting his favourite

French château influence, with touches of Elizabethan country style such as brick chimneys, with Gothic trimmings and, Eleanor would rhapsodize, "just a touch of the Alhambra," pointing to the ornate balcony facing the east lawn.

The house was set back on the sloping lawn that led to the street and was enclosed by a three-foot-high wall of stone blocks. There was an enormous glass conservatory on the west side of the house and servants' quarters at the back. The driveway passed through the porte-cochère at the front and around to the coach house in the rear, which accommodated the Trevors' new Daimler automobile.

The Union Jack on the flagpole in front of the porte-cochère was flapping in the strong wind that crossed the southern tip of Vancouver Island on the day of the garden party. From the branches of the Garry oak trees around the green lawns, red and white crepe-paper streamers fluttered, as they did from the tents and tables. At the entrance to the grounds, a lady seated at a small table graciously accepted the twenty-five-cent entrance fee from adults (children under twelve entered free).

All the ladies found it terribly amusing to take their turns at the booths, selling jewellery, toys, books, clothing and assorted knick-knacks collected from the best homes during the past year. A lady in a nurse's uniform was in charge of the "nursery booth" under a red-and-white-striped awning, with a sandbox, rocking horses and toys to keep the little ones happy, so that their mothers might move freely around the gardens. For the older children there was a fish pond, while a woman dressed as a gypsy told fortunes from tea leaves in the tent nearest the tea table.

Silver tea services at each end of the table were presided over by the lieutenant-governor's wife at one end and the mayor's wife at the other. Silver trays bearing dainty cucumber sandwiches and cakes were circulated by Mrs. Trevor's maids, dresssed in long black dresses and starched white caps and aprons.

A string trio played under one of the oaks, on loan from their regular teatime engagement at the Empress Hotel, and Eleanor had selected the music: Gilbert and Sullivan songs, "Merrie England," English country dances and tunes by Franz Lehar, with a final medley of patriotic songs at the conclusion of the afternoon.

Eleanor was the centre of attention. Her ankle-length dress was a wonderful concoction of layers of pink voile, edged with dark pink satin on every flounce, and a dark pink velvet sash. The enormous hat balanced on her red hair was of leghorn, decorated with an array of plumes, satin bows and huge tulle roses. She seemed to be everywhere at once.

Sir Neville and Lady Wallingford had arrived early and taken up a position as close to the tea table as decently possible. "Jolly good show," Sir Neville declared to Eleanor. "Very decent on your part to go to all this trouble for a bunch of . . . orphans." His wife gave him a gentle nudge, and he spilled his tea.

Eleanor gave him her widest smile. What a dear he was, really, for all his pretense at gruffness. "I'm so happy you're here, dear Sir Neville. It means a great deal to all the ladies who worked so hard to have someone in your position attend."

"I suppose it does," he muttered and helped himself to another slice of cake.

🐦 🐦 🐦

Adelaide Godolphin and her two young daughters took the streetcar up Fort Street to Rockland Avenue, then walked up the winding road, past the magnificent houses, until they came to Blenheim Oaks.

Adelaide had attended the garden party alone in the past, but she felt her daughters were now old enough to accompany her, and she was looking forward to showing them the best that the city had to offer. Julia was ten, pretty and sensitive, her fair hair shining and straight in spite of her mother's efforts with rags and curling tongs to put some flounce into it. For Julia, the party was a chance to see the kind of house she dreamed of.

Lilas at seven, with every curl accounted for and bobbing in its place, was chattering with excitement, skipping every step of the way.

Adelaide was very proud. Both wore their best white voile dresses with blue smocking and wide blue silk sashes, with matching blue bows in their hair, white ribbed stockings and black slippers. Adelaide had made the dresses herself. She knew how to stretch her limited means so that she and the girls were always dressed in the best of taste. If only their behaviour could be as elegant as their appearance, she would feel secure.

Today Adelaide wore her own best dress, of white silk with narrow blue rick-rack trim. Her blue sailor hat was set neatly upon her thin blond hair, which she augmented with a "rat" at the back, held in place by a tortoise-shell comb. Adelaide was a tiny, formidable woman, an American by birth, known for her strength of character, her intelligence and her sharp tongue. She made it her duty to endow her children with a strong set of values, to counterbalance the influence of her gentle, easygoing husband, Lewis. She was always careful, while holding up the manners of the rich as an example for the girls, to remind them of the evils of greed.

Lilas, the chatterbox, inundated her mother with questions. "Why couldn't Papa and Stanley come with us, Mama?"

"You know that Papa has to work on Saturdays. And Stanley has to mow Miss Oxenham's lawn. Anyway, a garden party is no place for a young boy. Now be careful not to scuff your good slippers. Julia, for heaven's sake, watch where you're going—you almost fell into that hedge. And do behave yourselves. Lilas, don't talk too much, and Julia, *try* not to bump into things. If you don't act like little ladies, Mrs. Trevor will send you home." The girls nodded and linked hands, cowed by the image of a stern lady ordering them from the party in front of everyone.

Adelaide gave them each ten cents to spend, a rare generosity inspired by the worthy cause. She paid the quarter for her entrance fee and was gratified when the lady at the table remarked on how pretty her daughters were. At first she kept the girls beside her as they walked cautiously up the driveway, observing the magnificently dressed ladies around the tea table. Then, assured that the girls were sufficiently awed by the surroundings to be careful, Adelaide allowed them to move away by themselves.

Lilas discovered the fish pond. It consisted of a four-foot-high sheet attached to two poles driven into the ground. The "fisherman" received a long stick with a string tied to it, at the end of which was a large safety pin. The contestant cast the line over the sheet, and a mysterious presence on the other side attached a parcel, wrapped in tissue paper and tied with pink ribbon, to the safety pin. The fisherman felt the thrilling little jerk on the line, and he or she pulled it up and over the sheet and grasped the present.

Lilas was enchanted. And the price was right—one penny for each try. When she felt the bite on her line for the first time, she jumped up and down. "Julia! Julia! I've caught something!" she cried, retrieving a small package containing a tiny celluloid doll. In succession, she fished up a packet of five marbles, a cotton handkerchief, a rubber ball, a miniature baby bottle and a nickel wrapped in waxed paper, which she immediately invested in five more chances at the pond.

By three o'clock the garden was crowded. Most men wore top hats, as bowlers in London had been relegated to the common folk and were going out of fashion. Victorians depended on stories from the *Colonist* or the *Times* to keep them abreast of current fashions, or information from socially prominent people such as Eleanor Trevor, who subscribed to the *Illustrated London News* and the *Tatler*.

Making a dramatic entrance was Major Lachlan MacCracken, hero of the Boer War, dressed in full battle tartan of the MacCracken clan. One step behind, as always, was his batman, Duffy MacRae, carrying his bagpipes. (It was said that Duffy, after cooking and serving the major's meals, stood behind his chair and played the pipes while he ate.)

"Isn't it delightful?" said Eleanor. "We might almost be at Balmoral!"

Under the only willow tree on the lawn, Doris Burman stood sipping her tea. Beside her, having just brought her a plate of sandwiches and cake, was her son, Harry. She did not possess the courage to come alone, and although she knew there was little to interest Harry, who was fifteen, he escorted her because his father hated affairs such as this.

Doris was forty and looked every worried year of it. She was stout and sallow, her pale brown hair streaked with grey pulled back under her unbecoming green velour bonnet. Her only extraordinary feature was her dark grey eyes, deeply set in her heavy face. She wore a white shirtwaist blouse and a heavy green woollen skirt and jacket. It was not that she was poor—her husband, Matthew, was the manager of the Bank of Victoria and they lived in a large house in James Bay—but Doris had little sense of style and always felt out of place.

Her mother had come to Victoria in 1862 on one of the "bride ships," the sole Irish lass on a boatload of Manchester girls. That made Doris doubly ashamed of the fact. Most such women went to work as domestics, but Doris's mother married a young Irish miner within a week of her arrival. Their marriage was happier than many in similar circumstances, but Doris resented her unromantic lineage. Doris also felt inferior because she was Catholic, while the cream of Victoria society belonged to the Anglican faith.

Still, her marriage was a good one. Scholarly, Catholic Matthew Burman, whose father had been an accountant with the Hudson's Bay Company and an early citizen of Victoria, had a respectable career. Matthew was not only a clever businessman, he was also a curious and sometimes free-thinking intellectual. He was proud of his mother-in-law's bride ship arrival, considering it an integral part of the island's history. He had a wife of good character, one who would leave him alone to concentrate on business and upon his private obsession, a book he intended to write about the native chieftain, Maquinna, and the history of Vancouver Island's west coast. Doris respected, though did not quite understand, his focus. "Him and his Indians," she would say to her son, "as if anybody cared."

They were blessed with only one child. Today, Doris and Harry stood together beneath the willow, Doris envious of her surroundings, Harry indifferent. He was tall for his age. His dark brown hair was combed low on his forehead and carefully parted on the right side, showing only slightly beneath his straw hat. His eyes were deep set and dark grey like his mother's, and his skin was as pale as hers. There was a sense of concentration about him like his father, and he made excellent grades, but he tended to look at everything as though he disapproved of it. Perhaps this explained why he was not popular with his schoolmates.

Today Harry wore a navy blue suit, with long pants and a vest, and a dark blue wool tie. When not waiting on his mother, he stood with his hands clasped behind his back, watching everyone gloomily, as though he were attending a funeral.

Julia recognized Harry Burman. She knew him from South Park, the neighbourhood middle school she attended, although now he went to Victoria High. Once she had dropped her books in the hall and he had picked them up for her, and she had been flattered that an older boy—indeed, any boy—would do such a thing. She attempted a smile in his direction, but he did not return it.

Julia knew what she wanted to see. She offered her nickel at the entrance to the large greenhouse, where she could see Mrs. Trevor's collection of flowers and plants. The lady taking the money, however, was not at all certain that a small girl should enter alone. "Hothouses," Eleanor had told her, "are no place for children." Still, she took the nickel and allowed Julia to enter.

It was like a jungle, Julia thought, and evoked the thrilling adventures that she read about in the *Girl's Own Annual.* There were fuchsias, heliotrope, hibiscus and jasmine blossoms such as she had never seen. Surely this was what India was like. She imagined the possibility of meeting a maharaja.

Many signs in the greenhouse admonished PLEASE DO NOT TOUCH, but when Julia saw a needle extending from a thick, dark green cactus, she could not resist the temptation to discover if it was as sharp as it looked. She put a finger on it and found that it was.

She was startled, and more than a little guilty, when she heard a loud voice directly behind her. "Just as mean as they look, eh?" Julia turned to see a plump, ruddy-faced woman, exceedingly plain and not at all well dressed by Godolphin standards.

"I'm sorry," Julia said meekly.

"Nothing to be sorry for, child, unless you've pricked your finger." Julia felt like Alice in Wonderland speaking to the Red Queen, especially after someone summoned her in what seemed like affected shrillness from across the greenhouse. "Mrs. Butchered? Please, may I have your kind attention in a matter of the utmost importance?" What a name for a person who tends flowers, Julia thought, as the woman walked away abruptly. Finally, she went out into the brilliant, cool world of the garden party to look for her sister. She found her at the fish pond, of course. "Come on, Lilas," said Julia, attempting to take her sister's hand, "we must go and find Mama."

"I want to fish!" Lilas retorted.

"Don't you want some lemonade and cookies? I'll treat you."

"*No!*" Lilas exclaimed in a tone that quite surprised the fish-pond ladies. Julia took her by the arm, but Lilas resisted, so Julia fell against the sheet, and the whole thing collapsed. Lilas gave a dramatic shriek on seeing her beloved fish pond destroyed and herself disgraced because of her sister's clumsiness.

Eleanor Trevor, chatting with the mayor's wife, glanced over. "Oh dear," she said plaintively. Adelaide had also heard the noises and assumed the worst. What if Julia had broken something of value? She put down her cup and saucer and edged through the crowd.

Julia was lying unhurt on her back, engulfed by the sheets, when she looked up into the face of the most beautiful lady she had ever seen and saw not only beauty but sympathy. The woman was in her mid-thirties, Julia guessed, dressed in a white linen eyelet gown, and beneath her white bonnet golden ringlets cascaded over rounded white shoulders. Her eyes shone with humour and kindness, but it was her smile that Julia would not forget.

"I'm sorry," whispered Julia. "I'm very clumsy."

"Don't ever say that, dear," said the vision. "It could happen to anyone. Are you hurt?"

Julia shook her head. Despite the sympathy of the lovely lady, she was deeply embarrassed and knew only too well the reaction she could expect from her mother. Above her, she heard one of the fish-pond ladies say, "I do believe that's Anna Aalgaard, Sveinn Arnason's daughter."

Mrs. Aalgaard, satisfied that no damage had been done, brushed the grass from Julia's dress, patted her on the head, picked her white parasol up from the lawn, and called out, "Albert, dear, please find a lemonade for the little girl."

Albert Aalgaard was not quite thirteen but carried himself with the poise of someone much older. He was tall, slim and blond, his eyes a darker blue than his mother's; there was a certain animal grace about him, so different from her comfortable solidity, but the smile was the same. Albert wore white flannels with the crest of the University School emblazoned on the jacket pocket and a straw boater hat.

As Adelaide Godolphin arrived, tense with anger, Albert appeared with a glass of lemonade in each hand. "I brought one for your little sister too," he said, smiling down at Julia. "I'm sure she wants one."

Anna looked at Adelaide, who was some six inches shorter. "Is this your daughter? She's a lovely little girl. Please don't scold her. It was an accident, you know." She gave Adelaide the full benefit of her smile, twirled the frilled parasol, and moved gracefully away, followed by Albert, who flashed his smile over his shoulder at the girls before he disappeared into the crowd.

"Who's that boy?" Lilas gulped her lemonade, having forgotten her grief, oblivious even to the fact that the ladies had now carefully folded the sheets from the disassembled fish pond.

"That's Albert Aalgaard," said one of the ladies. "Isn't he nice? His grandfather owns Arnason Island. What a handsome boy, and so well mannered!"

Lilas put down her glass and gathered her prizes together. "I think he's Prince Charming from *Cinderella*," she stated. "I always knew he was real."

The ladies laughed, but Julia knew her mother was still furious.

"Girls," said Adelaide, "we are going home!"

Eleanor Trevor, sensing that the time had come for a diversion, signalled the band to play her favourite tune, "Rule, Britannia!" Then, taking her place in front of the tea table, she made her carefully prepared speech, welcoming her guests and thanking them for their support of the great cause and for their patriotism in coming despite their deep sorrow over King Edward's death. When she concluded, to much applause, the musicians struck up "God Save the King," and the party was declared officially over.

CHAPTER TWO

A Boy's Life

Stanley Godolphin began his Saturday chores as he always did, at Miss Oxenham's home on Dallas Road. While he both hated and feared Miss Oxenham (Lilas had declared that she was really the witch from *Hansel and Gretel*), he loved her odd old house and the open stretch of front lawn directly across the road from the beach and the Strait of Juan de Fuca.

Before he began his work, he crossed the road and stood amid the Scotch broom, looking down at the short strip of rocky beach below him with its piles of driftwood. The water was quiet, despite the wind. The waves lapped lightly against the pebbles lining the shore, and Stanley gazed at the waves and the stretch of water beyond, where the light shimmered as though the sun were pulling on strands of silver.

A few yards out from shore, about twenty seagulls gathered on a raft of kelp. Stanley smiled as he watched, and imagined them as aquatic Fathers of Confederation, like the ones he'd seen in a picture in his history text-book. They sat, bobbing, silently staring at each other, until the mood was broken by the cry of another seagull farther out who had discovered a fish just below the surface and was diving for it. The meeting on the seaweed instantly broke up, and with much flapping and squalling, they rose, wheeled, and flew out to join their brother.

Across the strait on the American side of the water, the Olympic Mountains rose above the haze, still with touches of snow on their peaks, while westward the strait continued on toward the great, mysterious Pacific Ocean and all the dreams of adventure it offered to the mind of a sensitive, eleven-year-old boy. He was so entranced with his thoughts that he forgot about Miss Oxenham, and it was five minutes after ten when he turned back and looked at the house where he should have reported at ten.

Miss Oxenham's father was an Englishman who had "struck it rich" during the British Columbia gold rush of 1858. He had built his eccentric house on Dallas Road, one of the first to be constructed there. The architect's identity was unknown. Some said it was old Oxenham himself, for the house was definitely unconventional, with no order or plan about it, the promise of many rooms offered in all manner of ways, none of which seemed to have any connection with the others. There were gables and additions and rococo trimmings along the uneven roof, and there were unexpected balconies and windows that made no sense at all. Exactly what had become of the old man was unknown. The rumour was that he had gone farther north in search of another fortune and simply disappeared. No one in Victoria knew anything of his wife. They only knew he had an exceedingly unattractive daughter.

Miss Oxenham was tall and thin, with a face so ugly it was fascinating. She had an enormous mouth, large pointed teeth and a hooked nose around which her piercing dark eyes darted constantly in suspicion. She reminded Stanley of a parrot. She was well into her fifties, and had never married. In fact, it was quite impossible for Stanley to imagine anyone wanting to marry her. Her only charming physical asset was a deep, resonant speaking voice, and though she rarely used it to speak pleasantly, a listener could neither forget it nor refuse to listen to it.

She always wore black, out of respect for her missing father, and, despite her dislike of ostentation, at least one piece of the exquisite jewellery that he had given her. Her favourite was a pair of long, dangling diamond earrings that, though beautiful, looked totally out of place with her high-necked bombazine and taffeta dresses and her plain features.

She never entertained and seldom went out, except to St. Andrew's Presbyterian Church on Douglas Street, where she had met the Godolphin family. She had also purchased furniture from Macauley's store, where Lewis Godolphin worked, and had spoken to him at the store about employing his son to work around her house on Saturday mornings.

Stanley arrived at the back door, and Miss Oxenham answered. "You are six minutes late, Stanley."

"I'm sorry, Miss Oxenham," he said meekly, cap in hand, aware that humility was the only stance that would be acceptable to her.

"You have been dawdling again. So many young people these days waste time in dawdling. In my day we were never allowed to dawdle, and consequently we made only the most valuable use of our time."

He nodded, used to such sermons, as his mother also considered tardiness a mortal sin.

"Shall I start in the front yard, Miss Oxenham?"

"Yes. You know that I always want you to start with the front yard. Begin at once and don't waste any more time."

She slammed the door, and Stanley went eagerly to the shed behind the house, happy to have escaped with so short a lecture. He hung his jacket and cap on a nail, then hauled out the lawn mower and took it around to the front.

Stanley leaned against the mower and looked out at the strait. He saw a ship headed westward and thought how wonderful it would be if one day he were aboard one of those freighters bound for India, China, or Australia, to an adventurous life. He would return home to Victoria with presents for his parents and sisters. He tried to imagine his mother saying,

"I always knew he had it in him," but he found it difficult to visualize.

"Stanley!" Miss Oxenham was on the wide veranda at the front of the house. Stanley stood rigidly, his thin hands grasping the handle of the mower, his dreams having burst like a bubble. "Come here, Stanley."

He left the mower and went to the bottom of the front steps, where the dragon loomed above him.

"What were you doing just now?"

He tried to think but couldn't remember doing anything at all. And that was the trouble. Yet if he answered, "Nothing," he would be considered impertinent.

"I guess . . . I just stopped working for a minute. I was looking at the water."

"The water will be there long after you and I are gone," she said in her deep voice, as though uttering words of great wisdom. "In the meantime, kindly look at it on some other occasion than when you are working for me. You already started late, remember."

He nodded and turned back toward the mower, but the voice stopped him in his tracks.

"Stanley!"

"Yes, Miss Oxenham?"

"What you were actually doing was daydreaming, was it not?"

"Yes, Miss Oxenham."

"Daydreaming is a partner of dawdling. They go hand in hand, and neither one will get you into anything except trouble. You're not in any kind of trouble already, are you, Stanley?"

He immediately felt guilty, trying to think of all the things he had recently done wrong or, more exactly, not done correctly. "I . . . I don't think so."

She came down the broad front steps and along the walk. She peered at him, her sharp eyes searing through his glasses and into his soul. "You have extremely good parents, Stanley. I hope you realize that."

He did, but before he could acknowledge the fact, she came even closer.

"They are good, decent people. You haven't done anything to disgrace them, have you?"

He looked at her in bewilderment. She stooped, leaning toward him. "A lot of boys your age have done very bad things. I'm sure you know that. I hope for your parents' sake that *you* don't do anything like that."

He felt himself growing hot. If only he understood what "that" meant. He was silent, filled with curiosity; perhaps if she continued to speak, he would learn something. "All men are born evil, Stanley. There are some, like your father, who have managed to overcome it and live decent lives. Unfortunately, he is an exception. We can only hope that you will be an exception too. But remember—the path of sin is your destiny as a male. Avoid it like the plague."

She bent even closer. He was aware of the diamond earrings swinging hypnotically from her ears. He knew that he was trembling, and that Miss Oxenham saw that he was, and he became even more frightened because she would be sure to attribute his reaction to his sense of having done wrong.

"Go back to work, Stanley." She drew herself up straight once more. "Remember what I have told you. Never forget it. And when you have finished the front lawn, continue around to the back." Very erect, she walked back to the house, up the stairs and through the front door.

Stanley continued to mow the lawn. He did not look again at the dark blue water across the road or the sharp white peaks of the Olympic Mountains across the strait. He concentrated entirely on mowing, except to wonder about the mysterious sin that he and all men were born to commit. At noon he was finished, or at least that was when Miss Oxenham came to the back porch and announced that he was. She gave him eight cents, deducting two from the ten he was promised.

Possessed by a guilt that he did not understand, he went directly home. Adelaide had left him a ham sandwich and a glass of milk.

At one o'clock, he went to the Whittakers' house at the end of the

27

block to do their yardwork. The Whittakers had come to Victoria from Minnesota, and had prospered after Mr. Whittaker had opened a hardware store on Fort Street. He and his wife were in their forties and had two daughters, Katie, who was ten and a friend of Julia, and Amy, who was three.

Mrs. Whittaker was in the kitchen baking when Stanley knocked on the back door. Katie was sitting on the back porch with Amy. Katie, brown-haired and plain, her chin in her hand and her elbows on her knees, was obviously downcast. "Julia's so lucky to get to go to the garden party," she sighed vaguely in Stanley's direction.

The Whittakers had a modest flowerbed with daisies and dahlias, a vegetable garden, a few raspberries and one rather scrawny oak tree. A wire fence, choked with morning glory in one corner, encircled the yard.

Stanley was struggling with the morning glory when he heard the cry. Amy had been chasing butterflies, and as she pursued one, she stumbled and fell. Her vanity was the only thing bruised, but she emitted a despairing howl. Stanley smiled gently, certain she was unhurt, and picked her up. Instantly, Amy's plump arms were around his neck as he carried her to the back door.

He could hear Mrs. Whittaker calling in panic. When she saw Stanley carrying Amy past Katie, who was still reading on the porch, Mrs. Whittaker cried again, "My baby! Katie, you selfish girl. Why can't you look after your little sister?"

Stanley decided that Amy had inherited her sense of the dramatic from her mother. "She's not hurt, Mrs. Whittaker. She just fell."

"Are you sure you're not hurt, my precious? Well, we'll go in the house and have a cookie. Amy will give you a cookie too, Stanley." Katie sulked while the three of them went into the kitchen, where Stanley was given a glass of lemonade. Mrs. Whittaker gave Amy two ginger cookies. "Give one to Stanley, there's a good girl."

Amy toddled over to Stanley, handed the cookie to him with her sticky little hands and gazed at him adoringly. He thanked her, smiling, basking for once in warmth and approval. He could still feel her moist, fat little arms clasped around his neck. He could not remember ever having such physical contact with his own sisters.

When he had finished working on the morning glory, with some success, he went home, happier than he had been for some time. Mrs. Whittaker had given him an extra five cents for rescuing Amy, so his day had been a profitable one after all.

CHAPTER THREE

Crime

A delaide Godolphin, like many Victorians, was an anglophile. She read the *Victoria Times* from cover to cover, and all the English newspapers and magazines she could obtain. She was also a European royalty buff and could speak with authority about the Mecklenburg-Schwerins and the Schleswig-Holsteins, the Tecks and Waldeck-Pyrmonts as though they were neighbours. She knew every member of the Romanoff, Hapsburg and Hohenzollern families by name and could tell you the differences between the Saxe-Coburg family and the Saxe-Coburg-Gothas. She had distrusted Kaiser Wilhelm II long before anyone else did, and only hoped that the new King, George V, realized what his cousin Willie was up to. In addition, she was an authority on all local gossip. If it went on, or was said to go on, in her neighbourhood, Adelaide knew all about it.

She had been born in New York. Upon the death of her father—a Welsh wine merchant who relied too heavily on his own wares, and passed away suddenly under suspicious circumstances—she preferred to sever all connection with her stepmother. Eighteen-year-old Adelaide mistrusted her father's third wife. She took her tiny inheritance (her stepmother having appropriated a good part of what her father had left her) and headed west to reconnect with her best friend at school, Lilas, who had moved to San Francisco with her parents.

Within two years, she had met and married young Lewis Godolphin, who had come from Cornwall, drawn by stories of California gold. They were married in San Francisco, but Adelaide decided that it was not a suitable city in which to raise children, while Lewis had heard stories of gold that might be found farther north. They moved first to Seattle, but Adelaide had heard much about Victoria and its charming "English" atmosphere. Surely one could raise children properly in such a place, away from the temptations and rougher ways of the newer towns of Seattle and Vancouver. Lewis deferred to Adelaide, whom he adored.

When the Klondike gold rush of 1898 arrived, Adelaide was already pregnant with Stanley, and they had moved to Victoria for a less adventurous life. Julia was born in 1900, and Lilas in 1903. Lewis took a job as a carpenter for Mr. Macauley, a Scotsman, and after four years, Macauley acted against his natural impulses and raised Lewis's wages. He knew that the shy, bearded, gentle Cornishman was a treasure. He could not only mould wood as if it were clay, he was an artist, and his designs were soon popular with the expanding population of Victoria, which by 1910 had reached forty thousand people ("excluding Indians and Orientals," as the census had noted).

In 1907, when the magnificent Empress Hotel was completed, Lewis was able to move his family to a two-storey house on Humboldt Street, within walking distance of his work. It was a well-built house that would become quietly handsome with a little labour. He trained Stanley to help him, and saw with satisfaction his son's proficiency. Adelaide decorated the house with the few possessions she had brought from New York and San Francisco, but primarily with her thrifty purchases from Spencer's department store on Douglas Street.

Their greatest treasure was the upright rosewood piano, which one of Macauley's clients had given Lewis for work he had done on his home. A piano was an emblem of family solidarity, an indication of their appreciation for the finer things in life, and musical evenings became a Sunday night feature of life in the Godolphin household. Adelaide had learned to play the piano in New York, before the advent of the stepmother. Lewis possessed a pleasant tenor, and although he was by nature a retiring man, he loved to sing for his family. Lilas sang like a bird, while Julia had begun piano lessons when she was seven. It was a happy life.

Lewis would sing Handel's "Where'er You Walk" and "Tit-Willow" from *The Mikado*, a great favourite of Lilas, while Julia loved to hear her father sing "I Dreamt I Dwelt in Marble Halls" from *The Bohemian Girl*. Stanley, however, had no musical ability at all. He was content to listen to his father and admire the talents of the females in his family.

🦢 🦢 🦢

In September 1913, Stanley Godolphin had just entered grade nine. He was supposed to go to Victoria High School, but the handsome new, sparsely adorned building on Camosun Street was not yet completed, so South Park School grew by a grade for the year. He was pleased to have avoided the harassment he expected from older students, but still he hated school more than he had any preceding year. His new teacher, Miss Ryseberry, was strict, unpleasant and unattractive, unlike Miss Devon, his former teacher and the only person who had made school tolerable for him in the past. He hated the other boys, their meanness, their rough habits and stupid ball games. The boys, sensing his dislike, returned it in double measure, teasing and bullying him, which was not difficult as Stanley was no fighter. He was not so much afraid as he was revolted by the idea of physical violence.

At the beginning of his second week at school, he came down the stairs from his bedroom, his schoolbooks held together by a ragged leather strap slung over his shoulder. He wore a white shirt, brown bow tie, brown woollen jacket and brown plus-fours. He moved slowly and stopped at the door to the kitchen. It was Monday morning, washday. Already his mother, who always rose at six o'clock, had finished her first load of washing. She spoke to him without turning around. Her children believed she had "eyes in the back of her head."

"Stanley, you're late again. Your sisters have already left. Why didn't you come down to breakfast when I called? Do you think I've nothing better to do on Monday morning than to keep calling you?"

He didn't answer. He was looking up at the rack of frilly white underclothes belonging to his sisters: the bloomers, camisoles and petticoats. Somehow he averted his eyes from the second rack, where his mother's plainer undergarments hung. As for his and his father's long woollen underwear, they repulsed him.

"Stanley!" Her voice was sharper. He tore his gaze from the ceiling and from the "unmentionables," as his mother called them, and looked at her.

"You listen to me, young man. You're in high school now, and you've got to do a lot better than last year. You're always daydreaming. I tell you, Stanley, if you get a bad report at the end of the month, I'm going to speak to your father."

He knew from past experience that this would result in a sad, gentle, vague lecture from his father. The real menace lay in the palm of his mother's small hand and the sharpness of her tongue.

He was silent. If he used the excuse that he had slept in, it could mean anything from castor oil to a trip to old Dr. Muddsley. Besides, he had not slept in. He had been lying in bed in his little room across the hall from his sisters'. He had heard whispering, giggling and the rustle of their skirts as they dressed. He had heard his mother call, several times, but he had been thinking about sex. This was normal enough for a boy his age, as he would be fifteen in November. His problem was that he knew nothing about it, and the prospect of finding out anything at home was bleak.

He did not know the circumstances of his or his sisters' conception or birth, nor had he any idea of what his parents did in bed; he assumed that they talked over the events of the day and then went to sleep. His mind had never been opened to any other activity. The changes taking place in his own body were puzzling and embarrassing to him. He had heard boys at school talking, but it all sounded ugly and disgusting to him. He thought he disliked all men with the exception of his father, who was a truly good man, a kind man with dignity, who would never indulge in such awful things.

Lying in bed after his sisters had gone downstairs, he began to think of Miss Devon. How beautiful she was, with her slim pale neck above the high white collar of her blouse, and the tormenting thoughts that he could no longer dismiss came to him. What was underneath? What if all those layers of clothes were gone; was there something beautiful to see? Did she wear simple cotton underclothes, or frilly garments like his sisters? And when they were off, what then? His sisters' bodies had been so carefully hidden from him that he had never seen them naked, even when they were little babies.

When he escaped from his mother's lecture, he scarcely noticed that she had handed him his lunch pail and then had pressed an apple into his hand as he went out the door, admonishing him to "eat something, for heaven's sake." He walked down the back steps, around the house and onto the wooden sidewalk, down Humboldt, over to Douglas Street, passing Beacon Hill Park until he arrived at school.

He entered Miss Ryseberry's room at nine-twenty, and she immediately questioned him about his tardiness. Did he have a note from his mother? He did not and had been afraid to ask for one. Miss Ryseberry sent him to the principal's office, where the severe Mr. Patterson placed the first demerit mark for the new term on his chart. Afterward, Miss Ryseberry wrote out a brief note to Mrs. Godolphin, informing her of her son's behaviour. "You will bring that back to me tomorrow with your mother's signature. Now take your place, Stanley. You have already interrupted class."

He took his seat, ignoring the grins of his classmates, opened his history book and tried to pretend he cared about the Stuart kings of England.

After school, walking down the dark halls that smelled so strongly of Lysol, avoiding other students, he stopped outside the door of Miss Devon's classroom. He could see her erasing the last of the writing from the blackboard, picking up chalk, putting everything in its place. She was very beautiful. He loved the movement of her long slim arms in the tight-sleeved white blouse. Soft curls of her gleaming red hair always managed to escape the net that was meant to imprison them and shape them into the severe bun at the back of her neck.

He was not the only one to be stirred by Laurel Devon. "Much too pretty for a teacher," everyone said. Actually, Miss Devon was a born teacher, intelligent and analytical, although she was inclined to be severe with her pupils lest anyone believe that her looks denoted weakness.

Stanley seldom listened to her; he only wanted to look at her, as he loved to look at anything beautiful—his sisters, flowers, birds, the sky on a windy day and the water in the harbour and in the strait.

Laurel Devon turned away from the blackboard and saw him at the classroom door. "Hello, Stanley," she said politely but without warmth. "I hope you are enjoying high school. Miss Ryseberry is a very fine teacher."

He did not reply, shifting his weight to one side, a habit of his when he was nervous. She came closer to him and he could smell her lilac sachet.

"I hope you are working hard, Stanley."

"I . . . I miss you," he said simply.

"Well, it's very nice of you to say so, Stanley," her voice sharpening somewhat. "But I know you're going to be a busy young man with all the studying you will have to do this year, and you do need to study more, Stanley."

He nodded but did not move. He was looking at her white neck, and then down to the cameo at her collar, and then to those mysterious curves beneath her blouse.

"You'd better be getting home now, I think. And I must get to work marking these papers. Thank you for coming by, Stanley, and good luck this year." She closed the door of the schoolroom almost in his face, as he still had not moved. Then Stanley turned away and went slowly and sadly into the school grounds. She was lost to him forever.

Laurel Devon went to her desk and began marking papers, but she could not concentrate. I should have a talk with his parents, she thought, but you didn't discuss such matters with parents. Besides, to bring up the subject of sex—well, it might be interpreted as being in her mind instead of Stanley's. She thought, uncertainly, that he would never do anything that was not right.

Stanley walked slowly across the dusty school grounds. It was warm for September, and he felt hot and uncomfortable. He walked in the opposite direction from where the older boys lingered. At the other end of the park were the swings where the younger children played, waiting to be picked up by parents or older siblings. Just for a moment he smiled. They were so happy, the little ones, so much nicer than children of his own age, and friendlier than adults.

In the row of swings he saw Amy Whittaker, now six years old and in grade one at tiny Beacon Hill Elementary, a couple of blocks away. She had evidently come with some friends and their mothers to the South Park playground, where she would meet her sister for the walk home. After he passed, he heard a cry. Turning, he saw that Amy had slipped off the swing onto the ground and then had been struck by the swing on its return. He was beside her in a second, picking her up and brushing dirt from her dress. She was crying but not badly hurt, mainly frightened and offended that such a thing could happen to her. One of the boys laughed and called her a baby.

"I want my mummy," she whimpered. "I want to go home."

Stanley swept her hair out of her eyes and then examined the scrape on her knee, visible through a tear in her stocking. Amy looked at her knee too and began to cry again. "Come along," he said and told one of the older children to tell Amy's sister that he was taking Amy home.

Hand in hand they walked out of the schoolyard. Amy was extremely proud to be under the protection of a big boy, and Stanley was so kind. They walked away from the school, pausing for a moment across the street from the park to observe some ducks waddling along the edge of the road.

Outside the Whittaker house, Stanley stopped, straightened the ribbon on Amy's hair and flicked off some dirt that still clung to her dress. They went around to the back door and knocked. Mrs. Whittaker, her voluminous apron flour-covered, answered the door. Just as Mrs. Godolphin always seemed to be washing or cleaning, it appeared Mrs. Whittaker was always baking.

"Amy, baby! What happened?"

Instantly Amy began to cry again and her mother seized her as though to ensure that she was still in one piece.

"It's all right, Mrs. Whittaker. Amy fell off the swing at school. She was shaken up a bit and scraped her knee, but I don't think it's serious."

Mrs. Whittaker opened the kitchen door and ushered them inside. "Thank you, Stanley. It was kind of you to look after my baby."

After that day, Stanley walked Amy home from school as often as possible. Katie was expected to walk her little sister home, but Katie had not proven dependable, and Mrs. Whittaker declared she felt more comfortable when she knew her baby was with Stanley.

Stanley too was happier. Amy made him feel needed, important. He would talk to her about the seagulls that clustered on the edge of the school grounds, searching for remains from children's lunch pails, and about the peacocks in Beacon Hill Park.

On a Friday afternoon in late September, Stanley and Amy started home along Douglas Street. It was warm, but the weather was changing. One dark and forbidding cloud hung directly over them, and rain began to fall in big drops. Stanley pulled the hood of Amy's coat over her head. "Come on, Amy, let's run away from the rain."

"Rain, rain, go away," she shouted, skipping along the sidewalk. "Come again another day, little Amy wants to play . . ."

The drops came heavier and faster. Across the street in the park was the broad trunk of a Douglas fir, and around it a hexagonal arbor with wooden seats protected by a mushroom-shaped dome of cedar shakes. "Amy, let's go over there. We've a long way to go before we reach home." Amy allowed him to steer her across the deserted street to the safety of the arbor. When they were seated, Amy snuggled up to him, her little legs not quite reaching the ground. He could see that she was not at all afraid but was enjoying the drama. "There won't be thunder, will there?"

"No. We only get thunder when it's really hot."

If Stanley said so, Amy was satisfied. He put his arm around her. He looked down at her little face turned up to him, devotion shining in her brown eyes. He felt the warmth of her small body. The hood of her coat had fallen away and the brown curls were damp and askew. He looked down at the little legs in their brown ribbed stockings and brown boots, her ankles crossed. How tiny she was, and how utterly beautiful. His right hand touched her chest.

"Why are you looking at me, Stanley?"

"You're so pretty," he said gently. "I think you must be pretty all over."

She was silent, digesting this new thought. His hand was on one ribbed stocking. His throat felt tight, and his pulse throbbed.

"Amy . . ." he began.

"What's the matter, Stanley? Are you okay?"

Her directness relaxed him slightly and he smiled. "Yes, but it's still raining too much to go home yet. Amy, would you take off your coat for a minute? You won't catch cold, and I want to see the nice dress you have on."

Ever susceptible to flattery, Amy carefully unbuttoned her coat. "You can see my dress. It's a new one my mama made for me."

She slipped off the coat and stood before him in her brown velvet pinafore dress over a ruffled white cotton blouse. For a moment he hated himself. How could he be so sly with Amy when he had always been so afraid in the presence of others? But that was why he loved her—she gave him confidence that no one else had given him. He knew he would never dare to approach an older girl this way.

He knelt down in front of her. "Amy, you're like a beautiful little princess. Do you know that?"

Amy had long thought so herself, but it was very nice to hear it from someone like Stanley, who was a big boy and ought to know about such things.

Very slowly, trying to keep his fingers steady, he lifted her skirt. "That's a beautiful petticoat," he heard himself say, aware that as long as he appeased her innocent vanity, he was all right.

"It's real taffeta with a satin ribbon," Amy told him proudly.

He raised the petticoat and saw the white bloomers above the ribbed stockings. Now the pulse pounded painfully in the place where he didn't understand it. He had never felt so overwhelmed by it before. He believed he was on the verge of some tremendous revelation and he could not turn back. He looked up at the curious, adorable face above him.

He looked over his shoulder at the street, still running with water, and he could hear the raindrops hitting the branches and the cedar roof above him. There was no one in sight.

He pulled her petticoat up and her bloomers down and her panties down, and with his eyes wide leaned forward and kissed her just above her pubic bone. "That tickles," Amy said, somewhat uncomfortable, but still giggling. He kissed her again, hugged her and felt his cheek against her soft belly. Suddenly Stanley felt as though he might be sick. He stood up uncomfortably, pulling Amy's clothes back on as he did so.

"Are you all right, Stanley? You shouldn't tickle me like that." It was a friendly reproach.

"No, I guess I shouldn't. It's just because you're so very pretty, Amy. You're pretty all over."

Amy was puzzled but not really concerned. Stanley was so kind. Her sister wouldn't have stopped tickling her.

"Let this be our secret, Amy," he whispered, "always." She nodded. "I think the rain is stopping. Let's start for home. I don't want your mother to worry about us." They joined hands and ran out of the park onto Douglas Street. Amy was skipping again.

Stanley was overwhelmed by a mixture of ecstasy and guilt. How wonderful it had been, and how terrible. He did not know how to deal with his new-found knowledge. Yet when he delivered Amy to her back door, it was just like any other day.

🐜 🐜 🐜

In most houses, Saturday night was the traditional bath night, but Mrs. Whittaker made a habit of bathing Amy on Fridays. Although they had a perfectly good bathroom upstairs, on cooler nights she would bring a small enamel tub downstairs and put it on the linoleum in front of the kitchen stove. After dinner, with a good fire still burning in the stove, Mrs. Whittaker would shoo the rest of the family out of the kitchen. She still thought of Amy as her baby.

She spread the big hooked woollen bath mat between the tub and the stove and undressed her little girl. It was warm and cozy in the kitchen; the iron stove almost glowed with heat. Amy had a small painted celluloid duck that she still enjoyed playing with, sometimes setting it on top of the Ivory soap bar and watching them float around the washtub. After the bath, she stood on the bath mat, feeling the heat of the stove on her body. While Mrs. Whittaker dried her daughter with a big bath towel, Amy looked at herself. "I'm pretty, aren't I, Mama?"

Mrs. Whittaker smiled. What was considered vanity in an older person was merely sweet in one so little. "Of course you are, my darling."

She looked at her mother, a birdlike, curious look on her face, her head cocked. "I'm pretty all over, aren't I?" Mrs. Whittaker was embarrassed.

Really, the things children said. She did not answer but continued patting her with the towel and reached for the powder.

"Stanley says I'm pretty all over," said Amy, now looking down at her body with new appreciation.

"That was kind of Stanley." She reached for Amy's flannel nightgown. "It shows that Stanley appreciates how well dressed you are."

"Oh no, not just my clothes," Amy said. "He meant me, without my clothes."

Mrs. Whittaker was on her knees. She did not move and she could not believe what she had just heard.

"Child, what are you talking about?"

Amy smiled with satisfaction. "Stanley thinks I'm just like a princess, and I'm so beautiful he kissed me." She turned to her mother who was still kneeling, rigid, staring at her. Amy patted her small crotch. "Right here," she said. "Stanley said it was a secret kiss, and he hugged me real hard."

Mrs. Whittaker's colour was ashen. She began to tremble. She did not move and she could not speak. Amy started to cry. "Mama?" Her mother began to shake, and Amy let out a dramatic wail.

Mr. Whittaker peeked into the kitchen and averted his eyes as he wrapped Amy in the towel. Then he knelt before his wife, who was clutching her hands to her chest. He thought she had had some kind of stroke.

"Jane, Jane, what is it?" She did not speak. He helped her into a kitchen chair, looked at Amy, still white with fear, and said, "Go upstairs to your sister, child." He tried to keep his voice calm. "Tell her to put you to bed."

As Amy left, Mrs. Whittaker started to cry.

"My dear," he asked softly, "what on Earth has happened?"

Sitting in the kitchen chair, still unable to look at her husband, she explained what Amy had told her.

🙥 🙥 🙥

For the rest of his life, Gordon Whittaker always felt that the hardest part of the whole sordid business was having to face Lewis Godolphin. Whittaker's hardware store was not far from Lewis's workplace at Macauley's Furniture, and the two men often walked home together. Whittaker, the more aggressive man, admired the quiet intelligence he found in Lewis and had nothing but respect for him.

How could he now tell this man that his only son was some sort of a pervert, that the boy had committed a criminal offence? This was the sort of act only whispered about behind closed doors. True, the child was not harmed, but who could tell what scars might be left on her innocent young mind, and who would have thought that the boy could have done such a monstrous thing? Perhaps he had already committed crimes against other children, and what might he be capable of in the future?

Julia was practising the piano when she heard the knock and answered the door. Stanley was in his room, while Lilas was helping her mother with the dinner dishes. Mr. Whittaker was brusque when he asked to speak to her father, and he did not smile. She ushered him in silence to the upstairs parlour where her father was sitting and then went down to the kitchen to tell her mother.

Adelaide was pleased. It was nice for Lewis to have the company of another man occasionally, particularly such a respectable man as Mr. Whittaker. She would leave them to chat for a while and then suggest that they have a cup of tea.

Lewis was working on his stamp collection and smoking a cigar. He was surprised to see Gordon Whittaker. They shook hands and the visitor seated himself in the high-backed red velour chair across the small table. It occurred to Lewis that Mr. Whittaker was not well. He kept clenching and unclenching his hands as though his circulation was giving him trouble. Lewis was about to offer him a drink when Whittaker spoke.

"Lewis," he said tightly, "I have come to see you on an extremely grave matter. I want you to be prepared to hear some bad news." They had never before spoken on a first-name basis. Lewis looked at his guest in astonishment, unable to imagine what bad news Whittaker could bring him. "It's about your son, Stanley."

Nothing could have surprised Lewis more. "Stanley?" His mouth actually remained open in wonder.

Then Lewis realized that Whittaker had yet to look at him directly but was staring at his own clasped hands. "Your son has committed a . . . a lewd and indecent act." Lewis remained silent. It was impossible. Could Whittaker have gone mad? He had always seemed like a level-headed fellow, but this made no sense at all. Whittaker continued, still staring at his hands. "A lewd and improper . . . an immoral act against my daughter."

"Katie?" Lewis asked very softly, trying to look into his neighbour's eyes.

Whittaker's voice was the barest of whispers. "Amy."

Lewis got up and went to the window. He pulled back the heavy green drapes, pushed aside the white curtains and looked down into the street. There was nothing to be seen out there. He would not have seen it if there were.

Whittaker also got up. A few tears ran down his cheeks in relief at having spoken those first words. He went to the window and put his hand on Lewis's shoulder. "I'm sorry, Lewis, believe me. My wife and I . . . it's been terrible, but believe me, I'm just as sorry for you."

Lewis looked at him and saw that whatever Stanley had done, it was true and there was nothing he could do to change it. "Tell me," said Lewis, and Whittaker told him. When he had finished, Lewis turned back to the window. This time, when he looked down he saw the picket fence in front of his house that he and Stanley had constructed together. There was no traffic on the street, and there were no people. The street lamp at the corner was on. Because of his son, they would never look the same again.

Then he remembered the little girl. He let the curtains and the drapes fall back into place. "The child. How is she?"

Whittaker sat down again; some of his control had returned. "She's all right, thank God. She's too innocent to understand, it but when she's older she . . ." Suddenly he began to cry, as though a dam had burst within him.

Lewis, for a moment, felt the stronger. "I must tell my wife," he said.

"No!" Whittaker reached out a hand. "Please. Not here. I can't bear it. It's enough that I had to tell you. Besides, we haven't finished. We must talk further."

"Further?" Lewis stared. "Is there more?"

"We must talk about what is to be done." Lewis was silent, and Whittaker could see that he did not yet understand. "Something will have to be done about your boy." Lewis felt a heavy weight on his chest. The shock was wearing off. The end of the world had come and gone and now reality must be faced. Yes. Something would have to be done about Stanley.

"I must tell you that my wife is ready to press charges. The boy could go to prison, you know. At least reform school."

Oh God, thought Lewis. He needed Adelaide's strength.

"I don't want to do it and I won't if you can think of another solution," Whittaker said quietly. "But the boy will have to be sent away. You can't allow him to mix with . . . with decent people. It's not fair to other children. For all we know it may have happened before. Certainly it will happen again, and he would not likely get a second chance. Next time it could be worse."

Lewis sat down in his chair, his knees giving away. He buried his face in his hands. Once again, Whittaker touched Lewis's shoulder. "Talk it over with your wife," he said, "and let me know tomorrow what you decide. I promise you that my wife and I will do nothing until then."

Whittaker took his leave, retrieved his hat in the front hall and closed the door quietly behind him.

CHAPTER FOUR

Punishment

Lewis remained alone for several minutes. He tried to pray and was conscious that he was not very good at it. He had never quite got on to confiding in God and yet he told himself that he believed in God's existence. Now God was unreachable when Lewis needed Him. He gave up, went to the door of the parlour and called downstairs to his wife.

Adelaide was almost finished with the dishes. Julia was still pounding out scales, and Lilas was sitting on the sideboard by the kitchen sink, drying dishes and singing "Je suis Titania," a rather elaborate aria. When Adelaide heard Lewis call between Lilas's cadenzas, she smiled, undid her apron, hung it up and went upstairs, assuming the gentlemen would be wanting their tea.

When she saw that Lewis was alone and observed the expression on his face, she knew that tea was not the answer. She entered the room, closing the door behind her. Whatever was wrong, the children must not hear of it.

"What is it?"

He drew her into the room and then began to sob, dry, terrible sobs, sounds she had never before heard him make, while he held her.

She drew herself to her full height, reaching up to put both arms around him. "All right now," she said firmly. "Tell me what has happened."

He sat her down in the chair where Whittaker had been, and then knelt before her, looking up at her, never taking his eyes from her face. He told her, as simply as possible, the story Whittaker had told him.

She was silent for almost longer than he could bear. Two bright red spots had appeared on her pale cheeks, and her blue eyes flashed with anger. "What will people say?" she whispered. "We'll be disgraced forever."

It was something that had not occurred to him.

"Addie, dear. Think of the boy."

She was on her feet then, almost pushing him out of the way. "'Think of the boy!' He's a bad, wicked boy! How can he do this to us after we brought him up so well? I always thought there was something wrong with him. I told you how I worried about him. Now I know what it is—he's evil. He's a . . . Can you imagine what everyone in Victoria will say? Our son is a fiend!"

Lewis sank back on his heels as his wife swept past him. Before he could stand, she was out of the door and running across the hall to Stanley's room. She flung the door open with such force that the doorknob put a permanent dent in the striped wallpaper.

Stanley was sitting at his desk doing his homework. His mother was upon him in a moment, turning him around with her left hand grasping his shoulder, while with her right hand she slapped him across the face with all her considerable strength, knocking him against the desk, sending his glasses flying, spilling the ink and sending books and papers to the floor.

"You evil boy!" she screamed. "You've ruined us all! You've disgraced your family. Your sisters will never be able to hold up their heads again. You've finished us!"

"Adelaide!" Lewis shouted as he came into the room, raising his voice for perhaps the first time in his life. "Stop it! He's just a boy!"

She let go of Stanley and turned on him; he was stunned by the look in her eyes. "'Just a boy? Just a boy?' He's a demon, that's what he is—a sex fiend. He should be thrashed within an inch of his life."

Stanley sat on the chair watching the ink slowly dripping across the edge of the desk onto the floor, staining the green carpet. He felt sick. Something was wrong with his mouth—it was warm inside. He touched it with his hand, saw the blood, stood up and then the room began to get darker.

Lewis caught his son just as he fell, and carried him the few steps to the bed. He looked down and saw that the boy was not only unconscious but as white as marble.

"My God," said Lewis. "You may have killed him."

Adelaide stood with her back to the desk. "If I have, he's better off dead than to live like this."

From downstairs, Julia was calling, "What's wrong, Mama? What's happened?"

The sound of her daughter's voice brought Adelaide to a quieter level. "The girls must never know about this. They'd better stay over at Miss Cooke's tonight. We'll tell them that Stanley has taken ill and it may be contagious."

Lewis stared at her. How could his wife be like this? Yet without her, he knew he would not have been able to cope at all. Lewis sat beside his son, holding one of the boy's hands. He felt he did not know his son at all, and wondered if he had ever really understood anybody.

Alone in her room at the end of the hall, Adelaide was still in a rage. Why should such a thing happen to decent people like her and Lewis? They had a good life and they had been good to others. Now this. She wondered if Stanley had "bad blood" in him, but if so, from whom? Her fury was such that she wanted to scream, to break the long mirror standing in the corner of the room. If she could not kill her son with her bare hands, she must do something. On her night table stood a wooden robin that Stanley had carved out of driftwood and given to her as a birthday present. She picked it up and flung it against the wall. If it did not break, she thought, it would burn.

She looked down at the bird and was surprised to find that there were tears streaming down her cheeks. She took a fresh handkerchief from the box on her dresser, picked up the wooden bird and sat with it in her hand while she composed herself, as time ticked away on the little pink French marble clock she had brought with her from New York so long ago.

Stanley came around after a while, his eyelids fluttering strangely. Lewis took off the boy's shoes and socks, pulled the covers up around him, poured some brandy into a glass and offered it to his son. Stanley declined. Then Lewis poured more into the glass and drank it himself.

Stanley looked at his father but said nothing, and Lewis couldn't find any words either. Soon Stanley closed his eyes and went into a deep sleep.

Lewis sat beside him all night. The boy did not stir. Lewis went through his whole life during those long hours: his childhood in Cornwall, crossing the Atlantic, meeting Adelaide in San Francisco, their wedding and finally the happy times in Victoria with Adelaide and the three children. The musical evenings, the walks on Dallas Road and in Beacon Hill Park—oh, the park. His retrospective came to an end. The park would never be the same to him. He would never again go into it.

At last he sat up straight in the chair, finished the brandy and realized it was for him to decide what would become of his son. The boy could not go to prison nor to reform school. He must keep the Whittakers from pressing charges and he must act quickly to prevent them. Yet there could be no escaping the fact that their lives would all change. He understood that Stanley could no longer continue to live in Victoria.

At sunrise he left Stanley, went to his bedroom and lay down beside Adelaide, who was on her side, staring at the wall, her eyes wide, her mouth still set. They did not speak. Lewis slept for a while. When he awoke, he thought he had a solution: he would call his friend Sveinn Arnason.

🐦 🐦 🐦

The next morning, Victoria and the rest of the world went about their business, and so did Adelaide Godolphin. One could not put aside Saturday-morning shopping because one's son had committed an unspeakable crime. It was all the more important that she dress well, hold her head up and make an appearance in the street. She served breakfast for Lewis and herself, making each move with care and deliberation, lest the fact that she had not slept at all betray her in some way. "I shall take the girls shopping as usual. It's better this way. Then no one will think there's anything wrong."

Lewis shook his head. "You had better let Julia stay home. Take Lilas with you, but Julia should stay here."

She stared at him as if he were totally incompetent. "Are you crazy? Leave her with him? What are you talking about?"

"I have to go to work, and I must also make arrangements to take care of Stanley."

She was so accustomed to making the important decisions about their activities that she was silent, surprised both that he had a plan and at the firm manner in which he spoke.

"I'm going to telephone Sveinn Arnason and ask him if he'll give the boy a job in one of his logging camps up-island."

"Why should he? Arnason's a decent man. Why should he be responsible for someone like . . ." She could not bring herself to utter her son's name.

"Would you prefer that the boy go to prison?" His voice was cold.

"Do you think the Whittakers will permit him to do otherwise?"

Lewis pushed back his chair. "Yes, if I handle it immediately. That's why I must make the call today. We can't leave the boy alone, so I think Julia should stay here."

"What can I tell her? Last night I said it might be meningitis and that it could be infectious. How can I bring her back today?"

"You had better think of something else to tell her. He'll probably sleep all the time anyway. But someone must stay in the house with him."

She could think of no other solution. For the first time in their marriage, Lewis left the house without kissing her goodbye.

Shortly after noon, Lewis left Macauley's and went to the Empress Hotel. There had been more rain in the early morning, and the streets were still wet. The chill off the water made him turn up his coat collar and hurry his pace. He could dwell no longer on his son; he could only act to resolve the problem. He must get the boy out of town, away from Victoria and everyone who knew them. Stanley was young, but boys younger than he worked in logging camps and in the coal mines of Nanaimo. Lewis himself had worked in the tin mines of Cornwall when he was twelve. Perhaps the experience could save Stanley, in more ways than one. It could strengthen him physically, being out of doors and working with his hands. In that isolated location, he would meet a new breed of people, who could open up new worlds to him.

Inside the Empress, it seemed as if warmth and safety rose to meet him. The magnificent Edwardian lobby was crowded with well-dressed people; the string trio was playing for the luncheon guests. The feeling of well-being, of security, of an ordered society struck him, and he felt as though he had no right to be in these surroundings. He thought that everyone who saw him must know immediately that he was the father of someone who would have no place in a society such as this—ever.

He gave the operator at the desk the number of the Arnason Inne on Arnason Island, then went to wait in the anteroom for his call to come through. Two other gentlemen in the room were making long-distance calls. Both were businessmen who spoke in crisp tones, loudly discussing stock purchases and contracts, to make sure that their points were clearly heard.

Lewis picked up the receiver of his designated telephone and heard Anna Arnason Aalgaard. She had a lovely voice, even over the poor connection. The speech training she had received at school in London did not entirely obliterate her natural Icelandic inflections.

"My dear Mr. Godolphin!" exclaimed Anna, as though they were the best of friends, although they had not met more than twice. "What a nice surprise to hear your voice. I'm sorry that dear Papa isn't here right now. He's in Victoria and won't be back until Monday morning. May I take a message?"

"Is there any place I can reach him in Victoria? It's very important that I speak with him today."

"Oh, I'm sure that's not a problem, Mr. Godolphin. Papa is staying at the Empress. Why don't you go over and see him there?"

Lewis thanked her and managed to politely discontinue the conversation. He returned to the operator's desk, paid for his call and went to the desk clerk to ask for Sveinn Arnason.

Sveinn sat in his luxurious suite on the third floor of the Empress and poured a whisky for Lewis, who took it, but after the first sip realized that Mr. Macauley would be sure to notice that he had been drinking on a workday. He would have to make up a good story before he returned from his lunch hour.

Sveinn was sixty-three and handsome, with thick blond hair blending attractively with the grey, heavy with the years and the comforts that his life had brought him. He was an imposing man, and now his jovial good nature focused on Lewis with sympathy.

They had met when Sveinn began to order furniture from Macauley's for one of his hostelries. He liked the tall, bearded Cornishman with the face and disposition of an artist, a man so very different from himself. Privately, Sveinn thought that Lewis might have done better for himself than to continue working for old Macauley, but he realized Lewis was not an aggressive man, nor an ambitious one. It was not Sveinn's way, and he thanked God for that. His life had brought him grief, but it had also brought him his wonderful daughter, Anna, a fine grandson, and much wealth.

Lewis told Sveinn only that his son had gotten into some trouble over a girl, and that the girl's family might cause trouble unless the boy was sent away. He could think of no other solution than to ask Sveinn if he could give his son a job as far away as possible.

Sveinn poured himself another drink and smiled.

"You Victorians! You're all such innocents. If every boy in this town who got into some trouble over a girl was sent away, half the male population would disappear!"

Lewis did not reply, and Sveinn saw that there was some deep hurt that would not be revealed. He offered another drink, but Lewis declined.

"I could take him over to the Inne. Anna could always use extra help, with Albert away at boarding school. What would you think of that?"

Lewis shook his head. Arnason Island, lying just a few hours away off the east coast of Vancouver Island, was still too close. "I was thinking of one of your northern camps. It would be good for the boy. I'm sure he'd work out well."

"I've a new camp that just opened up at Winter Harbour. We could use him there. I don't know how strong the lad is. It's not an easy life."

"I think, if you agree, that we should try it." Lewis was feeling the whisky now, but it was not helping, only aggravating his sense of loss and depression.

"All right. Put him on the *Princess Maquinna* on Monday night. I'll see that the captain keeps an eye on him. He'll have a good trip. The *Maquinna*'s a fine ship. He'll need a good pair of work boots. And tell his mother to see that he has lots of warm clothes."

They shook hands and Lewis went back to work, wondering how to explain the whisky on his breath.

ᗕ ᗕ ᗕ

There was no musical evening at the Godolphins' that Sunday. Adelaide broke her own rule about working on the Sabbath and decided to wash the kitchen floor so, she said, it would be clean for Monday. As always, there was no point in anyone questioning her actions. Lewis spent most of his time alone in the upstairs parlour, smoking cigars, staring at nothing.

On Saturday evening, he had gone into the room for the first time since the previous night, and had seen his stamp collection on the small table, untouched since he was interrupted by Gordon Whittaker. He closed the stamp album, took it over to one of the drawers under the oak bookcase and shoved it as far back in the drawer as possible, as though the album was somehow touched by evil. He never took it out again.

Julia slept both nights at Miss Cooke's, where Lilas was now firmly ensconced, thoroughly enjoying herself, despite her claimed conviction that her brother was dying. She regaled Miss Cooke with endless chatter and sang as long as her little voice held out.

On Saturday, however, Julia was told that she must stay in the house while her father was at work and her mother and Lilas went shopping.

"Your brother's still sick, but Dr. Muddsley said it's not catching. Don't go up to him, though, unless he calls, and he most likely won't," Adelaide said.

"What's wrong with him?"

"We don't know. Don't ask me any more questions. Practise the piano until Lilas and I get back."

Julia was not afraid of becoming sick. She had heard her mother's voice that fateful Friday night and it was not the voice she used when children were ill. Something else was wrong, and she worried about her brother.

Just once Julia went upstairs in the silent house, more carefully than she had ever done before, conscious of her tendency to be clumsy. She walked on tiptoe. The door of her brother's room was open; he was lying on his bed, his body facing the wall. She looked around and saw that his schoolbooks were on the floor and there was a great blue stain on the green carpet. It was unlike her mother to leave any room in the house in an untidy condition.

"Stanley?" she whispered.

He did not answer.

Satisfied that he was asleep, Julia went cautiously downstairs again and back to the piano.

On Monday evening, Lewis went to his son's room and awakened him. He did not know that Julia was next door and had stepped into the hallway so she could hear. Stanley sat up in bed, blinking at the light, as though he were in a strange place. "What is it, Dad? What's the matter?"

Lewis relaxed a little. Then he remembered what he had to do, and the weight in his chest returned.

He must explain to his son the enormity of his crime. Into his mind came a memory of an incident from his childhood in Cornwall, how a man had raped a child and then bashed her head in with a rock. The miners had tracked him down and hanged him on the nearest tree after beating him almost to death. Everyone agreed that the man deserved it.

"Stanley," Lewis said, his throat dry, "we're going to have to send you away."

There was no answer, no expression of fear, only a perplexed frown.

"Now this may turn out to be a good thing for you, son. We all pray that it will. I'm sending you up-island to work in a logging camp—one of Sveinn Arnason's. He's a good man, and if you work hard and don't . . ." The words were sticking in his throat now. "Don't do anything but work hard. That's all you can do now."

"I don't understand. Why must I go away? What's happened?"

"It's because of . . . little Amy Whittaker. What you did in the park."

Lewis was now more ashamed for himself than for his son. Why couldn't he look the boy in the eye and discuss this wretched thing? But he knew he could not.

"Oh, that," Stanley said simply. "I didn't think she would tell."

Lewis winced. "Of course she told. She's just a young child."

Something that was almost a smile appeared on Stanley's face.

"That's something that must only happen between adults, Stanley. Married adults, and very privately."

"I'm sorry," Stanley said. "I didn't . . ." He could not find any words.

Too late, his father found his. "You didn't understand. And that's my fault. I never explained. I couldn't explain. And I too am very sorry. But you molested that girl, and you must never, ever do that again."

Julia stood alone in the hall. She was heartsick. She did not entirely understand the word *molest*, except that it was a terrible thing to do, but she also couldn't imagine her brother doing anything cruel or evil. In that moment, she felt very much a child. Then she heard Lewis and Stanley rising, and went downstairs, where she was supposed to be helping her mother with some sewing in the den. She paused in the parlour, though, and watched as her father and brother came down the stairs. Stanley wore his heavy brown coat and cap, and the woollen muffler she had knitted for him as a gift last Christmas. He looked pale. Then she saw the battered suitcase her father carried.

"Stanley," she said, "where are your glasses?"

Father and son looked at her and then at each other. They had both forgotten the glasses, still lying in fragments on the floor of his room.

"I'll have them repaired and sent to you," said Lewis. There was no indication that Stanley heard him. His face was blank.

"Where are you going?" Julia asked.

Lewis looked away from his daughter, put a hand on Stanley's shoulder and guided him out the front door to the porch. They were on the path, almost to the picket fence, when they heard her voice.

"Stanley!"

She stood in the doorway, silhouetted by the light in the hallway, a slim, fair-haired schoolgirl in a dark blue dress.

"Stanley," she called into the night. "I'll miss you."

Lewis felt a tremor go through his son's body as though it were in his own. The boy was looking back at his sister, and for the first time since Friday night, it was as if a light had gone on inside him and he was alive again. He raised his gloved hand weakly and waved. Then he looked up at his father and nodded, as though giving him the signal to continue. They walked away toward the harbour in silence.

Julia closed the door and went back into the hall. She was sure she would never see her brother again, and she was furious at her parents, her mother in particular, for keeping the truth from her. She had never experienced such emotion before. She felt certain that what was happening was wrong, that her brother had been unfairly judged. She would never, she told herself, do such a thing to another person.

Then she saw her mother staring at her. There was wonder, anger and frustration on Adelaide's tense, white face. Only for a moment did she look at Julia. Then she returned to the den, slamming the door behind her.

CHAPTER FIVE

Passage

Publicity material for the *Princess Maquinna* proclaimed that she was named for the daughter of a powerful Nootka chieftain. Though there had been irregular service by boat to the west coast of Vancouver Island in the past, it was only recently that the British Columbia government and the Canadian Pacific Railway considered there were enough thriving villages, logging camps and canneries to make a regular service profitable.

The *Princess Maquinna* was instantly popular. It was considered daring to make the "West Coast Tour" for those who had no economic reason to do so. Every ten days the *Maquinna* left the Belleville Street dock in the Inner Harbour at eleven o'clock on a journey that would take her to Port Alice on the northwest coast of Vancouver Island and back to Victoria in seven days, making twenty-six scheduled stops and, weather permitting, occasional unscheduled ones.

As visitors were allowed on the ship until five minutes before sailing, Lewis boarded with Stanley and met Captain Gillan and the first officer, both of whom greeted them with the utmost courtesy. Captain Gillan was a big, bearded, jovial man who welcomed each passenger coming up the gangplank. Officers stood at the foot of the gangplank and on deck to assist the ladies. Besides the captain and first officer, there was a white-uniformed stewardess to look after the children and render any other necessary assistance.

The night was cold and moonless, but the ship glowed with rows of lights across her bow and along each deck. Inside, there were more bright lights and a string quartet playing lively selections from *The Pirates of Penzance*.

The *Princess Maquinna* was no simple ferry, but an impressive steamer, elegantly equipped to give the highest standard of service to the ladies and gentlemen on board. The table linen, china and glassware were worthy of the finest homes. All meals, including afternoon tea and midnight supper, were included in the price of passage. Musicians performed two concerts each day, during tea and dinner, and at shipboard dances.

There were close to a hundred passengers on board. Some were adventurous Victorians who wanted to see the famed wild west coast, so different from the scenery on the CPR routes to Vancouver and Seattle through the sheltered waters east of the island. Many passengers were visiting relatives who were brave enough to live in isolated villages, working as missionaries, lighthouse keepers and postmasters or in general stores. There were also merchants aboard to supervise the loading and delivery of supplies to canneries, logging camps and small settlements. A few passengers were prospectors, convinced that gold could be found if only one looked hard enough. There were also a dozen or so Chinese and Indians aboard, headed for work in the mills and canneries. They were not allowed to purchase staterooms but bedded down on the floor of the second-class lounge, wrapped in their own blankets, and ate their meals only after the other passengers had eaten.

Inside the main lounge there was a festive air. For Lewis, looking down at his son's white face, the weight in his chest seemed heavier than ever. He scanned the other passengers to see if there was anyone he recognized or who would recognize him. The thing Adelaide feared most was that their secret would be discovered, despite their agreement that they would inform everyone that Stanley was being sent north for his health. The Whittakers, he knew, would never mention the subject. Mr. Whittaker had declared his satisfaction that the boy was being sent away and had persuaded his wife, with some difficulty, to accept the situation. He had already decided, however, to sell his business and move to Vancouver. They would never, he told Lewis, feel comfortable in Victoria again.

Lewis saw a few vaguely familiar faces, people who at one time or another had been to Macauley's, but no one with whom he was really acquainted.

The second officer approached. "Captain Gillan told me you are the young man going to work for Sveinn Arnason. Congratulations!" He extended his hand to Stanley with such sincere enthusiasm that a ray of colour crept into the boy's cheeks, and for a few moments Lewis felt the tightness in his chest ease.

"We thought you'd probably like some company on your trip, so we've put you in with one of our crew, a nice young fellow, not much older than yourself, I should think. He's a midshipman, and something of a character. I think you two will get along fine."

The ship's whistle blasted through the night, startling everyone and causing a few children to cry. It was the warning signal for all visitors to depart. Lewis hesitated, then impulsively seized Stanley and hugged him. He wanted to kiss him, but he could not. Instead, he fumbled in the pocket of his overcoat and brought out a crisp, new Dominion of Canada five-dollar bill. He pressed it into the boy's hand.

"Write to me," he said huskily. "Better send the letters to Macauley's. You know the address?"

Stanley nodded, the old bewildered look crossing his face again. He stood in the lounge, surrounded by the milling crowd, and watched as his father went out to the deck and hurriedly left the ship.

Lewis stood on the dock, watching the bright lights and hearing the music and the cheerful voices as the *Princess Maquinna* slipped her moorings and glided slowly away from the wharf. He had never understood the term *broken-hearted* thinking that it was only found in women's novels. Now he knew what it meant. He leaned against a wooden shed and wept.

≈ ≈ ≈

The second officer touched Stanley's arm. "I'll show you to your cabin, lad. Then when you've put your gear away, come up and have some supper. Ours is the best on any CPR ship." Once they got to Stanley's cabin, the officer reminded him not to forget his key. "The dining room's on B deck aft. You'll see the directions right enough. When you get there, ask for me, Officer Petersen."

Stanley entered and found himself in an inside cabin on C deck. It was a small, hot room, with an upper and lower bunk, two folding seats, a wardrobe, a washstand with a pitcher and basin, and a chamber pot tucked away in underneath. He put down his suitcase and noticed that there was a knapsack lying on the lower bunk. Before he left, he looked at himself in the mirror and thought he appeared different, his facial features somehow exaggerated.

The midnight supper was luxurious. A wonderful chandelier hung in the centre of the room. There were two long buffet tables on the starboard side, heaped with food: cold salmon, roast beef and turkey. For dessert, there was fruit salad, chocolate cake, crème caramel and raisin pie.

Stanley stared at the table, fascinated, and his mind focused. He knew it was Monday night. Tomorrow was a school day. He wouldn't miss it. There was little to miss except his father. He regretted the shame he had brought on him for an offence he still did not fully understand. Then he remembered Julia. She had said she'd miss him, and as he left she had looked at him with affection and longing that truly moved him. He would miss Julia very much.

He calmed down and looked at the food again, this time with interest. He had scarcely eaten for days. He took a plate and filled it with everything the table had to offer.

Stanley poured himself a glass of juice and was immediately met by a short, greasy-haired, freckled youth in uniform who was helping the stewards serve the food. "Hey, you the Cornish bloke?" Stanley hesitated. "Godolphin—that you? That's a Cornish nyme, y'know. Me'n' you are cabinmytes, did y'know?" Stanley shook his head. He could see Officer Petersen waving to him, indicating his place, and was glad to join the table.

The string quartet had now switched from Gilbert and Sullivan to Strauss and "Tales of the Vienna Woods," hoping to inspire a peaceful late supper and a feeling of security. They would soon leave the Strait of Juan de Fuca and enter the treacherous open seas of the west coast, navigating a stretch of water that was becoming known as the Graveyard of the Pacific.

It was the rule on board that officers would sit with the passengers. Beside Stanley was banker Matthew Burman. Also at Officer Petersen's table were a middle-aged couple who had been missionaries in China and two young American men headed for Tahsis in search of gold. Despite the officer's attempts at sociability, there was little conversation at the table. Stanley ate heartily at last.

At 1:30, he returned to his cabin. His cabin mate was reclining on the lower berth, smoking a cigarette and wearing striped pyjamas, an article of clothing that Stanley had never seen before. He had not realized that men wore anything other than nightshirts to bed.

"You blokes sure get all the chow. Us working bastards just get wot's left over." Stanley did not respond. "Well, don't stand there. Myke yerself comf'table and tell me wot it's all about." Stanley continued to stand in the centre of the room, not sure what was expected of him. He had already used the lavatory down the corridor, knowing he could never use the cabin's chamber pot, at least not in the presence of another person. Now he had to undress in a strange room with this strange boy, who continued to stare at him unblinkingly.

"Is it true? Yew're goin' to work for Sveinn Arnason?"

Stanley nodded. He did not know why, but apparently there was some kind of importance attached to the Arnason name.

The boy whistled. "'E's some toff, that one. I seen him. E's been aboard 'ere a few times. Big rich Swede, 'e is."

"My dad said he's Icelandic."

"Syme thing." The boy proffered a crumpled pack of cigarettes. Stanley shook his head.

"Me nyme's Reggie. Wot's yours?"

"Stanley."

Reggie looked at him. "Figgers. Well, this 'ere Sveinn Arnason is rich. Stinkin' bloody rich. He gyve me two bits one time. Not bad for a Swede." He lay back on his bunk and began to blow smoke rings upward. The vessel lurched occasionally, and the small airless cabin was filling with smoke. Stanley stood very still, feeling faintly sick.

Reggie went to the cabinet, drew out the chamber pot and from it produced a small bottle of whisky. "'Ere, have a swig. This'll put 'air on yer chest." He laughed and took a long drink from the bottle. "An' from the looks of ya, ya'll need it."

Despite the boy's speech and appearance, Stanley noticed Reggie's crooked yellow teeth when he laughed, there was something engaging about him, a cheerful optimism and interest that Stanley had not encountered before.

Stanley took the bottle and sniffed at it cautiously. He took a mouthful, and coughed. His natural politeness made him realize that if he were to share a cabin with this boy, he should co-operate as much as he could. He took another swallow and felt warmer inside and less apprehensive.

"Thanks, Reggie, thanks very much."

Reggie hastily retrieved the bottle. "Hey, y'got any shackle?"

"Any what?"

"Shackle, lolly, wot Americans call dough. Dunno what you call it— money, I reckon."

"I've got five dollars my father gave me. Why?"

"Never mind." He made a face at Stanley's ignorance. "Y'll probably need it." He put his cigarette out, drained the bottle and turned over in his bunk. "Put th' bleedin' light out, will ya?"

Stanley put out the light, undressed in the dark and climbed into the top bunk. He had not expected to sleep, but after he pushed into the cool, starched white sheets that held him as though he were in the grip of a straitjacket, he remembered no more.

Five hours out of Victoria, there was a loud blast from the horn as, having rounded Rocky Point, passed Race Rocks and almost cleared the Strait of Juan de Fuca, the vessel reached her first stop at Port Renfrew. Stanley woke up, and for a moment he had no idea where he was. Then he heard bells clanging, the ship shuddered and everything seemed to be in motion—chains rattled, footsteps scurried along passages, rough, unfamiliar voices shouted and heavy scraping sounds echoed from below.

He looked down and saw Reggie below him. "What is it?" he asked. "What's happening?"

Reggie had just used the chamber pot and was reaching for his uniform. "'Ello, don't get the wind up. It's only Port Renfrew. Nothin' to see 'ere, but we workin' blokes gotta earn our chow. You toffs can sleep in."

Stanley stared. "It sounded like . . . well, I thought maybe we were sinking."

Reggie shook his head, lit a cigarette, blew an impressive smoke ring and went out, slamming the cabin door.

Stanley lay back on his pillow and went to sleep once more. It was almost six o'clock when he woke again. The ship was pitching strongly. He slid out of his bunk and dressed with difficulty, as the ship's movement made it impossible to stand up and pull on his pants. He combed his hair, washed his face and went out on deck to meet whatever fate had in store.

The *Princess Maquinna* was alongside Clo-oose, a village facing directly onto the Pacific Ocean. Stanley climbed the stairs and went onto the deck, where crew members were hustling about on assorted unknown errands. He stood on the starboard side not far from the bow and saw the village in the first light of morning, the sun rising over the row of houses on the beach and the trees behind them. On the beach there were about twenty Indians and half a dozen white men, the Indians preparing to embark in canoes while the white men moved toward their rowboats.

The vessel gave a sudden, violent shudder, the engines increased their noise and Stanley became aware that they were turning. Perhaps the Indians on shore were dangerous and Captain Gillan had decided to retreat, Stanley thought, as he remembered his mother's dramatic tales of the savages of the west coast.

"You'll have a better view from the stern." The voice behind him was flat and detached. Stanley turned and saw Matthew Burman barely touching the handrail, looking toward the shore.

"What's happening? Are they going to attack us?"

Matthew rolled his eyes and smiled. "Come with me, boy. I'll show you a sight you've never seen before, and perhaps never will again."

They went to the stern as the vessel turned, churning the dark water, pushing determinedly against the heavy swell. When they arrived, the ship cut her engines and rode the waves, her stern toward the shore. "There," said Matthew. "Now we shall see a sight." Below them, the ship's freight doors opened, not far above sea level. Two dugout canoes and a rowboat had put out from shore, but the rowboat was no match for the canoes and turned back, while the canoes were paddled over the pitching surf toward the *Maquinna* as though they were part of it.

"They're going to sink!" gasped Stanley. He was afraid, as he had never experienced even the possibility of death.

"They never sink," said Matthew. "*We* might, if we were foolish enough to try it, but *they* won't. Do you see the old man in the stern of each canoe?

Watch how he handles the short paddle. He's the one who keeps them afloat. The boys with him are along to pick up the freight and to learn how to handle the craft, just as the old man learned from his father."

"Why did the captain turn the ship away from the shore?"

"Captain Gillan knows what he's doing, and he'd better, if the *Maquinna's* going to keep a regular run this winter. You see, if he hadn't, and we were broadside to the waves, one good roll would not only flood the hold but might smash the canoes against the ship. Believe me, it's happened. There've been plenty of fools who thought they could run a ship. But if they'd listened to the Indians in the first place, they'd have had no trouble. The Indians named this place 'Clo-oose,' which means 'safe landing,' and they meant it."

Matthew suddenly raised one hand, and Stanley saw the old Indian in the first dugout raise his own hand in reply.

"You know him?" He had never seen a white man wave to an Indian.

Matthew nodded. "I know them all." He looked down to where the crewmen of the *Princess Maquinna* were now tossing bales to the young Indians, who stood, balancing gracefully, in the canoe. "Watch how they time the action. You see how they balance? Each throw and catch must be coordinated exactly to the swells. See how the old man keeps control at all times?"

"They don't look like any Indians I ever saw."

"You probably haven't seen any but our poor Songhees. These are Nitinats. They're a different nation."

Stanley was mystified.

"The Songhees," Matthew sighed. "There won't be a dozen left in twenty years, the way we treat them. But these Coast Indians, there's hope for them, if we could only learn to leave them alone."

The old man in the first dugout turned the canoe, and it moved skilfully away on the dark blue waves to allow the next canoe to come alongside and receive its share. On shore, the white men and the Indian women and children waited to unload the bales from the first canoe. "Why are there white men on the beach?"

"A few white people live here. That big man by the canoe is Dave Logan. He runs the store here and he takes care of the mail and just about everything else. The Indians trust him. Captain Gillan told me that when there's fog here, all any vessel needs to do is give a blast and Dave stands on shore and yells back. Guides the ship with his voice. The Indians say that as long as they've got Dave, they don't need a foghorn. But this area's pretty hazardous in winter. I don't know if the *Maquinna* will be able to call regularly. None of the other coast ships could."

"How do they get supplies?"

"The ships put everything off at Port Renfrew, then the Indians pack it overland. But it's a slow business in winter. Christmas often doesn't come until late January."

"I wouldn't like that," said Stanley, and he could smell the tree and the warmth of his own home. He pulled the muffler that Julia had made for him more tightly around his neck.

"Most of us wouldn't care for it," said Matthew. "Too used to our creature comforts, our Victorian idea of civilization. But these people out here—well, Christmas may not come on time, but at least they know how to live." There was bitterness in his voice. The second canoe departed, the *Princess Maquinna* immediately engaged her engines again and began to nose back out to sea, and Matthew Burman turned and walked away.

After breakfast, Stanley went out on deck again. He remembered he had once wished he could run away to sea. He stood near the stern, watching the seagulls swarming near the galley, crying and fighting as the remains of breakfast were flung from the open portholes. Although he had little to do, the unfamiliar sights helped the day pass quickly.

At dinner that night, Stanley sat at the same table as before, this time with Chief Petty Officer MacTavish. Only the two Americans and Matthew Burman joined them. The missionaries did not appear; Mrs. Mackintosh, despite having crossed the Pacific to and from China, and before that from Scotland around the Horn to Victoria, was not a good sailor.

"She's been through a lot, that lady," the officer was saying. "She and her husband were caught in the Boxer Rebellion, you know. Did you notice the way she wears her hair?" Matthew Burman nodded and concentrated on his food. "The yellow bastards sliced off her right ear," said MacTavish, certain that this kind of anecdote would interest someone of Stanley's age. "So she wears her hair dressed very low over both ears, or where both ears were, so you won't see the hole on the right side."

Stanley's food was suddenly less appetizing, as his old horror of violence shook him. Matthew paid no attention, other than to frown as though his meat was not cooked to his taste.

The Americans were more attentive. "We should have gone in there and wiped out those Chinks altogether," said one. "Some of our navy boys were there and I'm told they blasted as many as they could."

MacTavish nodded. "She's a brave woman. Her husband's the new chaplain at a church up near Quatsino. She's got a beautiful singing voice, her husband says, so she'll do fine."

"Next thing that'll happen," said the American, "is that she'll be scalped by an Injun. Then what'll she do?"

Matthew Burman stopped eating, his fork poised halfway from his plate to his mouth, and his eyes flashed. Officer MacTavish changed the subject, addressing himself to Matthew. "I understand you've made this west coast trip many times before, sir, although this is your first trip on the *Maquinna*."

"That is correct," said Matthew, his voice cool.

"But you're a banker, are you not?"

Matthew twisted his roll into small sections, carefully buttering each morsel separately and eating one piece at a time between sentences. "Also correct, but I thank God I am able to make a trip such as this at least once a year. I have clients up the coast who depend on me to advise them. I can't find anyone else I trust or who cares to make the trip. Fortunately, it suits me. In fact, when I retire I intend to write a book about the history of the coast." He looked sharply at the Americans. "I am bound for Friendly Cove to see one of my oldest friends." Once again he paused. "The present Chief Maquinna."

The red-haired American stared. "You got an Injun for a friend?"

Matthew looked pleased. "Chief Maquinna is my client, and I give him whatever financial advice he requires and I am able to give."

"Didn't think Injuns owned anything, or had any money to invest."

"A man must live," said Matthew. "You'd be surprised."

"Chief Maquinna?" asked Stanley. "Is this ship named for him?"

"The Canadian Pacific, in a rare example of acknowledging the past of this place, gave the ship the Maquinna name. Some say it's named for his daughter, but I doubt they thought that much about it."

Having silenced the table, Matthew concentrated on his plate of roast beef, mashed potatoes, peas and carrots, which he dissected with concentrated precision, but then he spoke again, addressing one of the Americans. "To you, my friend, Chief Maquinna may be something less than a plain man in a poor Indian village. To me, he is a descendant of rulers who controlled a vast and powerful civilization for thousands of years, who showed grace and generosity when James Cook arrived, who held on to his land and his pride through three years of Spanish occupation."

"I didn't know there were ever Spanish people on the island," Stanley interrupted. "We didn't learn about them in school."

"Nor did you learn about Maquinna, I'm sure."

🐦 🐦 🐦

It was raining hard when the *Princess Maquinna* docked at Friendly Cove on Nootka Island. Everyone in the village was there on the wooden wharf that jutted out from the promontory, some with umbrellas, some with sou'westers and assorted headgear, some with newspapers on their heads, while others ignored the weather completely.

They were used to the rain. The coming of the *Princess Maquinna* in any weather was cause for a celebration. It meant supplies from Victoria: canned goods, sacks of flour, potatoes, clothing. There was very little grown on Nootka Island; the few attempts at farming had failed, and it was still essentially a maritime society. The sea otters were gone, the pilchards were extinct and the great whales were less numerous, but the salmon still ran, and along with lesser fish and marine life, they were sufficient to support the residents of the island. Some worked in the canneries and logging camps, at Tahsis or Muchalat, but the majority still fished for a living.

The current chief, who was a descendant of the great Maquinna and shared his venerable name, stood with his hands in the pockets of his black mackintosh, his collar up and his rain hat pulled as low on his head as he could manage to get it. He was a short, heavy man, with no distinctive qualities except his prominent cheekbones and something in the way he held his head.

Chief Maquinna had received little formal schooling himself, but he made sure that his sons regularly attended the mission school on the island, and they were well aware of their heritage. He had visited Victoria twice, and had helped to construct the famous sea serpent canoe *Heitl-hei-yachist*, which was more than forty feet long, with a beam of five feet, six inches. Eighteen of his men, sixteen paddlers and two steersmen, manned the canoe. He had sent Chief Atliu and his daughter, both from Nootka, with five others to appear with the canoe at the St. Louis World's Fair in 1906, so that all might know of the greatness that was still part of the coastal tradition. So impressive was the huge canoe that a rich American bought it and donated it to a museum in the United States.

Maquinna had done what he could to carry on the tradition of his people, but he was under no illusion that this land was still his. He and his people could survive only by co-operating with the newcomers, but survive he intended to do. He hoped for more jobs for his people, more money and the opportunity for better education. And for all that he desired these things for his sons, he wanted them most for his daughter, Sa-Sin.

Stanley, standing on the upper deck, saw her first as she ran along the beach toward the dock, as though she had heard the ship's whistle from a distance and was hurrying so as not to miss the arrival.

He had never seen anyone like her. She was wearing long black pants and a black mackintosh that reached to her knees, but the coat was flying open to reveal a brilliant red sweater. She was hatless and her long black hair hung loosely over her shoulders, while the rain, to which she seemed oblivious, streamed over her. She ran with a freedom Stanley had never witnessed before. Even in the rain, she seemed to dart over the rocky beach like a bird. As she neared the dock, she shouted and waved, looking upward toward the ship. Stanley saw that Matthew Burman was waving to her in return. So were many members of the crew.

"She's a beauty," Matthew said calmly. "Every year more so."

Stanley asked who she was.

"She's the present Princess Maquinna. Her name is Sa-Sin, the hummingbird. I think she's very well named, for the daughter of the great Maquinna who welcomed Captain Cook, but I understand that she wants to be called Elaine."

"That's not an Indian name, is it?"

Matthew chuckled drily. "I gave her a book of Tennyson's poems, and she picked the name up from it. She'll be heard from some day, that girl. She'll make sure of that. I'm thinking of having her come to Victoria to finish her education, if I can talk my wife into letting her board with us."

The banker had his suitcase and umbrella beside him, and patiently extended his hand. "Goodbye, young man. I hope you've learned some things on this trip that you'll remember. You'll be fine with any crew assembled by Sveinn Arnason. He's a good man. You might remember me to him when you see him up at Winter Harbour."

Matthew went down the gangplank to the dock.

At breakfast the next morning, Stanley felt tired and cross, having spent a restless night.

"Do white people ever marry Indians?" he said to the young officer at the table.

The Americans laughed. "You don't want to be no squaw-man," said one.

The officer came to Stanley's rescue but, like Matthew Burman, he was addressing the Americans. "The first governor of British Columbia, James Douglas, was married to a woman whose mother was Cree. Douglas himself was part black. His mother was a Creole. They were very happily married. I understand she had some problems with prejudice, but that didn't seem to hinder him much."

The American scoffed and shook his head.

🐦 🐦 🐦

That night, the *Princess Maquinna* was once again in open water. The wind was up and the ship tossed in the heavy seas.

Stanley awakened suddenly. He had been dreaming of Sa-Sin, the way she moved and laughed. He had imagined he was with her on the beach, but she broke away and ran, faster than he could ever hope to run. He watched her rushing toward the dock where there was a ship moored, and the crew were watching for her. It was to them she ran; she had forgotten about him. All at once the ugly, domineering face of Miss Oxenham, her diamond earrings dangling hypnotically, appeared in front of him. "All men," he could hear her deep, resonant voice vibrating in his mind, "are born evil." Then suddenly Amy was smiling at him, her head to one side. He sat up in bed, and for the first time he was genuinely seasick.

Stanley remained in his cabin most of the day. Officer Petersen brought him tea, and it was almost five o'clock before he dressed and went out on deck, alone. He could feel the salt spray stinging his face as he looked toward the dark coastline, the mountains already crested with the first snows of the season.

The following morning, the vessel rounded Cape Cook and headed toward the more sheltered waters of Quatsino Sound. Officer Petersen came to the cabin and told Stanley he had better pack and be ready to land. They'd go first to Winter Harbour, then his stop at the nearby Quatsino village.

While Stanley was carefully packing his belongings in his suitcase, Reggie came to the cabin. He was chewing on an enormous wad of gum, which made him even more difficult to understand than usual. Reggie thrust a small bottle into his hand. "A goin' awye present fer ya. Cheers 'n' all that."

Stanley felt a small twinge of regret at leaving his peculiar cabinmate. "Thank you, Reggie."

"That's awrite, myte. Jest yew watch out f'r them Injun gerls. Or mebbe they better watch out for yew, eh?" He jabbed Stanley in the ribs. "Keep yer pecker up!" Stanley decided that he would never go to England because he would not understand the language.

When he had finished packing, he went out on deck. He looked down and saw some Indians and a few white men on the dock. Although the Quatsino camp would hardly offer the luxury and hospitality he had found on the *Maquinna*, Stanley felt somehow he might be safe in this wild country. If he encountered such kindness as he had found from Officer Petersen, Mr. Burman and Reggie, he would return it by working hard and learning all he could. It was not until he unpacked his suitcase on his primitive new bunk that he realized the five dollars his father had given him was gone.

CHAPTER SIX

The Immigrant

Sveinn Arnason arrived in British Columbia from Iceland in 1871. He was twenty-one years old. As a boy, he had heard stories told by returning sailors of the exciting life in great countries that lay far from Iceland, and he had made up his mind before he was fifteen that the wild British colony on the Pacific Ocean, with its Indians, luxurious furs, giant trees, land for the taking and even its gold, should one day be his destination.

His father would not part with him until he turned twenty-one. Sveinn was frustrated by the wait, but he loved and respected his father. His mother was dead, and his younger brothers needed to be old enough to be of help to his father. But when his time came at last, there was a huge party in the small fishing village, and next morning, with a splitting headache, young Sveinn departed for England, where he boarded a sailing ship bound for the west coast of North America.

He was a handsome boy, tall, with huge shoulders, blond and blue-eyed. He had a cheerful, direct quality that charmed everyone, despite his evident shrewdness and ambition. He enjoyed the sea to the fullest, yet he knew it was not for him. Although he was a very able fisherman, he was determined to try other work, and he was practical in his thinking. There was something desperate in his shipmates' obsession over gold. Timber, on the other hand—surely that could be reliably lucrative. Thousands of gold-seekers would need places to stay. The idea fascinated him for, almost without knowing it, he was a natural builder.

His sailing vessel put in at Victoria in March of 1871. Although the gold rush of 1858 was long over, the town was still filled with settlers and fortune hunters. Under James Douglas's earlier governorship a stable society had been built, founded on the principles of Victorian law and morality, but the social pretensions of Victoria did not appeal to the young Icelander. This was not the wild country he was looking for.

Within a week he had found a small vessel about to circumnavigate Vancouver Island to carry supplies to isolated villages. Also on board were a surveyor interested in speculating in land, a doctor who made the trip twice a year to call at the villages, a missionary bound for Quatsino Sound and a half-dozen gold-seekers.

The vessel began with the outside run. Sveinn was fascinated by the wilderness, yet his practical nature saw little opportunity in it. The seas were too rough, the land would never yield to farming and the Indians were unfriendly. The circumnavigation of the island took almost a month, and by the end of the voyage he had made up his mind as to his destination. He returned to Victoria, found a small boat that plied the protected passage between Vancouver Island and the mainland and boarded it for the Comox Valley about halfway up the island's east coast.

In the early 1860s, settlement of the valley had been encouraged by James Douglas, who governed the colony of Vancouver Island until it merged with the colony of British Columbia in 1866. When Sveinn arrived, there was nascent agriculture, the promise of coal mining and a burgeoning logging industry.

Sveinn took a job in a logging camp, quickly excelled at the work and, unlike his fellow loggers, saved his money. Ships from Seattle sailed up the coast carrying liquor and prostitutes, and those ships took the loggers' money away.

The area's Coast Salish Indians had been savaged by smallpox a decade earlier, after years of suffering the raids of the more powerful Kwakiutl to the north, but some persisted, including the Comox people from whom the valley's name was taken. A few of the young Scandinavians were attracted to the Indian girls, and some even informally "married" them, but the clergymen would not legitimize these relationships. Rape of Indian women was not uncommon, and violence sometimes erupted when members of a victim's family tried vainly to demand some form of punishment.

Sveinn took no interest in these distractions. He was sometimes ridiculed for the monastic life he chose, but at the end of his first year he had saved enough to purchase a tract of land from the government, and he began to prompt envy and finally respect. He built a large house from the Douglas fir, red cedar and maple trees he felled himself, and showed great attention to detail, ordering curtains and carpets from suppliers in Victoria and San Francisco. No sooner had he moved in than he began to build still more rooms, which puzzled the community, until they realized that the young Icelander had built the valley's first hotel.

From the day it opened, anyone of means who arrived in the area stayed at the Arnason Inne—traders, speculators, government agents, clergymen and surveyors. Only the travelling prostitutes were unwelcome. The loggers found Sveinn's prices higher than they could afford, but at one end of the building a large room was soon appointed with a bar, tables and chairs and, finally, beer for the white men permitted to enter.

Sveinn purchased one of the first government licences to serve alcoholic beverages, which he imported from Victoria, and he was as strict in the management of the establishment as he was with his own life. Men soon found that Sveinn's cheerfulness was no sign of weakness.

At the beginning of his third year on Vancouver Island, in 1873, Sveinn wrote to his father, asking him to select a girl willing to come to the New World to be his wife. She must be Icelandic, preferably from his own village. She should be strong and good-natured, someone who would want a large family and be able to work hard. In return, Sveinn offered far more advantages than most young settlers. An innkeeper's wife would be an enviable position for a young girl.

It was November before he received his reply. A packet arrived from his father, containing letters from his own family, a letter from Gudrun Johannesdottir, the daughter of Johannes Holmfridson, and a miniature. It depicted a young girl, not beautiful, but with intelligent grey eyes, a small, turned-up nose, straight brown hair and the promise of a smile at the corners of her mouth. Her letter was neat and carefully worded, and she described herself with modesty. If Sveinn would accept her, she wrote, she would be happy to leave on the next available vessel.

Her picture and her letter delighted him almost equally; there were innocence and sincerity in both. His father praised Gudrun highly, and advised Sveinn that he could not do better anywhere in the world. Sveinn sent his letter of acceptance to Iceland on the same ship on which her letter had arrived.

In the summer of 1874, twenty-year-old Gudrun Johannesdottir arrived at Comox. She was the youngest of five children, the only girl, and grew up emulating her brothers. She wanted to make her father as proud of her as he was of his sons, and they were all in thrall to her remarkable smile. It seemed to start at the centre of her lips, the upper lip covering the lower for a moment, and then the corners lifting upward, until the little, even teeth showed and unexpected dimples appeared. It displayed such warmth and merriment that she was irresistible.

Gudrun remembered Sveinn and she was deeply flattered by the prospect of becoming the wife of a handsome innkeeper in this new land of British Columbia. When she arrived and looked from her ship at the crowd on the newly constructed Comox government wharf, she had no difficulty picking out the man she had come to marry. She waved eagerly and smiled.

The men around Sveinn were satisfied. Not a raving beauty, perhaps, but with a smile like that, all indications were that Sveinn was a lucky man.

He gave a shout, raced up the gangplank and on to the deck, scooped Gudrun up in his arms and carried her down to the wharf.

"Mr. Arnason," she said in her low, gentle voice, "please don't forget my dowry."

Sveinn laughed and sent one of his friends to board the ship and see to Gudrun's possessions, while he escorted her to the Arnason Inne.

Captain MacDermot married Sveinn and Gudrun in the front room of the Inne that night. He blessed them, drank a toast to them and immediately sailed under a full moon into Queen Charlotte Strait and around the northern tip of the island to begin the treacherous run down the west coast. On a reef off Nootka Island, in a storm, the vessel foundered and sank, with all hands lost.

🐟 🐟 🐟

It was a happy marriage for Sveinn and Gudrun. Gudrun won everyone's love and respect. She worked hard to ensure that the Inne's services were beyond reproach. Sveinn added a wing and lowered his prices so that he could offer reasonable terms to the loggers who often desperately needed accommodation. Gudrun could cook meals for two dozen men at a time and have them all asking for seconds. She sang as she washed the clothes and bedding. Before a year had passed she was able to tell Sveinn that by late next spring they would have a child.

During the long winter months, Gudrun often sat by the fire when her work was done, sewing a quilt for her baby. Sveinn had insisted she employ an Indian woman for some of the heavier chores, but it was difficult to keep her inactive. There was nothing to indicate any weakness or cause for concern.

The day before Gudrun gave birth, she stood on the slope behind the Inne. Wandah, her Indian helper, was hanging up the washing on the cord

77

that extended from the back porch to the nearby maple tree. The sun shone as Gudrun watched the white linen flapping in the wind and the robins moving across the yard, heard the crows' hoarse voices, saw an eagle circling above. She was radiant at the thought that their child would soon be born into this world.

They were returning to the Inne when Gudrun faltered, and Wandah helped her back, then ran to the home of the midwife, Lucy Fitz-Lacy, to seek her help. After Gudrun had been settled in a bed in a room near the water and linens of the kitchen, Lucy dispatched Wandah to the harbour to inform Sveinn that the time had come.

The bar was closed for the day, but Sveinn had promised free drinks for everyone the moment his child was born, so little knots of fishermen and loggers gathered to await the news. It was to be a long wait. The moon rose and fell, and the ship in the harbour sailed with the next morning's sun before the faint wail of the baby was heard.

At last Lucy came out of the room where she had remained for more than twenty-four hours. She looked very old. Sveinn was waiting as he had been for the whole time, without sleep. Lucy was brief. The baby was a girl. And Gudrun was dead.

There were no free drinks on that day in the spring of 1875. Only Sveinn Arnason drank, as he had never done before. He broke bottles against the bar. He eventually collapsed under a table, and when he awoke he drank again. He would speak to no one until Lucy marched into the room with a cup of thick coffee. Two days had passed since Gudrun's death. She had prepared the body for burial, and there was another matter.

"Mr. Arnason. Your daughter needs you."

Gudrun's funeral was held that afternoon. Everyone who could be there was present—whites and Indians, missionaries and sailors, loggers and fishermen. The day was as beautiful as the one on which she had entered the last test of her life. She was buried on the slope of the hill rising above the water, to one side of the Inne. Sveinn stood alone, in his Sunday suit, his head bowed not only in grief but in some measure of shame. That night he opened the saloon and kept his promise. Drinks were free, but Sveinn was not present.

The next morning Sveinn Arnason, in his best suit once again, appeared before the man who served as magistrate, postal inspector and defender of the law. Sveinn carried something that could have been a parcel, except that it was wrapped in a white shawl. The birth of his daughter needed to be recorded, and a baptism arranged, if possible in the Lutheran faith. She was to be named Anna, after his mother.

❧ ❧ ❧

Anna Arnason was ten. She had finished her chores, which meant washing the last of the dishes used by a dozen or more diners at the Inne. She helped Lucy and her father prepare the dinners, and served coffee while her father looked after the bar. An Indian woman employed to assist with the dishes had left the Inne, and Sveinn as yet had not found a replacement.

Anna did not care for the Indians; she did not see in them the virtues she admired in her father. Yet she objected to the disregard for human dignity she sometimes saw outside the Inne's doors. Drunken white loggers often treated their Indian "brides" with grave disrespect and fights occasionally took place in the street.

Perhaps it was the intensity of the noise that stirred her that fateful evening while she was doing the dishes. She pulled on her boots and winter coat, wrapped the red wool scarf that she had made herself around her throat and went out the Inne's back door to learn the cause of the shouting and cursing.

Not far away, where the village thinned out and the tall trees encroached, some white men were beating a small chap who looked completely defenceless and was screaming in a language that Anna could not understand. The men were holding him by his hair. At first she thought he was an Indian, but as she came closer she saw in the dim light that the

79

victim was a Chinese boy being held by his pigtail. The men were drunk, and she worried for his life as they kicked him.

"What did he do?" she cried. Running forward, she pushed one of the men who had not answered her. He shoved her away, knocking her to the ground.

She was accustomed to thinking of the whole village as belonging to her and her father, and she was furious. She scrambled to her feet, ran to the Inne and grabbed the rifle that was kept in a cupboard just inside the back door. Satisfied that it was properly loaded, she hurried back out to where the men were continuing their assault.

Anna raised the rifle and, as her father had taught her, pointed it into the air and pulled the trigger.

The men turned. The last thing they expected to see was a ten-year-old girl with a loaded rifle. "This Chink is a thief," one said, "and he's got to pay for it."

"You let that coolie go," ordered Anna, "or my next shot won't be over your head." She had heard Sveinn make that threat once when there was a fight outside the Inne, and she thought it sounded effective.

"He's a thief," the man repeated. "Now you run along to your mama."

Anna levelled the gun directly at his face.

"Give me the coolie and I'll let you go. If you don't, I'll shoot you, and nothing will happen to me because I'm a little girl and I'm Sveinn Arnason's daughter."

Fortunately, Sveinn had heard the shot and arrived just in time to hear his daughter's final threat. He took the gun from her tight grip. "All right," he said. "What's happening here?"

"Papa, these bastards were going to kill this poor coolie. I want them to give him to me."

"What could you possibly want with a coolie?"

Anna looked at him with an expression he could not resist. "We need the help."

This was how Anna Arnason, aged ten, won the undying devotion of Wong Lee, aged twenty-two, formerly of Canton, China, and from that point on a member of the Arnason family.

CHAPTER SEVEN

The Island

From the day Sveinn Arnason recognized that Gudrun was dead and Anna was alive, something changed in him. His ambition didn't wane, but his enthusiasm for it was tempered. Yet Sveinn was not bitter. He simply closed the pages of the book of Gudrun and devoted himself to the book of Anna. She was now first in his life, as assuredly as though she had been the first-born son in a dynasty.

Sveinn Arnason became a popular and successful figure in those early days of the island's history. Comox grew and prospered, and so did Sveinn. He bought land as far north as Campbell River and as far south as Nanaimo. He acquired the first logging camp he had worked for, and opened many others. He was careful to build as much as he could in these communities, so he could control and profit from their growth.

By the time Anna was twelve, Sveinn had ceased to be an innkeeper and devoted all of his attention to his land holdings. And to Anna. She would be his only child, for Sveinn had vowed never to marry again. They had their differences, for they were very much alike, particularly when it came to their stubbornness.

Anna was almost the image of her father. She was a big girl, blond, blue-eyed, beautiful and strong. She inherited only two characteristics from Gudrun. She loved to sing, and sing she did, as she was naturally cheerful. The other inheritance was the smile, which was exactly like her mother's, although in Gudrun it had lit up a merely plain face.

Lucy had become Anna's nurse and then the housekeeper for the Inne. When Anna adopted Wong Lee, he became and excelled as the cook. As Anna approached her teens, Sveinn began to worry about her future. He was already a rich man, but her education—at the mission school and through Lucy's tutoring—was not ideal. Sveinn sent her to school in Victoria for a year, but she disliked it to the point of open rebellion and was sent back to her father as "clever but unmanageable."

When Anna was fifteen Sveinn took her to England. On the journey, Anna walked the decks daily, making friends easily, while Sveinn, who liked work more than unfocused social activity, tended to stay in his stateroom. It hadn't helped that they had a major quarrel over Sveinn's insistence that Anna attend school in England for at least a year. "Papa, I do not wish to become a silly woman," she said firmly.

"No one is asking you to be silly! Only learn to act like a lady instead of a logger."

"There's nothing wrong with loggers." Anna's smile was not in evidence.

"That may be, but it's no way for a woman to behave if she wants a husband of honour and purpose."

For once, Sveinn had his way. After three weeks in London, they parted, both holding back their tears, and Sveinn returned to Vancouver Island alone.

Anna returned to the island just before her eighteenth birthday. She had acquired more poise and her speech was more carefully articulated, but she was the same Anna, warm-hearted and impulsive as ever.

When she returned, Sveinn suggested they move to Victoria, but Anna had different ideas. "It's not real, Papa," she declared. "It's just an imitation of London."

Fate, however, intervened, when Sveinn was returning from the town of Vancouver, having concluded a deal to sell lumber to a new yard in Burrard Inlet. He was on his own launch, a recent purchase he called the *Anna*, thirty-six feet long with a crew of three. They had crossed the Gulf of Georgia, but impending nightfall and rough weather obliged them to seek shelter in a natural harbour on a small island just south of Nanaimo.

They had no way of telling whether the island was inhabited. By dawn, the wind was down, but Sveinn's curiosity delayed them. He rowed to the beach and found a path that wound its way upward over rocky, moss-covered ground, below the smooth red bark of the arbutus trees that formed an arbor on the way to the crest of the hill.

He found himself on an open plateau with a view of a large and beautiful bay and the mountains of the mainland beyond. Turning west, he saw the gentler slopes of the southern part of Vancouver Island. To the north, the land rose above him, perhaps as high as two hundred feet.

Sveinn took what seemed to be a path up through the Douglas fir, hemlock and cedar, and when he came to its end he stopped, amazed, as he looked at a house such as he had never seen before. A sprawling, brown, mock-Tudor structure, with sandstone blocks at its foundation, and even some brick in unexpected places, stood before him. Its construction was a touch eccentric, but surely this was a place of some importance. Yet the signs of ruin and decay were everywhere. The place appeared deserted. What a marvellous place for an inn, Sveinn thought.

He walked slowly toward the front steps, looking about him, excited by the possibilities, feeling that the house had a meaning for him and for his daughter. As he approached, he was startled to see, seated alone on the vast veranda, a very old man, dressed in white, wearing a pith helmet and high boots. His thin hair might have been fair at one time, but now it sprang in wisps of grey from under his hat. He did not seem surprised at the sight of the big blond man emerging from the forest in front of the house.

"Ye're a Scot, I ken. And if ye're not, I'll not sell t'ye."

Sveinn paused, choosing his words carefully. "I'm not a Scot, I'm Icelandic, and I'm not interested in buying." Even as he said the words, he felt a sudden guilt. The moment he had seen the house, he knew he wanted it.

The old man's eyes narrowed. "I dinna believe it. Icelander, maybe. But ye'll be wantin' this place. Ye want it a'ready."

Sveinn was now standing at the top of the steps leading to the veranda. He could see the ghastly yellow-grey of the old man's face and the skin stretched tightly over the bones. He could have been a hundred years old.

"I was caught in the storm last night, and was lucky to find the cove down below. I don't even know what island this is."

"It's my island, laddie. It reminded me of Scotland. I bought it when old Sir James was in charge. There's a grand Scot for ye. I knew Guv'ner Douglas well."

"Are there other houses on the island?"

"Nay, the island's mine. And I won't be selling it to none of you Victoria property men."

"Do you live alone, then?"

There was silence as the old man rocked back and forth, watching Sveinn.

"How do you manage for food and supplies?"

"I manage. But I am not long for this world, so it dinna matter much."

Sveinn shook his head. They were both silent.

"Are ye married, mon?"

"My wife's dead," said Sveinn shortly.

"My wife died crossing the Atlantic to join me, so ye have me sympathy. Ye'll have sons, I should think?"

"One daughter. But she's worth a dozen sons."

The old man watched Sveinn and nodded, rocking rhythmically in his old chair. Finally he spoke. "Why wud ye bring a young lass to a deserted place like this? D'ye want to keep her all to yersel'?"

Sveinn looked back across the clearing in front of the ruined old house and out to the foam-flecked blue waters of the gulf. A pathway led from the front stairs down to the left to where the wide harbour lay.

"I would turn the house into an inn if I had it, and I would make this island famous for its hospitality."

The old man cackled. "Maybe there's Scots blood in ye somewhere. Ye're thinkin' o' makin' money, I can see. I'll be wishin' ye good day now, Mr. . . . Ye didna say yer name."

"Arnason. Sveinn Arnason. I live up in Comox." Sveinn held out his hand and took the Scot's bony fingers in his.

"I'm Ferguson. Jock Ferguson. And this is Ferguson's Isle. I'll nae see ye again, Mr. Arnason." He pronounced the name as though it were a Scottish one, rolling the "r" and drawing out the syllables. Before Sveinn could speak further, the old man rose, turned and went inside, closing the door firmly behind him.

The seas were flat when the launch pulled out of the narrow cove and headed north. An island—that was the answer. An island, close to Vancouver Island, with Vancouver across the Gulf of Georgia, and the American cities—Bellingham, Seattle, Olympia—to the south. Anna would be the hostess of a great old house, one with prestige, so the best people would be their guests, including young men of substance. He was visualizing the place he had just left refurbished, with tennis courts on the grounds, croquet and horseback riding, and down in the harbour there would be fishing trips and beach parties for the guests.

He tried to put it out of his mind, remembering that there were many other islands to be had. Besides, he had not consulted Anna. But he was convinced that their future lay in buying an island and turning it into the finest resort on the coast.

He had almost succeeded in forgetting about his plans, throwing himself deeper into the lumber business, closing deals and imagining new ones, visiting the small communities on the northern part of the island.

But three months later he received a letter from a Victoria law firm. Jock Ferguson had died and had left his island and all that was on it to Sveinn Arnason.

"I don't understand, Papa. What did you say to him?"

Sveinn had no answer. He had only told the truth—what he would do if the island were his. Yet something had passed between him and the old man, some unspoken sympathy, perhaps in the fact that they had both lost a loved one.

In June of 1895 the Arnason Inne on Arnason Island opened for business. Sveinn had worked for a year rebuilding the house. The original leaded-glass windows still faced the ocean and offered the view from the large, fir-beamed dining room. There were now fourteen bedrooms and four bathrooms, an enormous kitchen, a parlour, library, sunroom and excellent servants' quarters.

It would be many years before the Inne became a truly popular and profitable travel resort—Sveinn was occasionally too far ahead of his time—but he could afford to wait. However, the appointments and hospitality were such that visitors came from throughout the Pacific Northwest, for two-week vacations or for weekends, on yachts or passenger boats, and stories of the great fishing soon spread as far south as California.

CHAPTER EIGHT

The Sailor

Anna was happy at the Arnason Inne. She worked harder than anyone, perfecting every element, overseeing Wong and Lucy in the kitchen, enchanting the guests with her beauty and good nature. She was so capable that Sveinn was free to come and go as he wished. Whenever the opportunity arose, Sveinn invited the eligible young men he encountered on business trips to visit Arnason Island. Surely, one of these might find favour with his daughter.

One day in early March of 1898, the winds from the mainland blew heavily across the gulf, and just as Sveinn had once found shelter in the cove of the island, so did another sailor. Anna had seen the small craft bucking the heavy weather, but she lost sight of it as it disappeared around the point.

She and two boys who worked year-round at the Inne were preparing for the Easter vacationers in April when something compelled her to leave them suddenly and go to the front door. As she opened it, she saw a man coming up the road to the Inne. It was her first sight of Nels Aalgaard.

He was lean and lithe and hard-muscled, with keen, dark blue eyes, thick brown lashes, brown hair and a neat beard. It was a pleasant, handsome face. When he spoke, his voice was unexpectedly soft, with only the hint of a Swedish accent.

He had entered the Strait of Juan de Fuca aboard the steamer *Calcutta Merchant*, bound for Victoria from Shanghai. He had heard from other sailors about Vancouver Island and the many small islands crowded along its eastern shore. One poetic old Irishman he had met in a Macao bar had compared them to the Scilly Isles off the coast of England and had warned Nels not to go there. One look at those green islands, he whispered, and a man would become so enchanted he would stay forever.

Nels had read of the Greek hero Ulysses and the enchantress Circe, but he did not believe he would succumb to any lure. Certainly, he was no Ulysses, and if there were some local Circe—well, Nels knew how to handle women, and how to escape from them too. He had set his own pattern for his life and so far he had been true to it. He was twenty-four, and by the time he first saw the Pacific coast of North America, at Cape Flattery, he was more than halfway around the world. He intended to explore for a few months and then return to the China Seas. He could speak some Cantonese and was sure that there was a future there for him, in honest trade, with some smuggling on the side. He could not imagine a stable, peaceful existence and had so far made sure that such would not be his fate.

He finished his job with the *Calcutta Merchant* after he helped discharge her cargo of tea and rice in Victoria. He liked Victoria well enough, but after a week he met a shipbuilder who had a sailboat ready for delivery to Vancouver. It was the job Nels was looking for. He had his master's papers for small craft, and his easy charm and obvious understanding of the sea persuaded the shipbuilder that Nels was capable of delivering the yacht. He could cruise the islands on his way to the mainland and then look around Vancouver, perhaps ride the rails to the east on the Canadian Pacific Railway. It would not be the first time that he had travelled that way. He believed in never paying for a journey if he could do it on someone else's dollar.

He caught a glimpse of the Inne up on the headland while he was looking for shelter from the weather, and decided that he would do some exploring until the wind subsided. On the wide veranda, he saw Anna Arnason.

～ ～ ～

Sveinn returned the next day from a trip to Vancouver. His daughter came to the door to meet him, her eyes sparkling in a way he had not seen before. "Papa," she said, kissing him, "such a surprise. We have company." Behind her, Sveinn saw the young sailor and knew that whatever was to happen, he could not prevent it.

The three of them lunched together in the dining room, and Nels explained his arrival. The sun shone through the few remaining clouds, and though the alder trees were still bare, it could have been a day in May. "I was wondering," Nels asked softly, addressing himself to Sveinn, while his eyes kept straying to Anna, "if you could use an extra hand around here?"

"Nels has been halfway round the world!" said Anna rapturously. "He was telling me of his adventures last night. I almost didn't believe him. And Wong adores him because he can speak Chinese. You should have heard the two of them talking to each other."

Sveinn noted that the young man at least had the grace to look out the window, embarrassed at Anna's enthusiasm. He could hardly believe that Anna, so cool and level-headed, so swift to appraise suitors and find them wanting, should be chattering like a sheltered schoolgirl. Then he saw the sailor's own affection in the way he looked at his daughter.

"Won't you have to get that launch to Vancouver?"

Nels looked as though he had just remembered the purpose of his journey, then turned his dark blue eyes directly on Sveinn. "I could be back here within the week, I suspect. That is, if you'll consider hiring me."

"We really do need a gardener, Papa. You said just last week that we needed a man to improve the grounds this season."

Sveinn offered Nels work, and soon after his return he had to admit the young man could do just about everything. He was strong, good-natured, willing and courteous. Yet Sveinn was nervous: as long as Nels and Anna were together, his eyes never left her face, but when he looked below at the water and the waves, Sveinn saw another longing.

He's a sailor, thought Sveinn, and no woman, not even Anna, will keep him away from the sea. He could not bear the thought of Anna being unhappy, or that any man should have it in his power to reject her.

During the Easter vacation, Nels charmed the visitors, taking them fishing and hunting grouse, playing backgammon and pool. Nels was also an artist, although he insisted it was a hobby no sailor could afford. The next day, Anna ordered canvases and other supplies from Victoria. In what spare time he had, Nels began to paint a portrait of Anna. She wore the pale blue satin evening gown she had purchased at Worth's in Paris, her blond hair loose over her shoulders instead of pinned back in the usual chignon. There was an edging of white lace at her neck and wrists, and her only jewellery was a long strand of pearls that Sveinn had given her.

Before two weeks were out, with the painting not yet finished, Sveinn found them on a window seat in each other's arms.

That night, Nels joined Sveinn in the little den off the dining room that Sveinn had come to adopt as his own, and spoke of his feelings for Anna. "I can't explain it," he admitted. "I recognized this place as soon as I saw it. Perhaps I dreamed of it at some time because it was as if I had finally come home. And that was before I saw her. I thought I knew what I was doing with my life, but evidently there is a stronger force. I've never thought about a God before. Now, since I found this island, I'm thinking."

Sveinn knew about fate and his island. He looked at the young man, with his lean face and sea-blue eyes, the scar on his left cheek (the result of a fight in a bar in Dacca), the tattoo of the mermaid on his right forearm. He meant to stay, Sveinn believed, but intentions can change.

"She's a girl of strong feelings," said Sveinn. "Did she tell you how she acquired Wong?"

Nels nodded, smiling.

"If she's set her heart on you, then there's nothing I can do to stand in your way. But I won't see her hurt in any way. Remember that."

"I couldn't hurt her," Nels said simply. "I love her too much."

"What future do you see for yourself here?"

"I thought," the gentle voice was even quieter, as he looked beyond Sveinn, out the smaller window toward the sea. "I thought I'd buy a boat—just a small one—she needn't be more than a twenty-six footer. Well, the fish are there, and maybe we could sell to the canneries on Vancouver Island, or to the markets. That could supplement the Inne's income off-season. And Anna's been talking about putting in some guest cabins."

Anna and Nels were married in the garden during the first week of June. Sveinn gave his daughter away, although Anna thought she was bringing him his son. A Lutheran minister from Victoria performed the ceremony. Lucy had baked an enormous cake. There was tea and champagne, and the hundreds of guests included the first summer tourists, who were understandably delighted. Sveinn had insisted on formal attire for the bridal party, so Nels wore his first suit and waistcoat, ordered from Victoria, while Anna was magnificent in a white peau de soie dress and a lace veil, made in Paris and purchased in Vancouver.

Sveinn offered them a trip to Europe or at least to California as a wedding gift, but Anna and Nels declined it. So Sveinn, realizing that perhaps he was fortunate after all, gave his son-in-law a thirty-foot fishing boat, while he presented Anna with the deed to the island itself.

For Sveinn's forty-eighth birthday, Nels presented him with a landscape of the Inne, painted from the deck of his boat. Sveinn put it in a place of honour in his study.

By the end of the first year of their marriage, Anna had given birth to a son.

꙳ ꙳ ꙳

Albert Aalgaard squatted beside the water on his favourite ledge of rock, just above the treasures of his tide pool and a smooth stretch of sand where he sometimes napped in the late afternoon.

He was seven, and he knew how the natural world worked. It was almost six o'clock in the evening; he knew this because the sun was just above the arbutus trees to the northwest, just as he knew that in winter, if you could see the sun at all, it would disappear behind the mountain, as he called the hill near the Inne, sometime after four. In a few minutes his mother or Lucy would call him to come in to get cleaned up for dinner, which was a silly idea for already his hands were beautifully clean, washed by the water in the tide pool. Now that he thought about it, his clothes must be clean too, because they were very wet. Some splashing in the tide pool was necessary for his many important experiments, but the grown-ups never understood any of this.

He picked up the white sun hat that lay on the rocks and noticed it was wet too. He must have dropped it in the pool. He thought that the hat made him look foolish, but his mother insisted he wear it because of sunstroke, which had sounded rather exciting but wasn't, especially if you got so dizzy you threw up. He was really not sure which he hated most, the sunstroke or the sun hat. His father had promised to find him a real pith helmet—the kind men wore in India and China and Africa—next time he went to Victoria. He could hardly wait.

There. Lucy was calling, and he slowly got up. It had been a pretty good day, on the whole. He had seen seven purple starfish and two orange ones. His grandfather always gave him a penny for every purple one and two cents for an orange one on the condition that he did not try to pry their legs off the rocks with a stick. He considered saying that he had seen seven orange ones and two purple ones to collect sixteen cents, but there was nothing on the island on which to spend the money anyway.

He studied the cool water in the tide pool, thinking that he should have brought his toy boat. He must remember to bring it tomorrow. This would be a nice place to float it. Then he heard Lucy call more sharply. He reached down, skimmed his fingers across the still water, said goodbye to the invisible crab-king who presided over the pool, put the detested sun hat on his head and wandered up the hill to dinner.

As he went he started to think about what's important. He thought about the things his family had told him. It's important to come when you're called.

His grandfather had just talked to him about something important. He had always delighted in his father taking him in the horse and buggy to meet the passenger boats that came once a week in summer. The people who came to the Inne sometimes brought their children and he ran into trouble here, for he was inclined to let everyone know that this was "his" island and the visitors were paying for the privilege of visiting it and the opportunity to play with him. He was surprised at the anger of his parents when they heard of this. But after a chat with his grandfather, he thought he understood better.

The little unhappiness Albert had known was over a skinned knee, an upset stomach, a bad storm—the really bad ones came in November. His father explained that storms were part of life near the sea, part of a wonderful pattern of nature, sometimes terrifying, sometimes beautiful, but always a miracle.

He did not count the death of his baby sister as unhappiness. As he had never seen her, he could not feel the loss. He was only sorry for the grief of his grandfather and Lucy, who seemed to be the most upset. His mother and father were calmer. Grown-ups could be very mystifying.

Long before he lost that sister, while his mother was putting him to bed, she had told him there was to be a new baby. Anna had looked down at her son's face. The deep blue eyes were his father's, but the rest was hers, particularly that smile they had both inherited from Gudrun.

"Well now," said Anna, the way she spoke sometimes to guests who had made a complaint, moving her head carefully, "would you like a girl or a boy?"

Albert didn't have to think about that for long. "A girl." He did not want another boy around. Another boy to share his mother? Never.

Anna clapped her hands. "A girl. Why, that's exactly what I would like."

"Mother," he said, "Grandfather told me about where babies came from, but I would like to know what you think."

"Oh, he did?" Anna arched her brows and then smiled. "I might have known it. Well, whatever he said would be right. Grandfather knows everything."

"He told me about how the seeds get planted and that babies come out of the mother. Will this baby come out of you?"

"Indeed it will. I assume he told you that's how you got here. You didn't think the stork brought you, I hope."

"A stork?"

"You must understand, dear, that many children believe that the stork brings babies."

He did not understand. "Why would anyone believe that?"

"Because their parents tell them. Some parents, in fact many people, Albert dear, do not like to talk about their bodies."

He looked at hers admiringly. "Why not?"

She knew that her and her father's open views were not part of the Victorian mindset. Even her schooling in London, dominated by the most rigid moral views, had not persuaded her to change them. She had lived in a part of the world where there was no place for illusion.

"Well now, let's see," she said. "For many years, people have been very modest. That is, they hide the private parts of their bodies. You remember the day you came into the dining room without your clothes?"

He laughed. "People looked so funny."

"It wasn't funny to them, Albert. There are many people in the world who believe that it is right to hide not only their bodies but also what their bodies do. Your grandfather, your father and I happen to believe that such

95

matters are so beautiful that they should not be secrets, yet we must respect the ideas of people who are afraid, or let us say who do not believe such wonderful things should be talked about. You will have to be careful with whom you discuss personal matters. Do you understand?"

When it was time for his sister to come out of his mother, his father took him for a long walk along the edge of the ocean and told him that phosphorus in the water sometimes makes it dance with light as though there is moonlight coming up from below. After they returned to the Inne, Lucy came down the stairs very slowly. "The child's dead," she said and walked out to the veranda.

Nels glanced out toward the sea and then down at his son, who was holding his hand very tightly. "Let's go and see Mother."

Anna was very pale, her long golden hair tangled against her white gown. There were lines around her eyes that Albert had never seen before, but when she opened them and saw him, the magic happened. Her mouth pulled down at the centre, and then the curves began to move around the edges and gradually widened, her eyes brightened and her free hand stretched toward him.

"Albert, darling."

Albert went to her side with Nels, who bent down and kissed her gently on the forehead. "Albert, dear, I'm so sorry. She was such a wee little thing, just not strong enough to live in the big world. We shall make a pretty grave for her and bury her on the hill, with lots of flowers. Albert, dear . . . is that all right with you?"

CHAPTER NINE

The Great War

The first year of Stanley's absence was a depressing one for the Godolphins, each of whom reacted differently according to their natures. Lewis had aged, and might have easily passed for fifty rather than his forty-four years. Never a demonstrative man, he was quieter than ever, but he remained a kind and considerate husband and father and a conscientious worker. On weekends he took to walking alone along the ocean on Dallas Road. Adelaide was more tense and tight-lipped than before, sharper with the girls and Lewis, and spent even more time cleaning the house.

No one mentioned Stanley. Since the day Julia had stood in the doorway and watched her father and brother walk away, it was as if Stanley had ceased to exist. The day after his departure, dinner had been an unusually silent meal. Julia was on her way to her room when she looked in at her father, sitting in the upstairs parlour, smoking his cigar and staring into space. He looked very old.

"Father," she asked softly, "what's happened with Stanley—really?"

Lewis dropped some ash from his cigar on the carpet and immediately bent down to carefully retrieve it, using the edge of the *Colonist*. "I told you," he said shakily. "Your brother is ill. The doctor recommended an outdoor life for him, plenty of fresh air and exercise. He'll get all that up-island." He was not looking at her. Julia realized for the first time in her life that her father was lying. His distress was so plain that she was embarrassed for him, so she said no more, and went to her room, where she tried to concentrate on her homework.

Lilas was fascinated by the subject of her brother's absence. "Well, we know it isn't meningitis because if it was he'd be dead by now," she said that night as she sat on the edge of her bed opposite Julia. "And I happen to know it isn't TB because Marybeth Brodie in my class has a cousin who has TB and he got sent to Tranquille on the mainland and that's where all the TB people go and Stanley didn't go there. You know what I think?" She started to whisper. "There's a terrible incurable disease going around I heard about but you're not supposed to talk about so it must be very bad and it's called cancer."

"We'd better go to sleep," was all Julia could say.

Julia lay awake. Her gentle, awkward brother had done something so dreadful that he had to be sent away. But how dreadful could it be? She had looked up *molest* in the Funk & Wagnalls dictionary her father had bought from a door-to-door salesman. *Harass, trouble* and *vex* did not justify what had been done by her parents. She would talk to Katie, her best friend. Katie must know what had happened, but she hadn't been in school.

Within a week, Mr. Whittaker had put his business and his house up for sale. Mrs. Whittaker and the two girls had gone to Vancouver to stay with relatives until he joined them and they could begin a new life there. Julia got a letter from Katie. "Dear Julia," it read. "Well, you won't believe this! My father told us we are moving to Vancouver because he's got a big new job. I am already here and it's such a busy new city. I'm so excited, although Amy said she doesn't want us to go. She said the sweetest thing, you wouldn't believe it, she said she will miss Stanley. I'm so sorry I didn't get to see you before we left. I look forward to seeing you someday soon so I can show you our new home. Ever your best friend, Katie."

Julia wrote a letter in reply, but she was afraid to ask about Amy. Her mother insisted she'd mailed the letter, but Julia didn't believe her, and she never heard from Katie again.

If Stanley had done something to upset Amy, why would she miss him? There were no clues at school. Stanley had been such an outcast that his absence was barely noticed, and never discussed. At home, Adelaide devoted herself to her daughters as though Stanley had never existed. Julia, in turn, worked harder than ever at school and at the piano. At night, however, alone in bed with her own thoughts, she frequently wondered how Stanley was doing. She knew that if he had done wrong, he also had been wronged, and she promised herself that she would find more kindness in her heart than she saw in her mother's.

The war was also quite disturbing to Julia. The boys they knew, such as Harry Burman, did not come home for Christmas in 1914, and by the following year it was plain that those who survived would not return soon.

Julia's mother obsessed over the news, pored over maps, disparaged the generals. During the harsh battle of Ypres, which involved the Canadian expeditionary force, she would send Lilas after school down to the office of the *Victoria Times* to see if any familiar names were on the casualty lists posted in front of the building.

One of the most famed war cartoons of the day featured gallant little Belgium, depicted as a slim young woman with her back against a wall, facing a gigantic, florid-faced, bulging-necked bully in a spiked helmet with an enormous gun and a bayonet.

Lilas showed it to her sister. "I heard the Germans in Belgium are killing babies and girls and women, and worse," she said. "What's worse?"

Julia just sighed.

On May 8, 1915, came the sinking of the *Lusitania,* and rumours spread through Victoria that some local Germans had secretly celebrated the sinking. A German beer garden and brewery was vandalized, and someone broke the windows at Brenner's Candy Store.

"Poor Mrs. Brenner," said Lewis sadly. "She must have been terrified."

"Once a German, always a German," Adelaide said, serving the vegetables.

🐦 🐦 🐦

In the fall of 1915, Sa-Sin, the hummingbird, the descendant of Maquinna, Lord of the Moachats, who had welcomed James Cook, arrived in Victoria to stay with Matthew and Doris Burman in their Simcoe Street home.

Doris opposed the idea, but she had never seen Matthew so determined. He had made the arrangements with the girl's father without consulting her at all.

"We can't have an Indian living in the house," she told him over Sunday dinner, which they ate in the early afternoon after church. "What will people say?"

"What does it matter what people say?"

"That's so like you. You never consider our position."

"We're not claiming the girl as a relative," he stated in his usual dry fashion, picking away with his fork at his lemon pie. "We're merely helping her to a decent education. Outside of school, she'll work for you. You said just the other day you wanted another maid."

"So I do. But I never dreamed of having an Indian. They're not to be trusted."

"If I remember correctly, that little Irish girl we had last year departed with my gold cufflinks and your wristwatch," Matthew observed.

Doris winced. She disliked uncomplimentary references to the Irish.

"Besides," he continued, "her ancestors ruled a good part of Vancouver Island while ours were plowing potatoes back in the old country. The girl's a princess."

100

"Rubbish. That doesn't count anymore, even if it were true. These days an Indian is an Indian."

He looked at her with such a scathing expression that she ceased her attack and took a second helping of lemon pie. He would have his own way, she could see, and she would have to make the best of it somehow.

"Very well." She poured his tea. "I shall fix up the little room off the kitchen for her. I was using it as a sewing room, but I guess I can do my sewing elsewhere."

"What's the matter with the guest room?"

"The guest room! Really, Matthew! How can you expect me to put an Indian in our guest room?"

"Well, I don't want to make any extra work for you."

"It won't be much trouble to ready the back room, and it would be perfectly suitable, being off the kitchen. The guest room indeed! I can imagine what Harry would say to that when he comes home."

For a few moments they both fell silent. There had been no letters from Harry for more than a month, and the Canadian forces were being deployed more regularly in major battles. He had survived Ypres, but now the situation had worsened. She could not imagine the possibility of anything happening to Harry. He would be all right. He was much too sensible to let anything happen to him. Matthew was not so certain.

A few days later, another argument arose over the girl's name.

"Sa-Sin!" cried Doris. "What kind of an outlandish name is that?"

"It means hummingbird."

"Ridiculous!"

"Her brothers always call her Princess," Matthew said, with obvious relish at his wife's discomfort.

"Well, I'm not going to call any housemaid of mine Princess. Surely she must have some kind of English name. I thought they all did."

"Elaine," he said quietly.

"What?"

"Elaine. As in 'The Lady of Shallot.' Surely you remember your Tennyson?" He knew quite well that her education had never embraced anything in that category, but that she would never admit it.

"Of course," she said shortly. "But it hardly seems a suitable name for a maid. Why can't she call herself Mary or Mabel the way most of them do?"

"Because," he spoke quietly but the edge had returned to his voice, "her name is Elaine."

So the sixteen-year-old Nootka princess became a maid in the home of the Burmans. She attended Victoria High School during the week for grade eleven, while after school and on weekends she stayed busy with her homework and her household chores.

Doris and Elaine did not get off to a particularly happy start. Doris was most upset by the girl's appearance. She had expected a plump, plain girl and was disturbed by the obvious grace and poise of her new maid. As for Elaine, she had never enjoyed being with women, even her mother, and from childhood she had preferred the company of her father and brothers.

"How is she working out?" Matthew inquired at the end of the first week.

"All right," said Doris reluctantly. "She keeps herself clean, I'll say that for her, but I had to show her how to make her bed properly, and she has no idea of table manners at all. She's a regular savage in that respect."

"Well, the idea is she's here to get an education. I imagine manners could be included in that category." He picked up the *Colonist* and was about to begin his evening reading when he said suddenly, "She certainly is a beauty."

Doris was genuinely shocked. A man of Matthew's age and position referring to a young girl, and a young Indian girl at that, as beautiful was indecent. "*Some* types of men might find her attractive. We shall have to keep an eye on her." She was so angry she left the room and went to the kitchen where she spoke sharply to Elaine about not having finished the dinner dishes.

Elaine was indifferent to the reprimand. Since her arrival in Victoria, she had thrown up a shell around her personality. She did as she was told, without comment, methodically, and at her own pace. She was respectful to Doris, but without warmth. With Matthew, she was more open but still lacked the buoyancy of spirit she had possessed at Nootka.

For Elaine, her stay in Victoria was an exile. She respected her father's insistence that this education would serve her well, with all the changes and doubts that had come upon them. But even as a young girl, she had seen "education" begin to pull her community's families apart. She was angry that her position of privilege at home should bring her in Victoria a role as a second-class maid. Yet her father had insisted that she come, and her own curiosity did temper her anger. She was as smart as she was beautiful. She believed Matthew Burman's interest in her family and her people was genuine, but she found some of his questions peculiarly naïve. She was herself fascinated by this world, so close to but so different from her own.

Matthew understood some of this, and part of him regretted what he thought of as the "caging of the wild hummingbird," but he never discussed these issues with Elaine. She was, as he had hoped, an excellent student, and he focused on that satisfaction. Sometimes, in the evenings, he would attempt to draw her out, endeavouring to discover how much of her native history she knew, what tales might have been told by a grandparent, but he was looking for different stories than the ones she knew, and he would end up telling her about the great days when Maquinna was Lord of the Coast.

Julia Godolphin first saw Elaine on the opening day of school in September 1915. The two sat in the same class across the aisle from each other, and Julia was impressed by the girl's loveliness. There were a few other students of mixed blood in the school, but they formed their own circle. This girl was different. On the first day, most of the girls wore bright new dresses. Elaine wore a plain grey cardigan sweater and black pleated skirt, yet she drew more looks from the boys than any of the other girls did. There were no jibes directed at her such as the other Indians had to bear. There was a dignity about Elaine, and she wore it like armour.

CHAPTER TEN

The Dream

In the winter of 1916, the war continued with no end in sight. Canadians died by the thousands. More and more men were being called up; the number of volunteers had begun to decrease as the fierce battles and huge casualties were reported. Two hundred and fifty thousand men were needed, but only one hundred and sixty thousand had enlisted, and one hundred and twenty thousand of those had joined during the first six months when the fervour was at its peak. After a bitter struggle in Parliament, Prime Minister Robert Borden was forced to seek the conscription that his government had hoped to avoid. The war was no great adventure; it had quickly become an appalling reality.

At the Godolphin home, Adelaide fretted over Woodrow Wilson's cautious approach to any American entry into the conflict. "Believe me, if Teddy Roosevelt was in the White House today, America would have joined us and the war would be over. Sometimes I wonder if Wilson isn't pro-German."

Julia's days were filled with schoolwork, knitting and her piano lessons, which persisted even in such difficult times. Actually, the war had improved Canada's economy; the shipyards in Victoria flourished, and Macauley's Furniture thrived. Macauley had made Lewis assistant manager.

One evening after dinner, with the dishes done and Adelaide finishing up her work in the kitchen, Julia sat down at the piano in the living room to accompany her sister, as both girls were to perform in the school's Christmas concert. Julia was to play Chopin's "Marche Militaire," while Lilas was to sing "Una Voce Poco Fa" and "Kiss Me Again," accompanied by Julia.

They were in the middle of the latter number when there was a knock at the front door. Lilas broke off and ran to answer it. She opened the door and found herself speechless, perhaps for the first time in anyone's memory. The visitor was Albert Aalgaard, whom Lilas would describe to her friends as the most gorgeous young man she had ever seen.

Albert was not quite eighteen, very much like his mother, yet with his father's lean, lithe build and graceful movements. Yes, his eyes were the roving dark blue of Nels's, but the smile was unmistakably Anna's. To Lilas, he was the embodiment of the heroes in the magazine stories she loved, in his grey flannel trousers and navy blue coat with the crest of his private school on the pocket.

"I'm terribly sorry if I interrupted your recital," he said, introducing himself and flashing his beautiful smile directly at her. "You sing delightfully. You know, I was tempted to just stand here on the porch and listen, but my grandfather, Sveinn Arnason, asked me to come and pay my respects to your father and give him a message."

Lilas blinked her eyes several times and opened the door with a flourish. "Do come in, please. Papa will be so delighted to see you." She used the merest touch of a mid-European accent. "He is in the upstairs parlour."

"Julia! You will never guess who this is. It's Albert Aalgaard to see Papa."

"I see you don't remember our first meeting," Albert said to Julia. "But I certainly won't forget it. It was at a garden party at Blenheim Oaks and you fell in the fish pond—or at least fell against it."

Julia blushed, not only at the reminder of her awkwardness but at the manner in which Albert was looking at her. His quick glance took in every line of her young, slim body. Lilas also noticed Albert's appraisal of her sister. "Imagine you remembering that. Julia was so gauche that day. I nearly died of embarrassment for her, but then we were all just children."

"And now, naturally, we are all grown up," he countered. Lilas tossed her hair and flounced back into the living room, leaving Julia to take Albert upstairs to their father.

Lewis was equally surprised by his visitor, and the old fear clutched at his chest at the thought that the boy might be the bearer of bad news.

"First off," said Albert settling himself comfortably in the chair opposite Lewis, "my grandfather inquired after your health and said he hoped everything was going well for you at Macauley's."

"That's very kind of him. Please thank him. My wife and daughters are fine, and business is very good."

"Your daughters are *extremely* pretty. Do you mind if I smoke, sir?"

"Not at all," said Lewis.

Albert drew a slim gold case from his pocket, along with a matching lighter. "A little present, from me to me," he said, noticing Lewis's glance. "Your wife doesn't mind smoking?"

"Fortunately not, and our guests are always welcome to a cigarette, but only up here."

"It's about the same at our place, except when we have guests at the Inne who smoke and there's nothing we can do about that. Father smokes all the time."

"Is your father in the service?"

"He's a volunteer with the Coast Guard along the Pacific Coast. I think he really wanted to get back into merchant shipping, but the Atlantic run is pretty dangerous with the Jerry U-boats out there, you know, so Mother and Grandfather insisted he stay as close to home as possible."

"And what are your plans?"

"Well, I'll be eighteen next month so that pretty much decides it for me. I'm hoping it'll be the navy. I rather fancy the air force, but Mother doesn't like that idea at all."

Lewis nodded, relaxing at the young man's easy manner, although he found him remarkably mature for his years.

"Now," said Albert, "enough about my family. Grandfather sent me here specifically to report on your son. We've had to close down the Quatsino camp. It's next to impossible to get experienced men, with the war still taking them. The Indians can do some of the work, but not a job that requires much knowledge or experience."

Lewis wondered if this meant that Stanley, who had been away for three years, was being sent back to them. He knew Adelaide would never accept that.

"So Grandfather asked me to get your permission to let Stanley come and work for us on Arnason Island. We really need him, you know, since Dad is out with the Coast Guard and the two boys we had were called up this fall. We need someone to help around the Inne, meet the guests when vacation time comes, and work on the grounds. Grandfather says your son is good at that—working with nature, I mean. I think Mother would like him from what I hear, and believe me, that's what counts around our place. So, what do you say?"

The weight lifted from Lewis. Stanley would be closer to home, close enough that he would be able to visit him sometime, and at the Inne he would be among fine people. But new weight descended. There would be guests at the Inne—families, with children.

"Don't you approve, sir?"

Lewis recovered his composure. "Of course, of course. I couldn't be more pleased. And I'm most grateful to your grandfather. Please tell him so."

"I will." Albert was on his feet, holding out his hand. "I'll tell him you approve and Grandfather will send to Quatsino for him at once. I really must take my leave now. It's been such a pleasure having this visit with you."

At the door of the room, Albert stopped. "Please don't trouble to come downstairs, sir. Enjoy your cigar. I'm sure your daughters will see me out and I'd like to call again whenever I'm free, if I may."

"You'd be most welcome."

"Oh, and in the spring perhaps you and your wife would like to come to the Inne as our guests. Mother would want that, I know. And be sure and bring your daughters too."

At the door, he took Julia's hand. "Your father said I might call again. I'm so glad, because I scarcely know any pretty girls in Victoria."

He was gone, and Julia was sure she would never be the same again. She was in love.

❦ ❦ ❦

It was June and Julia was seventeen when she and Albert went on their first official date. Albert had called at the house on two occasions. On the second visit, Adelaide had served him tea, although she instinctively mistrusted and disliked him. "Natural maternal protectiveness," Albert decided. Adelaide could find no excuse, however, to deny his request to take Julia to afternoon tea at the Empress Hotel.

Now at last, Julia was seated at a table in the lobby, that enormous white and gold room, filled, as part of the afternoon ritual, with tea tables covered in crisp, snowy linen. There was the white and gold china, and the soft clinking of cups and saucers could be heard along with the equally discreet murmur of well-spoken voices, as the staff brought the tea, the crumpets and the "Empress cake" to each table. The string trio played sprightly music, which on this afternoon seemed to consist of only the most romantic selections by Offenbach, Oscar Strauss and Rudolf Friml.

Julia wore her newest dress, picked out for her by her mother at Spencer's and given to her for her last birthday. It was a silk dress of pale blue, which Adelaide had long ago decreed to be "Julia's colour." Her honey-blond hair was tied back with a blue velvet ribbon and crowned with a straw boater decorated with another blue ribbon.

Julia was observing the cleft in Albert's chin and the sudden creases that came when he smiled. "What are you thinking of?" asked Albert. She blushed. "Didn't you know that since the outbreak of war, girls have stopped blushing?"

She shook her head, but her colour deepened.

"I'm sorry. I've made it worse. Personally, I think blushing is charming—this whole 'new woman' thing they're talking about is ridiculous. And now they've got women voting! It's all wrong."

Something stirred within her, a faint anger. Her own mother approved of voting and women's rights. How odd that Albert, with his youth and air of sophistication, did not.

"Don't worry," he said, leaning across the table, his eyes twinkling as though he were oblivious to her discomfort. "It's been proven to be absolutely impossible to seduce a girl while she's having tea, especially in the Empress lobby. You're safe for now."

Julia tried to smile as though she understood, but she was unsure exactly what the word *seduce* meant. Somehow she must change the subject. "I remember," she said carefully, "that time when I first saw your mother, at the garden party. She had a white parasol with the most wonderful frilled edging all around it. I'd never seen one like it. I never saw one again either."

"Mother knows how to dress to please herself. She never follows any fashion, but she always manages to look marvellous. Mind you," he said, frowning, "there's a limit to eccentric fashion." He jerked his head in the direction of two elderly ladies sitting at the table next to them. Both were dressed in a style dating back to before the turn of the century. One wore a brown cut-velvet tea gown and a turbaned hat with an enormous emerald surrounded by tufts of peacock feathers set directly in the centre. The other wore a hat with a feathered bird perched on the broad brim and a dress of heavy brocaded grey silk with cream lace at the high collar and at her wrists.

"I wonder what would happen if that bird should suddenly take off. What havoc he'd create!"

"Oh, Albert! That's old Mrs. Hoskins, the one with the bird. She's terribly rich."

"Julia, darling, I don't want to *know* about them. I just want the bird to fly off her hat and skim over the cake and crumpets and maybe light on that old codger's bald head over there."

It was apparent that Albert did not share her romantic view of the Empress, yet he was so amusing and delightful and handsome that whatever he said was all right with her. She began to eat her crumpet, very cautiously, so that the butter would not drip over the side.

The trio was playing selections from *The Merry Widow* and the romantic strains of the waltz entranced her. Where would her relationship with Albert go? Would he one day take her hand and ask to marry her, as the heroes did in books and motion pictures? Or tell her he must speak to her father?

Then she remembered that her brother worked for his family. As she picked up her tea cup, she imagined this would somehow doom their romance, and her hand began to shake. Albert saw this and touched her shoulder.

"Oh, Albert, I'm sorry."

"Don't apologize, please." He was looking intently at her now. He paused for the longest time. "I think I'm in love with you."

He smiled then, and she looked at him, and felt that she could deny him nothing. Today, at least, there was only tea.

🙢 🙢 🙢

Albert had just begun his naval training when the war ended. Victoria celebrated with an Armistice Day Parade, yet it was a time of mixed blessings. The death toll was tragic; the physical injuries were appalling. Those who came home unscathed seemed somehow changed. The full price of the war had not yet been paid, nor was it even recognized during the time of rejoicing.

Eleanor Trevor's husband, George II, did not return to their home at Blenheim Oaks. Eleanor honoured him as a hero, and became totally devoted to their younger son, Georgie.

Harry Burman returned, "safe and sound" as his mother put it, with a shrapnel wound in his left shoulder, a medal for valour and elevation to the rank of lieutenant. He was also, to the astonishment of his parents, engaged to be married. He had met a young Irish nurse, Kathleen Ryerson, in France. Kathleen had returned to Dublin to visit her few relatives—her parents were dead—and prepare for her journey to Canada. She would not arrive until spring.

But it was Christmas, the first peaceful Christmas in four long years, and Doris was determined that Harry should be suitably hailed by all their friends. They would have a homecoming party to honour Harry and announce his engagement.

Matthew was not convinced, but Doris had her heart set on it. "We owe it to Harry," she said, "and to our position in Victoria. The boy's a hero. Think what it will mean to your customers to have a war hero in the bank!"

Matthew nodded his approval, resigned to what he obviously could not prevent.

CHAPTER ELEVEN

Home

Harry Burman's family home was exactly as it had been when he left it more than four years ago. The two-storey wooden house, painted dark brown with a weathered shingled roof, the single chimney against the east wall, seemed to stand in a world where there had never been a war. There was snow on the ground, but the front walk was neatly shovelled and he wondered who had done it, as that had always been his job. The entrance hall was as gloomy as ever. The only difference was that the small room off the kitchen was home to a new maid. In the past they had always had maids by the day and this was the first time that another person had lived in the house.

The first afternoon of his return, Harry sat in the living room, across the fireplace from his mother, exactly as they had always done, she to regale him with her gossip, he to listen. His father was in his study with his books. Saturday was a day Matthew was accustomed to having to himself.

Doris was telling him about marriages and petty scandals. Harry did not talk about the war. He had determined that the war was over for him, as well as for the rest of the world, and he would put it out of his mind forever. Only by doing this, he was convinced, could he be assured of a successful future and true happiness.

Then he saw Elaine.

She had come in by the back door as always, and placed the groceries on the kitchen table. Doris heard her and called out, "Elaine, you must come and meet my son." She came to the door, still in her plain long brown coat, a black shawl thrown back from her head and resting on her shoulders. It was snowing lightly outside and a few flakes remained on her black hair, which she wore in two thick, long braids.

Harry knew that his mother had an Indian maid. She had mentioned the fact with some disdain in her letters to him. He knew that the girl was some sort of chief's daughter from the west coast of the island, and that his father had made an agreement to give the girl a decent education in return for her working in the house. Harry did not share his father's interest in Indians, and he expected Elaine would confirm his low expectations of them.

Yet when Harry looked at Elaine he was instantly consumed by a lust he had never experienced before. The dark living room with its heavy mahogany furniture, the small fire in the fireplace, simply disappeared. The sight of this beautiful girl—taller than any Indian he had ever seen, with her high cheekbones, full lips and startling eyes, the very way in which she had turned her head to look at him—stunned him.

"Harry, this is Elaine. Elaine, this is Lieutenant Burman. I'm sure I told you in my letters, Harry, that she's been quite a help to me."

There was not the slightest flicker of acknowledgment in Elaine's eyes. As far as she was concerned, Harry was just another Burman. Even Matthew she now took for granted. She simply endured them. She saw the way Harry Burman looked at her and recognized the expression, but she did not care. She had seen the same look in the eyes of many men.

Harry was at a complete loss. One didn't shake hands with a maid, nor with an Indian. He stood up, turned to the mantel and took a cigarette from the box, lighting it with shaking fingers. He forced himself to say, "Hello, Elaine" and concentrated on his cigarette.

Elaine said, "How do you do," flatly, took off her coat and hung it in the hall closet, along with her shawl, and went back to the kitchen to unpack the groceries.

🐦 🐦 🐦

The party took place one week later. There were red and green paper streamers and red and green paper Christmas bells, hung in chains across the deep green drapes in the living room. Doris had done most of the decorating herself, even to the Christmas tree in the hall. She had thought Elaine might have some ideas as to the trimming of the tree and arranging the streamers. Indians were thought to like bright colours, she had heard, but the girl simply did what she was told and nothing else. Doris decided this was just as well. A forward Indian would not have been comfortable to have around the house. At least the girl was quiet.

Doris had splurged, as she called it, and bought herself a new dress. It was a rose taffeta from Spencer's, designed to diminish some of the bulk that the years seemed to be adding to her figure. She had even bought a dress for Elaine: a maid's uniform, suitable for formal occasions, black, with a starched collar. Any servant would have been proud to wear it, but Elaine said nothing. Really, the girl was not the least bit grateful for all she and Matthew had done for her. It was as if she still did not understand her place in civilized life.

Harry stood in his room, looking at his reflection in the mirror while he carefully adjusted his bow tie. He had grown a neat dark moustache and combed his hair forward to hide the fact that his hairline was beginning to recede. He made certain that no fleck of dandruff appeared on his shoulders. But he felt deeply uncomfortable. He looked around at the room he had occupied since his childhood, with its forest green rug and the neat white bedspread on the simple four-poster bed. Even the bookcase contained the same books: *The Last of the Mohicans*, a *Boy's Own Annual*, a few history books and his Catholic missal.

Nothing had changed. Except him. He had been a virgin in 1914 and had had his first encounter with sex when he went with a group of soldiers on leave to a Paris brothel. The woman he encountered was not young, and not especially attractive, but she was kind. When the young Canadian private failed to accomplish the purpose of his visit, she said it was natural, given the tensions of the war. Many men who came to her were like this. Harry had few doubts about his manhood. He was, he told himself, repulsed by the squalor of the room, the cheap perfume and his belief that she was not clean.

His first active experience came in 1916, again with an older French woman, the wife of a councilman in a small French town where the Canadian regiment was quartered. If she did not provide all the enchantment he had dreamed of, she at least taught Harry what was necessary for him to feel confident.

He met Kathleen in 1917, when he was in the field hospital after suffering the shrapnel wound. She was with a medical unit nearby and often visited the hospital tent, passing all the beds and greeting everyone with her warm smile and perhaps a joke. She was an attractive girl, with short brown hair, a turned-up nose and a charming voice with an Irish lilt that delighted the men. Harry Burman was not the only soldier who waited for her visits.

Her ease was all on the surface. She pretended not to be horrified at the sight of men whose faces had been horribly scarred, whose limbs had been lost. She focused all her energies on the patients' feelings, not on her own. Her parents had been killed in a housefire before the war, and she smiled gently when she told Harry about them, saying only that they were "happy now, for they are with God." She was a devout Catholic, and her sense of morality was as deep as all her other emotions.

She responded to Harry's marked attention very cautiously at first, knowing that wounded soldiers had a way of becoming attracted to young nurses, but as she learned that Harry was as serious about life as she was, that he was also a Catholic, with a desire for a home and family, she began to respond. When he told her about Victoria, so far away, and the respect he had for his parents, she was convinced that this was what God had intended for her—to get as far away as possible from the war, and from Ireland.

After the first cautious kiss, she was even more positive. Here was a good-looking young man, Catholic, of obviously high moral principles, with a solid future as a banker. What more could she ask for? They pledged their engagement, and Harry felt he could hardly wait to meet her in Victoria. He had done well.

Then he met Elaine. He could not fathom what had happened. He felt possessed. Perhaps this was some post-war sickness. A few more days and it would lift and he would be free. He went downstairs.

The party was getting off to a good start, Doris thought, not realizing that many of the younger guests had dreaded it because of the Burmans' reputation for being "deadly dull." Nevertheless, it was the first peacetime Christmas, and there had not been many parties of any sort in the past few years.

The living room was not large enough for dancing, but some of the young couples were waltzing in the hall. Fortunately, Sergeant Lloyd Morrissey, a Victoria man from the same regiment as Harry, proved to be a great asset as he played the piano well. Doris had insisted on having a piano in the house as a sign of their social status, although no one in the family had ever attempted to play it. Sergeant Morrissey, however, was able to play waltzes and all the most popular war songs, as well as some "ragtime" tunes. There was non-alcoholic punch to go with the sandwiches, biscuits and Christmas cake, and later, in honour of the occasion, wine would be served. Doris had tried to prevail upon Matthew to propose a toast, but so far he would not commit himself.

Among the young guests were Julia Godolphin and Albert Aalgaard. Doris had become more closely acquainted with the Godolphins during the war as Adelaide and her girls were members of her branch of the Tommy Atkins Knitting Club. Albert had been transferred to eastern Canada while he was in training, but now he was out of the service and attending Victoria College, and once again paying careful attention to Julia.

They had been to one dance at the Empress, Julia's first, an experience she would never forget. To waltz with Albert's arms around her, her fears of tripping over her own feet vanquished by his easy charm and skill, lifted her to the height of romantic fantasies. She had discovered the meaning of seduction, if not all of the actual activities involved.

Albert even had his own car, a Hupmobile roadster, a present from his grandfather. It was in the Hupmobile that he had arrived to collect Julia for the Burmans' party. This did little to ease Adelaide's attitude toward Albert, and even Lewis admonished them to be careful, before Albert honked the horn in farewell and took off.

"I don't like it," said Adelaide. "I don't like it at all. You mark my words, no good will come of it."

"Addie, dearest, what harm can there be in going to a Christmas party at the Burmans? I can't imagine anything more respectable."

"Well, just remember, I was right about the Kaiser when no one else was."

Lewis repressed a smile.

As Albert drove, he glanced at Julia admiringly, thinking how lovely she was in her dark blue cloth coat with the muskrat collar, over the blue dress, her elegantly slim ankles in beige silk stockings, her feet in narrow white pumps.

"Do you always wear blue?" he asked suddenly.

"Do you mind looking at the road and not my dress, until we get to the party?" Her voice had a slight edge to it, which amused him. She was generally so placid.

"Absolutely, madam. Anything madam pleases." He turned his attention to the road, on which there were fewer than a dozen cars.

Albert was making Julia nervous, as any indication of judgment by anyone always did. If they started out this way, the evening could very well not be a success. "I hope you understand that this party will probably be dull," she said.

"Don't worry, my dear. I'm an expert at livening up parties. From one end of Canada to another, thanks to college in Victoria and the officers' training camp in Quebec." Taking one hand from the steering wheel, he reached over her knees to the glove compartment, opened it and extracted a small silver flask. He took a fast swallow and handed it to her.

"What is it?"

"Gilbey's gin—the very finest. Direct from England via my grandfather's private collection. Don't be afraid. You'll love it."

She took a tentative sip. The sharp liquid had a taste totally unfamiliar to her. "It tastes like perfume."

"Do you drink perfume?" he said with a smile. "I didn't know that."

She relaxed a bit and took another sip. "I don't feel anything. Should I?"

"Later, my love. Give it time."

He reached the harbour and continued on toward James Bay, passing the ships, trimmed with lights glowing in the darkness, until they reached Simcoe Street and the Burmans' house.

Albert dispensed his charm to the Burmans, complimenting Doris on the merits of her son. "All Victoria is proud of him," he declared, certain that he understood mothers better than anyone else. He fared less well with Harry. The two young men were introduced, shook hands, but did not take to each other. The gulf between their personalities was much too wide to be bridged by a mere Christmas party.

Albert and Julia were dancing in the hall among a few other couples when Julia felt his arms tighten and he missed a step. He put his head closer to hers and whispered, "Who is that?"

She looked over her shoulder and saw Elaine moving among the guests, carrying a plate of sandwiches.

"That's Elaine. She's the Burmans' maid. She's an Indian princess from Nootka, and Mr. Burman had her come and stay with them and finish her education while she worked for them. She was in the last two years at Vic High with me, but I never got to know her. She was very quiet." She did not add that Elaine was also unfriendly.

Albert did not appear to be listening. He continued to watch Elaine, fascinated. Elaine wore the maid's uniform as though it were a ceremonial gown. She had coiled her braids around her head, adding to her stature.

"Albert! Albert!" Julia prodded him. They were blocking the other dancers.

"Oh, sorry, darling." He began to dance again, steering Julia around the floor, but his concentration was gone. In the corner of the hall, when the number was finished, the smile returned to his face, and he kept his arms around Julia. "I told you I know how to liven up parties, didn't I?" His voice was soft and amused. "Well, I've just had an inspiration."

She looked at him nervously. Albert's inspirations could lead to almost anything. "You must help me," he said. "Be a good girl and go and stand in front of the table with the punch bowl on it. Smile prettily at everyone and don't pay any attention to me."

Julia stepped obediently in front of the table while Albert moved around it, slipped his flask from his pocket and emptied the contents into the punch bowl.

"I told you not to worry about the party being dull," he murmured to Julia, leading her back to the hall, where it seemed that waltzes had been abandoned for livelier selections. "Now if I could just get a smile from the princess over there, the evening would be perfect."

"Elaine never smiles," said Julia. "I don't think she has a sense of humour."

"We'll see about that," said Albert. He left Julia on the dance floor, helped himself to another punch and went over to the table in the dining room where Elaine was methodically arranging the food. He reached for a piece of cake with his free hand and whispered to Elaine, his lips as close to her ear as he could manage. She gave him a swift glance, her eyes sparkled, and she smiled directly at him, then moved smoothly away. Albert was satisfied. He had registered.

"What on Earth did you say to her?" asked Julia curiously, hoping she was not showing the jealousy she felt.

"I told her that if she is bored she might want to know that I'd spiked the punch."

Harry saw Elaine's reaction to Albert. How could that fellow prompt a smile when he had tried all week to get some acknowledgment of his existence from her? He had asked her about her people, and attempted to help her carry the groceries, and she was barely civil to him. She was a constant torture. She ate her meals in the kitchen, while he and his parents ate in the dining room, but she waited on their table, standing close to him as she picked up his plate and poured his tea. He could barely control himself. He was desperate to touch her. Elaine did not appear to notice him at all.

Matthew had firmly resisted his wife's attempts to get him to propose a toast or make any sort of speech, so she decided to take on the responsibility herself. She went to the fireplace in the living room, cleared her throat, rapped on the mantel and spoke.

"Ladies and gentleman," said Doris, and she was surprised at how loud her own voice sounded in the crowded room. The music stopped instantly, and so did the chatter. Elaine was circulating with a tray of glasses of wine. Once Doris had everyone's attention, she hesitated momentarily, but she continued, determined to show Matthew how these things should be accomplished. "First, let me say that Mr. Burman and I want to thank you all for coming." Applause from the guests, and even a couple of "hear, hears," one of them coming from Albert. "We feel it is a great honour to our son to have you welcome him home in this manner. Now I have something special to say. I'm very proud to announce the engagement of Harry and Miss Kathleen Ryerson. Kathleen is in Ireland now but will be joining us in the spring, at which time there will be a wedding!"

There was considerable surprise at this, and Doris looked triumphantly at Matthew, hoping he recognized how accomplished she was at public speaking.

"Now I want to propose a toast. To my son, Harry, and his bride-to-be, Kathleen." Everyone raised their glasses to Harry, who stood by his mother, without a flicker of any warmth or pleasure at the toast. Nudged by Doris, however, he managed to speak. "Thank you very much. I'm sure that Kathleen would thank you also if she were here."

Albert watched him keenly. "Not exactly the picture of a happy bride-groom, would you say?"

"Harry was always like that," said Julia. "I remember him at school. I never saw him smile."

Albert shook his head. "It goes deeper than that."

He was an astute observer of human behaviour, despite his light-hearted manner. The years of sitting on the stairs of the Inne and watching the guests, as well as peering through cracks and keyholes at everyone he could, had sharpened his vision. There was something very wrong here.

Then he saw what it was. Elaine was accepting the empty wineglasses, placing them back on the tray, walking lightly among the guests. Harry's eyes were fixed on her and for a moment, only a fleeting one, his feelings were visible.

Aha, thought Albert. I am not alone.

He deliberately took his wineglass over to Elaine, put it on her tray, smiled at her and said, "Beautiful." Elaine looked at him and smiled. She understood his meaning.

When she had moved on, Albert looked back at the fireplace. Still standing before it was Harry with a new expression—that of the icy hatred he was acquiring for Albert Aalgaard.

☙ ☙ ☙

Instead of driving back past the harbour, Albert turned south toward Dallas Road.

"It's a lot farther this way," said Julia.

"That's the idea," he said, turning eastward on Dallas to where Beacon Hill Park met the road and the rocks and the water beyond.

The night was cold and clear, except for a few wisps of clouds through which the full moon seemed to be playing hide-and-seek. On the strait there were half a dozen strings of lights on the passing ships. The wind blew off the water. Julia shivered and Albert reached over and pulled the fur collar of her coat up around her neck. But her movement was not because of the cold; it was a spasm of excitement because she was alone with Albert.

He stopped the car, reached into his pocket and brought out the flask. "Damn, I forgot it was empty. Imagine wasting all that good gin on the Burmans' guests."

"I'd hardly say it was wasted. It seemed to have some effect."

"Maybe I've got some more." He reached again across her knees, letting his hand linger for a moment before opening the glove compartment and finding a small bottle of gin.

"I'm so grateful to Grandfather. You can't buy this stuff in Victoria, you know. Of course, Grandfather doesn't know I'm so free with the Inne's liquor supply, but if he or Mother find out, I'll explain that I needed it for public relations in Victoria."

"Albert, you shouldn't drink any more."

"Why not?"

"Because you shouldn't. For one thing, you still have to drive me home, and . . ."

"And for another?" He leaned closer to her, his hand moving along her leg. He kissed her on her mouth, gently. She stared at him, marvelling at her own secret response.

"That's the first time that anyone's ever kissed me."

"Then we must make sure that it isn't the last," he said and drew her into his arms, this time kissing her firmly, holding her to him. All at once he stopped and drew back.

"What's wrong?" She could not imagine what had made him stop, except to fear that it was her fault.

"You're so vulnerable, and I feel like I'm taking unfair advantage of you," Albert said. He stroked her hair. "It just wouldn't be right for me to seduce you, no matter how sweet and innocent you are."

He kissed her lightly on the forehead and started the engine.

"I don't understand," Julia said and looked out the window, hiding the tears that rolled down her cheeks. In the street in front of her house, he stopped and pressed her hand, then got out and opened the door for her.

"Now please don't cry, that's a good girl. I'm not going to kiss you again or your father is likely to come out with a shotgun. Your mother definitely will. It was a great party. I enjoyed it much more than I ever expected to, but I'd appreciate it if, when you tell your family about it, you leave out my contribution to the punch bowl." There was a light in the front hall, and he could see the small figure of Mrs. Godolphin inside.

🐦 🐦 🐦

Julia vowed that she would never become a music teacher, yet she worried that that was precisely what the future held for her. Most young girls, unless they were extremely wealthy or had married immediately on graduation, were taking jobs, usually as teachers, nurses or typists. Teaching piano appeared to be the most obvious way for Julia to keep herself occupied until such time as she married. If she did not marry, at least she would be assured financial independence and respect as a spinster.

She had almost a dozen students between the ages of six and twelve who came to the house, some on weekdays after school and others on Saturday morning. She did not really like teaching, but she was fond of children, often feeling more secure with them than she did with adults. Besides, she was determined never to leave the kind of impression on any child that the autocratic Miss McMurtrie had left on her. No knuckles would be rapped during her sessions. Adelaide, listening from the other rooms to her daughter's gentle voice explaining the intricacies of harmony or the importance of scales, would shake her head over Julia's lack of firmness. A teacher could never succeed without discipline.

On the Saturday morning before Christmas, with Lilas and her mother off on their weekly shopping trip, Julia dreaded the idea of teaching more than ever. She had a headache, and was struggling with her disappointment over Albert's behaviour, but she tried to maintain her patience with nine-year-old Ernest McGillivray, wishing that his mother had excused him from lessons over the Christmas holidays. Ernest had a tendency to play loudly to make up for his lack of artistry, and every note of the scale seemed to be hammered into her brain.

Finally and mercifully, Ernest's half-hour came to an end. She gave him his Christmas present, a book about famous composers of piano music, for which she hoped he would one day forgive her, while he presented her with a thin square box that would no doubt contain the traditional white handkerchief. She wished him a Merry Christmas and, remembering Miss McMurtrie, told him he had played well.

The day before Albert left to spend Christmas on Arnason Island, he had called while she was out and left a package for her. Adelaide had accepted it for Julia, had given him Julia's present, and wished him a courteous but cool Merry Christmas.

Julia's present from Albert was an exquisite pair of long, white kid gloves with tiny pearl buttons. Adelaide, noting the Paris label, considered the gift totally useless and unnecessarily extravagant. Julia had given Albert a plaid wool scarf, purchased at the best importer of Scottish goods in Victoria. These scarves were especially popular for young gentlemen to wear while driving automobiles. It was more expensive than Adelaide would have liked had she known the price, but Julia had saved a little extra from her classes, so she lied about what she had actually paid.

While wrapping the gift, she had a sudden sharp memory of another muffler—the one she had made herself as a gift for Stanley, and how he had been wearing it when he went away. She wanted to send him a gift now, yet it would have been difficult to arrange without her mother discovering what she was doing: Adelaide knew everything, or so it seemed. Finally, she slipped out and bought an elaborate Christmas card, and mailed it to him in care of the Arnason Inne. Inside she had written, "With all my love, your sister, Julia."

🐟 🐟 🐟

Eleanor St. John Trevor and her younger son, George III, had their Christmas dinner at the Empress Hotel, their first ever away from Blenheim Oaks, exchanging gifts over the plum pudding and coffee. Eleanor presented George with his father's watch. George gave his mother a silver bracelet set with emeralds that had cost him several allowances. He wanted so very much to make her happy again. She reached across the table and took his hand. "Thank you, darling," she said, and for a moment he could see the tears glisten in her lovely green eyes.

How lucky she was to have him, she thought—how truly fortunate. If he had been born just one year earlier the war might have taken him too. Plainly, God was on her side. He had taken away, but He had also given. George II had died a hero and a credit to his country, and here was darling George III, red-haired, freckled and a true gentleman: loving, thoughtful and devoted. He would carry on the tradition of the Marlboroughs, and the Trevors, too, she remembered to add in her mind.

"Merry Christmas, Georgie."

"Merry Christmas, Mother."

They stood up then at their table. It was precisely ten o'clock on Christmas night, and the quartet struck up "God Save the King."

🐟 🐟 🐟

In the spring of 1919, Lewis still went for his evening walks and Adelaide, although she saw no real necessity for him to do so, made no objection, busying herself with her sewing or reading the newspapers while he was absent. Their musical evenings were less frequent now. On Sunday afternoons Lilas would perform her latest arias, accompanied by Julia, but Lewis sang no more, and the girls, sensing that for some reason singing was painful for him, did not press him.

One evening at dusk, late in March, Lewis walked toward the strait, as was his custom, sometimes going down to the breakwater and watching the sunsets, the ships coming in and out of the harbour or the fishermen casting off the jetty. The weather was mild for March, but there was dampness in the air, and mist hung over the water; he walked as usual past Beacon Hill Park, where the first broom was beginning to blossom, bringing patches of yellow to the dark green foliage. There were few other strollers and only the occasional automobile.

Lewis had received his monthly letter from Stanley that morning, delivered to Macauley's as always. The letters were carefully written. The boy expressed himself well, Lewis thought, considering he had left school so young. It was apparent that he read whatever he could, and although books had been few at the logging camp, there was an excellent library at the Inne.

His description of his life on Arnason Island was as cautious and sparse as it had been when he wrote from Quatsino. He arose at six o'clock every day, he wrote, to enjoy the morning quiet and the variety of birds that abounded at that time. He displayed some pride in his increased physical strength. His jobs included clearing land, building cabins and maintaining the island road. When the tourist season came, he drove the newly acquired Arnason automobile down to the dock to assist passengers with their luggage and drive them to the Inne.

He mentioned no personal relationships other than an occasional reference to Sveinn, and the fact that Mrs. Aalgaard was very kind to him, and now that her husband had returned from his wartime duties with the Coast Guard, he was pleasant too, although they saw little of him as he spent most of his time fishing. Never did Stanley discuss his own feelings, other than his satisfaction over the opportunity to work out of doors. He always sent his love to his mother as though nothing was wrong, and to both his sisters—"especially Julia," he had added in today's letter.

Lewis remembered, bitterly now, that it had never been a custom in the family to speak of personal feelings. *Especially Julia*, he thought. Why did he find those words so significant? He walked along, hearing no sound except his own footsteps, the mist thickening into a fog that swirled off the water.

A gull's cry startled him and the bird landed on the railing by the sidewalk above the beach. Lewis stopped. Somewhere below, another sound wafted upward in the fog. Human voices. Lewis leaned over the edge of the stone wall. The tide was not yet all the way in and there was a strand of rocky beach, packed with driftwood. Yes, there was somebody down there. He heard a girl's laugh, a strange, eerie sound in the mist.

On the beach between two huge logs sat a man and a woman, facing the water. They were embracing. Not much of a place for a rendezvous, thought Lewis. No doubt about it, since the war morals had become looser and the young more reckless.

He looked down again despite himself, and something in the young man's voice struck a chord. He saw the back of his head—fair hair, and then a plaid muffler; surely it was the same as the one Julia had given Albert for Christmas? He told himself that the scarf would not be one of a kind, yet with the fair hair, the movement of the shoulders, and the familiar light-hearted laugh, it could only be Albert Aalgaard. Lewis was struck with sudden self-pity, the notion that his family was cursed in some way, and that happiness would always elude them.

The couple was moving now, the girl slipping down to lie on a blanket, the boy moving over her. They were silent. No more laughter. Then the red knit cap the girl wore fell back and Lewis saw the stream of long black hair. He could not see her face, only her hands from the sleeves of her black wool jacket as they went around Albert, stroking his hair, touching his neck under the plaid scarf.

A gull shrieked. Albert raised his head for a moment, and Lewis caught a glimpse of the girl's face, seeing with surprise that she was Indian. He moved back from the railing and continued his walk, more swiftly now as the fog rolled in. He could feel the swirls of moist air against his face. He must get home; Adelaide would be worried about him.

The last sound he heard from the water as he walked away was the heavy call of a foghorn, echoing off the strait.

CHAPTER TWELVE

The Newlyweds

Kathleen looked at herself in the mirror of the guest room of the Burmans' house. She was trying to convince herself that she was really here, in the city of Victoria, which, until she had met Harry last year she had not heard of. Now it would be her home for the rest of her life.

She kissed her image in the mirror, smiled at it, and stood back. She had had her hair bobbed in France, as being more practical, and wore it with bangs in front and a wave over each ear. She had no pretensions to beauty, but as long as Harry loved her, that was all the flattery she needed.

It had been six months since she had last seen Harry in France. She was surprised to find he was tenser than he had been overseas. Then she remembered that he always wanted so much to do the correct thing, and he was obviously trying to please his parents and adjust to his new life. Once they were married and in their own little house, he would relax and be as he had been when they first met: still a cautious man but able to confide his hopes and dreams to her, even laughing at her little jokes and encouraging her to sing to him. He would be a wonderful husband, she knew. Waving to her reflection, she left the room and went downstairs to participate in the wedding plans with Doris.

The wedding took place in mid-April at St. Andrew's Cathedral, with the reception held at the Burman home. Harry had chosen as his best man Sergeant Lloyd Morrissey, the piano player at the Christmas party, while Kathleen had yielded to her future mother-in-law's suggestions and accepted Mildred Burman, a niece of Matthew, and Julia Godolphin as her bridesmaids.

Her wedding dress had been her mother's; she had brought it with her from Dublin. It was of white silk with long, full sleeves, a high neck, tight waist and a wide skirt that ended in a train at the back. Doris had helped her choose the white veil, encrusted with seed pearls, which framed her face attractively and fell to the floor over the train of her dress. Mildred was dressed in pale yellow, Julia in pale blue. Both girls had matching floral wreaths in their hair.

Julia had seen Albert only once since the night of the Burmans' Christmas party. He had called on her to thank her for the Christmas present and inquire if she was pleased with his. Their brief visit was friendly, without tension, but he was soon on his way. The Burmans had sent him a wedding invitation and he wrote a note to Julia asking if he could escort her, adding that he had enjoyed the Burmans' last party so much that he wouldn't miss this one for the world.

The event was a success, and the crowning achievement for Doris was that both the *Victoria Times* and the *Daily Colonist* wrote in detail about the wedding and the reception. Doris had worked hard to make her son's wedding day the most beautiful day of his life, and she had to admit that she could scarcely have done it without Elaine. This time she really rose to the occasion. Doris had heard that Indians enjoyed ceremonies, and certainly the girl was more animated and cheerful than at any time since her arrival in Victoria.

Elaine had for once made a dress for herself, of dark red velveteen. Matthew complimented her on her appearance, and she even turned her head and for a moment smiled at him, in the way he had seen her smile long ago at Nootka.

Julia stood in the receiving line in front of the mantel in the Burman living room, watching the guests. Her parents had been invited, and her mother and Lilas appeared to be enjoying themselves. Lewis tried to enter into the spirit of the wedding, but Julia saw that his heart was not in it and wished there was some way she could reach him to give him comfort, to exchange confidences. Yet, much as she loved him, he seemed to be slipping away from the family.

When the reception line ordeal was over, Julia mingled with the guests. She found Albert, who was watching the proceedings with his usual amused demeanour.

"You're not planning to spike the drinks again, are you?" she asked.

"Not this time. It wouldn't be any fun. You look very lovely by the way, but I suppose you've already been told that."

"Not by you."

"My, aren't we bold today? Do weddings bring out this unexpected forward streak in you?"

She was not quite sure if he was laughing at her or not. "Doesn't Elaine look beautiful? I've never seen her look like this before."

Albert nodded, and for a moment he was silent. "What do you think of the bride? She seems a pleasant girl. Much too good for the stodgy groom, I should think."

"I like her very much. We've become quite friendly. It's the first time I've had a girl friend in years, ever since . . ." She had been about to say "Katie."

"Yes, since . . . ?"

"It doesn't matter. Anyway, Kathleen has a great sense of humour."

"Harry will take care of that, I'm sure," said Albert, and there was a long silence.

"I have to go and help Kathleen change," Julia said.

Kathleen stood on the landing halfway up the staircase and looked down at the guests crowded into the hall. She flung the bouquet over the banister, aiming it deliberately in the direction of Julia, and clapped her hands when Julia caught it. Lloyd Morrissey slapped Albert on the back. "Looks like you're next, old man!"

Julia caught a glimpse of her father. He looked flushed and angry, as though someone had touched a sensitive spot. She had never seen that look on his face before. Then Julia and Mildred followed Kathleen upstairs to help her change into her travelling outfit.

Soon Kathleen and Harry were gone, in a shower of rice and confetti, with much laughter and good wishes. They were to spend one night at the Empress Hotel and then go by boat the following day to Vancouver. From there they would take the train to California for a honeymoon in San Francisco, Matthew's wedding present to them.

After the wedding, Albert parked at Laurel Point, facing westward to where the sun was setting over the hills beyond Esquimalt, its rays catching the treetops. He put his arm around Julia and drew her close to him. "Your mother's right. Blue is your colour." He was looking at her with an expression that she had not seen before. "You're a beautiful girl, Julia. I'm very fond of you."

She was silent. He had not said he loved her. Should she tell him now how much she was in love with him? That the very sight of him meant everything to her? She would deny him nothing. When his dark blue eyes shot their glance over her body, her responses were almost beyond her control.

The moment now could lead to only two endings. He must either propose marriage or seduce her. Julia knew she would accept either.

"Julia, I have something to tell you."

It wasn't a good beginning for either a proposal or a seduction, she thought. She took his hand in hers and put her head on his shoulder.

"I'm going away to Europe."

If he had said he was going to jump into the harbour she could not have been more surprised. The war was over. People no longer went away.

"Why?"

The first hint of a smile touched the corners of his lips. "Trust you to ask the practical question, and the one that's hardest to answer." Albert paused. "You've always been my ideal, Julia. The perfect young girl, beautiful and pure."

"Don't say that! I'm not beautiful and I don't want to be pure. Don't smile, Albert! If you must go away, make love to me before you go. I want you to do it. Please, Albert."

He shook his head. "I can't do that. It's not right. Please believe me. It's not that I don't want you. I do. But somewhere, for once in my life I've got to do the right thing. Let me be honourable this time. Please, Julia. I love you too much to do this any other way."

She drew back then, and both her passion and her fear subsided, a tiny seed of pride growing in their place. "How long will you be away?"

"A year, maybe longer. I'm going to Switzerland to learn about hotel management."

"I'll wait," Julia said.

He was silent.

"Will you write to me?"

His smile broadened. "You may depend on it, my dear."

"Take me home, Albert."

He started the engine, reversed the car and drove back past the Inner Harbour, where the *Princess Mary* was already getting up steam for her midnight voyage to Vancouver. They drove to the Godolphins' without speaking.

"Goodbye, Albert," said Julia, and this time when he kissed her she did not allow herself to respond.

He stayed in the car and watched her go slowly up the walk to her front door, and thought he would never forget the sight of her in her long, blue bridesmaid's gown, the wreath of flowers in her hair, clutching Kathleen's wedding bouquet. He waited until he saw her mother at the door as she went into the house. Then he drove away.

Albert went back to James Bay and Simcoe Street. He passed the Burman home, where the lights were out. Harry and his bride were at the Empress Hotel; Doris and Matthew had retired. He drove the car around the block, his hands gripping the wheel tightly, and stopped in the street behind the house. Soon he would see her. Perhaps already she had opened the window of her small room, climbed over the sill and was on her way. He wondered if she would still be wearing the red dress. The night was cool but he was sweating. Surely this could not be what love was like. Did his father feel this way about his mother? He could not believe it.

He only knew that soon he would once again lose himself within that long, smooth, bronze body, the thought of which possessed him constantly. Tonight he must tell her, also, that this would be their last time together. He opened the glove compartment and drew out his flask. He would need it.

The footsteps sounded clear in the cool, silent night. Then she was there on the sidewalk, still wearing the long dress, but with her brown coat over it, and her hair hanging loosely down her back. He opened the door; she got in swiftly in one single, lithe move and closed it. Then they drove to the park.

❧ ❧ ❧

Harry stood in his dressing gown and pyjamas, looking out the window of the large Empress Hotel room that faced the harbour just across Government Street. This would be the night to bring him the peace he sought, to quell all the turmoil within him. From now on he would be able to concentrate on what his life was meant to be: to succeed at the bank, to raise a family, to be of service to the community and to be happy with Kathleen. He was nervous.

She came out of the dressing room shyly, wearing a long, white satin negligee, trimmed with white net frills along the edge and the sleeves. The plain round neckline emphasized her innocence, even as the smooth satin displayed the tender curves of her body. He went to her and put his arms around her. He must be very gentle, he thought, must control his haste and his needs.

He kissed her, and she looked up at him and smiled. "I love you, Harry," she said as he led her over to the bed. Harry was surprised by the depth of his passion. When it was over, and he had kissed her lovingly, he lay beside her, holding her in his arms.

"I'm sorry," he whispered. "I didn't want to hurt you."

Kathleen took one of his hands in hers and kissed it. "It was wonderful, Harry, and remember, it is just the beginning." He felt better then. She was right. They had the rest of their lives together. He could not tell her that as he made love to her he was thinking of Elaine.

🐜 🐜 🐜

In the first week of May, Kathleen was experiencing the full beauty of Victoria in the spring. She rejoiced at the warmth, the clear skies, the sparkling water always so close and most of all the flowers. It seemed as if every home had a neatly kept garden, usually with a small picket fence around the front, a green lawn at the back and a variety of flowers seldom seen in tiny Dublin yards.

Already, she had taken over the gardening from Doris, who was getting much too stout to work about the yard. She borrowed books on gardening from the library, learning the names of all these wonderful new species she had not known. She wanted most of all to have her own garden.

Harry had told her they would have their own home by summer, and she had looked for houses by herself, taking long walks around the James Bay neighbourhood and elsewhere, looking enviously at bungalows, especially if they were inhabited by young families. Kathleen would lean over a fence to talk to children playing in their yards; she could scarcely wait for the day when she would watch her own children play in her own garden.

She was fond of Matthew and Doris, but it was becoming increasingly necessary for her to get Harry away from his parents' house. Kathleen wanted to meet more people but realized that her husband was not particularly sociable. Even after church, his conversations were perfunctory. Kathleen also wanted some evenings alone with Harry. Matthew kept to himself in his study after dinner, but Doris took over the living room and dominated the conversation.

Harry was still kind and affectionate, but he seemed perpetually depressed. Kathleen tried to draw him out, to get him to walk with her, but on weekends he would simply concentrate on the latest books on banking and the financial newspapers. She told herself that he was suffering from war nerves, and became convinced that the only solution was for them to have their own home and family. A baby, she thought, would change everything.

CHAPTER THIRTEEN

Consequences

Matthew and Doris had gone to a funeral. Although the deceased had been an old and valued business acquaintance of Matthew, the fact that his funeral was held on a Saturday afternoon was bitterly resented by the banker. "I thought the fellow had more sense," he declared. "Must be his wife. Latimer knew how we men treasure our Saturday afternoons to ourselves."

Doris said nothing, but adjusted the black veil on her hat. Privately, she was rather glad to get Matthew out of the house with her for once, even if the occasion was not a pleasant one. She had tried to persuade Harry to come too, particularly as Kathleen had gone to Butchart's Garden with Julia, but he flatly refused.

With his parents gone at last, and Kathleen not expected back until dinner time, Harry was alone—except for Elaine.

It was inevitable, predestined, he told himself, that this should happen. He had been given the opportunity to see her, to talk to her, to declare his feelings and thus rid himself of the tremendous weight that continued to press upon him. Once she realized the extent of his desire, she would surely reciprocate.

He had decided that only her shyness and consciousness of her place, and his position as a married man, had kept her from confessing her own interest in him. The house was quiet, except for the ticking of the clock in the front hall. He crossed the kitchen and the hallway, coming to her room. Her door was open and for a moment he was afraid she had gone out.

Elaine had just washed her hair and finished braiding it. She was sitting on a straight-backed, armless chair, her hands resting in her lap, staring out the window into the back garden. She wore a simple black robe of worn, cheap silk, with a frayed black silk cord around the waist. Her bare legs protruded from the calf-length gown. Even the sight of her long slim feet excited him. Her full lips were parted in a slight smile, while her eyes, always large and luminous, were moist with tears.

"Elaine," he said, controlling his trembling, "I must speak to you."

The smile left her face and her features returned to their familiar expressionless look. She rose from the chair and stood by the little table. "All right," she said guardedly.

"May I come in?"

"I can't stop you."

He searched for some softening in her stare but did not find it. He must declare himself without waiting for her to thaw. Then she would understand. "You must know . . . know that I want you," he said, and it was difficult for him even to keep his voice steady enough to produce the words he wanted to speak. "That I both love you and want you. I'm convinced that you understand."

She said nothing but turned to the window and stared out into the garden. God, he had never realized her eyelashes were so long.

"You have a wife," said Elaine coolly. "She is pretty and she loves you. That should be enough."

He was in the room now, looking at the plain single brass bed. He saw the chest of drawers in one corner, the table and the single chair. She remained by the window.

He would not accept it. Somewhere inside her there had to be some feeling for him. It was only her guilt about Kathleen and his parents that kept them apart. Once he could persuade her that this moment was for the two of them—here in this room—she must surrender. Those full lips would part for him at last.

He had no plans. He had not been prepared for the gulf that was between them.

She moved across the room toward the door, with a look of hatred and contempt. It was the movement that did it, he told himself—the way she moved, her sudden recoil. It was her own fault. If she had kept still, it would have been different. He crossed the room and grabbed her in his arms, tried to kiss her and failed. He had not expected her to be so strong. They struggled, and he heard her hard breathing.

He threw all his weight against her and managed to put one leg behind her knees so that she lost her balance. He was on top of her at once as she lay across the bed, yet she continued to struggle and bite until she had almost driven him off her.

He caught her wrist in one hand and put his forearm across her neck. Suddenly she ceased to move and lay still. The change almost took him off guard. He did not dare move his body away from hers, his arm away from her neck. She remained motionless, her eyes closed, taking long, deep breaths.

He found himself wishing that she would continue to resist him but did not know if it was because the resistance excited him or because he was fearful of what he was doing. He was seized with anger, and found himself muttering every vile word he had ever heard and suppressed. "Bitch, cunt, cochon . . ."

When he had finished raping her, he raised his head and looked down at her. She opened her eyes. Her deep and silent hatred of him was still there, but it was no longer a threat.

Now, he felt, the fire inside him could rest and he could continue with his life without the passion that had so possessed him. If there was not to be love between them, as he had once hoped, at least now she had been his in one sense. He stood, pulled up his trousers and left her lying on the bed, silent.

🔶 🔶 🔶

The war had strengthened not only Canada's economy but her position as something more than a silent, assenting Dominion to whatever Great Britain's policy dictated. Prime Minister Borden fought hard for recognition of Canada's tremendous contribution to fighting and winning the war. Canada was about to become an economic power in her own right, and Toronto had become Canada's economic centre. Close enough to the capital, settled by Scottish and English, mainly staunch Presbyterians, the city was regarded, at least by itself, as strong, moral and wise—the bastion of security and supreme authority on the policies of Canada.

One evening in June, Matthew invited Harry into his study after dinner. It was a rare occasion. The two walked to and from the bank together every day, and this normally provided the time Matthew considered necessary to discuss business. But he had something special to mention to his son.

"I've had a letter from Jim Mulvaney. I don't know if you remember him. He and I went to Victoria High together and he worked at the bank for a couple of years. He went to Toronto before the war, and he's done well there. Anyway, to get to the point, he's made the suggestion that maybe you'd consider spending a year or so back East."

Harry looked up, surprised.

"Now it's up to you, of course, but he may have a point. The country's changed, no doubt about that. And it'll change even more over the next few years. There'll be closer ties to the United States, for one thing, and we've a lot to learn about what's going on there. Mulvaney knows you'll be taking over from me one day, and he figures the more you know about the new banking ways, the better. He's offering you a job at the Bank of Toronto."

Hope sprang up within Harry. Toronto! A new city and a new beginning for him, a chance to forget what his life had been since his return from France. He would be alone at last with Kathleen, with no guilt to haunt him. "I'd have to talk it over with Kathleen," he said.

"But you don't reject the idea totally?"

"No, I don't. He's right about the times. There's a lot of new facets in banking I'd like to learn. I'll speak to Kathleen."

He was surprised at her eagerness when he told her that night what Matthew had suggested. "Oh, yes, Harry, yes!" She threw her arms around him. "I thought you wouldn't want to leave Victoria. You said the other day you never wanted to go anywhere again. But we'll be back. And, Harry, when we do return, it will be with our baby. Just imagine!" She let go of him and whirled around the bedroom ecstatically. "You and I and our child, together!"

"You're sure now? Toronto isn't Victoria, you know. It's a big commercial city, and it's very cold in winter and hot in summer."

"I don't care. I don't care. I'll love every minute of it.'" She danced back to him, put her arms around his neck again and kissed him on the mouth. He touched her hair gently.

Perhaps God was giving him a second chance.

🐦 🐦 🐦

In the first week of July, the Burmans held a dinner party to celebrate Harry's birthday. It was also a farewell party, as Harry and Kathleen were relocating to Toronto for a year.

Kathleen was singing happily in the kitchen. Doris had prevailed upon Harry to go shopping with her, as it was a Saturday afternoon, and Matthew had firmly shut the door to his study. Kathleen had the opportunity to make Harry's birthday cake by herself, without any advice from her mother-in-law.

She had finished "Killarney" and was starting "When Irish Eyes Are Smiling" when Elaine came in the back door, carrying groceries. It struck

Kathleen that Elaine did not look well. "You look tired. Put your groceries down and I'll make you a cup of tea."

Elaine put the bags on the table and sat down, then turned to Kathleen and said suddenly, "I'm going to tell you something."

Kathleen was surprised. It was unlike Elaine to offer any confidence. "I shall be telling Mr. and Mrs. Burman later. But as long as you're here I may as well tell you first. I'm leaving."

Kathleen was filling the kettle with water. "Why? I thought you were happy here."

"Because," said Elaine, in her low voice, "I'm going to have a child."

Kathleen felt the water running over her hands and dropped the kettle into the sink. Her face drained of colour. Somewhere in her mind there was a door that she had kept shut and now it had opened. Elaine got up from the kitchen chair, put an arm around her and led her away from the sink.

"Here. You sit down. You look as if you need it more than I do."

"Why . . . why are you telling me?"

"I thought you should know. My condition is becoming obvious and I intend to go away, but isn't it better that you know the truth rather than think about it after I'm gone?"

Her voice was cold, but as she looked at the fragile figure in the kitchen chair, she went over to the cupboard where Doris kept the port, poured some in a glass and handed it to Kathleen. "Have a drink," said Elaine, and Kathleen drained the glass.

She looked at Elaine, taking in the increased fullness of her figure in the plain brown dress. "It's Harry's child, isn't it?"

Elaine did not answer, but walked over to the sink and looked out into the back garden.

"I didn't know," said Kathleen. "Except that there's been something wrong with Harry ever since I got here. Now I understand. It's you. Harry's in love with you. That's why he's so anxious that we move to Toronto."

"No," Elaine's voice was firmer now. "He doesn't love me. He loves you. And I don't love him." Again she looked at Kathleen and was struck by a momentary pity. "Just something that happened. But it's you he loves."

Now it was Kathleen who rose and went to the sideboard, where she helped herself to another glass of port.

"Where will you go?"

"I haven't decided. Not to Nootka. My . . . my father would hardly welcome me."

Kathleen whirled around suddenly. "The baby. What about the baby?" She was very pale, but two bright pink spots stood out on her cheekbones.

"What about it?"

"What *about* it? Elaine, it's a human life. It's Harry's child! I must know what you intend to do." Her heart raced, yet her mind was clear.

"I'll give it up for adoption. Probably through the Salvation Army."

"No," cried Kathleen. "No, Elaine! Don't you see what you must do? It's God's will. He's decided for us. You must give *me* the baby!"

Elaine frowned. "What for? I should think you'd want no part of me."

"I want the child!" Kathleen exclaimed. She poured still another glass. "I have a plan. God has made everything clear to me. It's like a miracle. You must listen to me, Elaine, and you'll see that I am right."

🐦 🐦 🐦

Dinner was served at seven o'clock, which did not meet with Adelaide's approval at all. She considered it an indication either of pretentiousness or of poor organization in the kitchen. She could not imagine why the Burmans did not dine at six, the way all civilized families did.

The reason for delaying dinner proved even worse, as drinks were served, something that Adelaide, an admirer of temperance champion Carrie Nation, thoroughly disapproved of. Victoria was, theoretically at least, under Prohibition, which also made the proceedings downright illegal. She was surprised that Matthew Burman participated in such activities, and wondered if she should withdraw her account from the Bank of Victoria and take it across the street to the Bank of Montreal.

Lewis accepted a whisky and soda, as did Lloyd Morrisey, the best man from the wedding party, who was obviously invited as a partner for Julia. Doris signalled Elaine, who came in with a tray bearing small glasses of sherry for the ladies. Adelaide sniffed disdainfully and refused on behalf of Lilas and herself. She hoped that Julia would have sense enough to refuse also, but she took a glass, and Adelaide had to be content with whispering, "Sip it, Julia," to her daughter.

Lewis had noticed Elaine. He had seen her at the wedding reception, but now he was doubly certain that this was the girl who had been on the beach that night with Albert Arnason. He looked over at Julia, who was at the moment speaking to Elaine. No, she had no idea, he thought. Yet he knew she was unhappy over the boy's departure. Lewis sighed and accepted a second drink when it was offered, avoiding his wife's glance.

The dinner was beyond reproach even by Adelaide's standards, with an excellent roast beef, mashed potatoes and gravy, new green peas and buttered carrots, preceded by a tasty cream soup with tiny shrimps, all served quietly and efficiently by Elaine.

There was much discussion over the forthcoming move to Toronto. Neither of the two families had ever been "back East," but Toronto was always in the news, and Harry and Kathleen were given advice about what to wear in the cold winters and how to get along with "straitlaced" Torontonians.

For dessert there was a recent innovation in ice cream, consisting of a square divided into three sections each of chocolate, strawberry and vanilla. Then Doris rose and switched off the lights while Kathleen went to the kitchen and returned with Harry's birthday cake.

Everyone sang "Happy Birthday" to Harry, who looked suitably embarrassed as his wife placed the cake in front of him, telling him to blow out the candles and make a wish. He hesitated too long, and Lilas took over impatiently, blowing out all the candles in one breath.

"Now," said Doris, "I would like to propose a farewell toast to my two dear children, Harry and Kathleen." Everyone murmured, "To Harry and Kathleen," clinking their glasses. Harry said, "Thank you" in his customary dry tone, without enthusiasm.

Suddenly Kathleen pushed her chair back and rose to her feet. "I want to propose a toast too," she said, her voice rising sharply. Her face was very flushed and her eyes glittered. "To Mother and Father Burman, for being so very kind to me and for treating me as if I was their own daughter."

Again the guests murmured politely, while Kathleen drained her glass.

"This is a birthday surprise for Harry and for Mother and Father Burman, and I wouldn't have announced it so soon except for it being Harry's birthday and the fact that we're going away and I'm so happy. I want to tell the whole world because I haven't any family left and all of you have made me feel that now you're my family. So, here it is. Harry and I are going to have a child!"

Harry experienced a few hours of elation, although he was astounded that Kathleen had chosen such a bizarre manner in which to announce her pregnancy. He knew how much she desired a child, and for himself the baby was an indication that God had truly forgiven him for his one act of unfaithfulness.

That night in the bedroom he began by scolding her playfully for having drunk too much. "That will have to be your last drink, my dear. From now on you must respect your condition."

She sat down on the bed. She had put on the nightdress she had worn on their wedding night and her eyes shone with a fervour he had not seen before. "Are you really happy, Harry?" she whispered. "I want you to be happy so much. Your happiness is even more important to me than my own."

"Yes, I'm very happy. I'm happier than I've ever been in my life." It gratified him that he could say this with conviction, even though he lacked it.

"You should be." Her light voice was even more intense. "Even happier than I am, really, because it's your baby, Harry, right from the beginning. Later, it will be mine too, when it's born, but now it's yours, and I can only imagine what it must feel like."

He looked at her, confused. She was making no sense at all. "You should calm down and go to sleep, Kathleen. You mustn't excite yourself further."

"I've made everyone happy, haven't I? Your parents, your friends, you, and I think I've even made Elaine happy too."

"Elaine?" he said sharply. "What's she got to do with it?"

"It's her child, Harry. Hers and yours. And when it's born, it will be ours."

Harry felt as though he was going to throw up. Seeing his distress, Kathleen at once became the nurse again. "Elaine told me this morning that she was expecting a child and she planned to leave. She had no idea where she would go, poor thing, and then she told me she would give up the child for adoption. Now, Harry, we couldn't let such a terrible thing happen to your child, could we?" She took his hand and began to stroke it. "I felt immediately that this was an act of God. He meant for us to have this baby."

"What makes you say it's *my* child?" he asked, not looking at her.

"I just know it. It came to me suddenly when Elaine told me she was pregnant. God opened a door for me and it was all clear. Elaine did not deny it when I asked her, but I knew it anyway. It's all right, Harry, don't look so stricken. I love you, and I will love your baby. Just imagine it like this: If you had been a widower with a child when I married you, the child would have been my stepchild and I would have loved it. But this one will be more like my real child because we're going to make everyone believe it's mine."

The enormity of what she was planning came to him. "How can you do such a thing? She won't…" He could not continue.

"Elaine will come with us to Toronto," she said, as simply as though planning the next day's shopping. "I shall tell Doris and Matthew that I need her help, being pregnant in a faraway city. Everyone will do as I wish because I shall be having the baby. Do you understand?"

He did not reply, and she smiled. "Oh, you don't have to worry about me being jealous. I have told you I love you. I forgive you. And I forgive her too."

"She won't come with us," he muttered.

"But she will; it's all arranged. Elaine will do what I say. After all, I am offering to take her child and provide for it and love it. It's more than she could do. After she's had the child, she can go back to your parents or to her home or wherever she wants. The child will be ours."

He stood up and began to pace, clasping his hands behind his back. "She's an Indian. How can you raise an Indian child? What if it looks like..." He could not say her name, nor could he refer to her as the mother of his child.

"Well, we'll worry about that when the time comes," she said practically. "But I've got dark hair, and so do you, and my own dear father was black Irish. I think the baby's going to be a girl, Harry. I hope you don't mind. Anyway, our next baby will be a boy, you'll see. I think I've chosen the name for our girl already. Sahndra. It's the name of a beautiful girl in an old Irish legend. Yes, Sahndra Burman sounds fine. Sahndra Mary. We must let God have a part in this too!" She was on her feet in a second and had flung her arms around him. Harry winced.

"Oh, Harry, darling. *Please* be happy. I am. Everything is going to be beautiful."

All he could think was that if Elaine wanted revenge, she had obtained it now. He would never cease to suffer because of his act that afternoon.

Once they were in bed, Kathleen went immediately to sleep, but Harry lay awake beside her, trying to sort out what was left of his life. Just before he himself slept, a new thought came to him. What if Elaine's complicity had not been motivated by hate? Was it possible that Elaine *wanted* him to have her child—their child—because in some way she loved him?

⌒ ⌒ ⌒

The winter of 1919–20 was cruelly cold, even for Eastern Canada. The heat, so much more humid than on the West Coast, lasted until late September. Then there were a few lovely weeks of crisp, cool weather, with the beauty of the leaves changing their colours from green to red and gold before beginning to drop. By October, the air was decidedly cold. Soon the snow began to fall, and it seemed as if the winter would never end, for it had begun in autumn.

Each morning, once the cold weather came, Harry donned his heavy black coat with the beaver collar, his beaver hat and fleece-lined gloves and left the house. He dreaded the cold, yet he was glad to escape from the house, for no matter how dreary or taxing his work was, anything was preferable to living under the same roof with Kathleen and Elaine.

They had taken a three-storey brownstone house on Yonge Street, from which Harry could walk to King Street and the bank. It was a narrow house, dark and sombre both without and within. The front steps stood close to the street, with a small square of grass beside them.

Nothing daunted Kathleen's good humour. She instantly set to work brightening up the house inside, declaring it to be a beautiful place. She had wanted to turn a downstairs room into a bedroom for Elaine, so that she would be spared the effort of walking up and down the stairs, but she stubbornly insisted on having the small attic room on the third floor, where she spent most of her time, avoiding both Harry and Kathleen as much as possible.

Harry's only escape was at the bank. His father and Jim Mulvaney were right: Canada was in a new position since the war, and Victoria was a long way from the nucleus of Canadian banking.

After the first flush of victory, and the excitement and optimism of the

148

armistice, Canadians slowly realized that the war had been responsible for the growth in the economy, and that industries relating to war were now unnecessary. Shipyards and munitions factories closed down. The jobs were gone and there were no new ones. Lines began to form in the streets at employment agencies and soup kitchens.

The banks were closely tied to the federal government's efforts to save the situation. New types of loans and industries must be developed. More active interest in trade and relations with the United States was encouraged. It was another world to Harry, and he applied his fullest concentration to the work, trying to wipe out of his mind the hours he spent in the house on Yonge Street.

Elaine steadfastly refused to eat with them, despite Kathleen's invitations. She ate in the kitchen and waited on them in the dining room. The sight of her, heavier now, obviously pregnant, was the hardest of all Harry's burdens. His illusion that she might have nurtured a secret love for him had vanished.

The odd thing, he could not help but note, was that her attitude toward Kathleen was very different. There seemed to be a kind of grudging approval, even though she steadfastly refused to be converted by Kathleen's intense program of motherhood. She was never rude or cold to Kathleen. She would look at her sometimes with the wisp of a smile, even shaking her head, as though it hurt her to temper Kathleen's fervent maternal mission.

Every Sunday, Harry and Kathleen went to St. Michael's Cathedral on Church Street, where Kathleen prayed for the baby. She was happy in the church. She felt safe. And she knew that God was on her side.

At Christmas, Harry bought a silver fox stole for Kathleen. It cost him a good deal, but he was compelled to buy her an extravagant gift, not only because it was their first Christmas together but because the circumstances were indicative of a special gesture. For Elaine, Kathleen bought a wine-coloured chenille dressing gown, large enough to envelope her pregnancy, yet with a sash that would allow her to use it afterward.

The three of them spent the day alone. They'd had no company at the house. Once, Kathleen had suggested inviting the Mulvaneys for dinner, but Harry had pointed out to her that it was impossible, that their secret would be revealed. Elaine assisted Kathleen in the preparations for the Christmas dinner but refused to join her and Harry at the meal. Her only reluctant concession was to meet with them in the parlour after dinner. Elaine stood in front of the gaily decorated Christmas tree, staring at it as though it evoked some memory that the others could not share. For a moment she looked vulnerable.

"Do you like the gown?" Kathleen asked eagerly. Elaine had opened the package, made note of its contents and covered it again with the tissue wrapping. She looked at Kathleen and again Harry saw the slight, reluctant smile. "Thank you," she said and then reached over behind the tree and brought out a parcel wrapped in tinfoil, which she handed to Kathleen. Then she took her own gift and prepared to leave.

Kathleen unwrapped the parcel. It was a fuchsia plant, with much greenery and just a few blossoms. The dark red flowers were the colour of Elaine's robe. Kathleen looked at it as though it was a treasure.

"Oh, how beautiful! Oh, Harry, look, isn't it wonderful? Oh, Elaine, thank you, my dear!" She went to Elaine in a rush and embraced her with unbridled affection.

At the end of the first week in January, Elaine went into labour. It was nine-thirty in the evening. Kathleen was working in the kitchen and Harry was trying to concentrate on his reading. Harry heard Elaine's voice calling Kathleen, rose and went into the kitchen where his wife was blithely singing while putting away the last of the dishes.

"She's calling you," he said shortly.

Elaine stood on the landing on the second floor in her white flannellette nightgown, her feet bare. She appeared to be perfectly composed, except that she clutched the newel post with all her strength. "You must send for the doctor," she said, and her voice was cool and deep. "It's time."

"It's too early," Kathleen gasped, almost pleadingly.

"I thought you were a nurse," Elaine said sharply. "Help me. Send Harry to get the doctor. Send him now."

Kathleen faltered. "Harry," said Elaine icily.

When Kathleen heard her husband's name, uttered with such unmistakable hatred, she found herself and ran into the parlour. "Harry, you must go and get Dr. Hammond. The baby's coming." Dr. Hammond lived some four blocks away. Harry pulled on his coat and left the house, grateful for the blast of wind that struck him in the face as he turned onto the street.

The baby was a girl, born just before the first light of the winter morning. The labour was not difficult, the child appeared strong and Kathleen recovered from her earlier panic. She had become a nurse once more, staying with the doctor and Elaine throughout the night.

"Elaine," she whispered gently when the doctor had left. "Wouldn't you like to see her?" Her hand touched the glossy black hair, pushing it back from the beautiful face, but Elaine jerked her head away.

"No," she said.

☙ ☙ ☙

Just one week later, after the Burmans had engaged a wet nurse, Harry and Kathleen took Elaine to the railway station and put her on to the train for Vancouver with a new, warm coat. She had wanted to go to the station alone, but Kathleen would not accept this, insisting that all three of them go to Union Station in a taxi. Elaine and Harry were silent, while Kathleen commented on the weather, and how she would always cherish the plant that Elaine had given her. Before she left, Elaine told Kathleen that she would write the Burmans a letter. "I'll make up something to explain why I'm leaving you and won't return to them. But I must do it my own way."

Tears suddenly welled up in Kathleen's eyes. "I'll miss you so much."

Elaine put her suitcase on the floor and stared at her. "I don't have religious beliefs. I don't believe in saints. But if I did, well, I'd almost believe you were one." She picked up her suitcase, started down the stairs and boarded the train without looking back. As they watched the train pull away, Kathleen said in a whisper, "She's gone."

"Thank God," Harry said. He and Kathleen walked through the station to the taxi stand and went home.

CHAPTER FOURTEEN

The Prodigal Son

Matthew Burman sat behind his desk in the study with the letter. Doris stood in the doorway. "Dear Mr. Burman," the letter read. "Perhaps you know already that I have left Toronto and returned to Vancouver Island. You may, if you wish, take this letter as my formal resignation. I would also like to take this opportunity to thank you and Mrs. Burman for your kindness and generosity to me. I shall not be returning to Nootka. Sincerely, Elaine."

Matthew looked at the envelope and saw that it was postmarked Nanaimo.

"Well?" Doris prompted him.

He read the letter to her in his arid voice.

"Sincerely!" She almost snorted with rage. "Why, that ungrateful girl doesn't know the meaning of the word. Sincerely, my foot. I told you all Indians were the same. Probably thought being in a house with a baby would mean extra work."

"That is not fair," said Matthew. "She worked well enough for you when she was here. And apparently Kathleen had no complaints."

"Indians!" she exclaimed and left the room, thinking her husband had learned a lesson.

Matthew looked at the letter again. It was neatly written and carefully phrased, a sign of her education. He felt a great sense of loss, even though he had lost any real connection he had with Elaine long before the move to Toronto. The relationship that he had hoped for, the exchange of ideas and opinions he had dreamed of, had not occurred. He had imagined she would provide him with insight into the character and personality of her race, but she never did.

Sa-Sin, the beautiful little girl who had run along the beach at Nootka, eager to meet him when he arrived on his annual visits, smiling, joking, flirting, had disappeared as soon as he brought her into his home in Victoria. Elaine, the cool, sombre woman—for she seemed to have become a woman immediately—had retained her dignity, but the joyousness in her had gone. Should he have left her at Nootka? He did not know. What, he wondered, was he supposed to tell her father?

He brooded over the matter for months. In June, Harry, Kathleen and Sahndra Mary arrived in Victoria. When he saw his granddaughter he knew at once that the child was Elaine's.

"My, she's very dark, isn't she?" Doris said, holding her granddaughter in her arms for the first time. They were all in the living room of the Burman house, enjoying the reunion and the excitement of the new baby. Matthew was watching Kathleen. The girl was either a great actress or somewhat touched—perhaps both. Plainly, she intended to pass the child off as hers, regardless of the baby's obvious likeness to Elaine. If she could handle it, fine.

It was Harry who baffled him the most. It had never occurred to Matthew that his son could have had relations with Elaine. Eventually, a dry amusement grew within him. He was the grandparent of a descendant of the great Maquinna. His liaisons with the Indians had achieved a truly curious completion.

"Harry was never this dark," Doris was saying querulously. But the truth was not within her realm of understanding; it would have been unthinkable. "Of course, my own dear father was very dark. He was such a handsome man, and didn't you say, Kathleen, that your father was unusually dark?"

Kathleen knelt on the floor by Doris's chair, touching the baby's glossy, thick hair. Her eyes were moist. "Oh, indeed he was. Black Ryan Ryerson, they used to call him. How he would have loved this moment. She's the image of him. But I'm glad you can see a resemblance to your own father too."

Matthew smiled and retreated to his den. Well, if the women were satisfied, it would work out. Harry and Kathleen seemed happy. No doubt there would be gossip among the neighbours, but that need not concern him. He would take a particular interest in the future of his granddaughter.

Harry and Kathleen purchased a small house on Battery Street, two blocks from his parents' home, and began to find some modest happiness. Victoria was experiencing one of its most beautiful summers, warm yet with cool breezes off the water. Flowers bloomed in profusion, and Kathleen at last had a garden of her own. Harry was installed as assistant manager at the bank.

Kathleen's little house delighted her. There was a small parlour downstairs, separated from the dining room by the front hall. A swinging door led from the dining room to a moderately sized kitchen, with sufficient space for a breakfast table and chairs by the window looking out onto the back garden. There were three bedrooms upstairs, and the main one was decorated in Irish green.

On Saturday evenings, Kathleen would put on the gramophone and endeavour to teach Harry to dance. He was amazed to find himself waltzing in his living room, holding Kathleen close, and laughing at his own clumsiness, and her assurance that he was a great partner.

Remarkably for Harry, he was enjoying his life. He had learned much in Toronto about the new Canadian economic situation, and was able to bring his knowledge to the aid of his father and the clientele of the bank.

He had gained in prestige among local businessmen who had seemed to dislike him personally. Harry had become a man to be reckoned with in Victoria's future.

He was convinced that he had put the past well behind him. His mother had spoken of Elaine's absence resentfully, but Kathleen had assured her that Elaine had chosen to return to the island to find her own place in life. "She was wonderful," said Kathleen. "I couldn't have managed without her."

Elaine was not mentioned again.

There was one reminder of her that angered Harry, but he could do nothing about it. Kathleen had brought the fuchsia plant that Elaine had given her back to Victoria, nurturing it with as much care as she gave to Sahndra Mary. She placed it on the windowsill, between the white lace curtains in the living room, so Harry could see it as he came home from work, with its exotic dark red blossoms like great drops of blood, so different from the delicate, light flowers in the garden.

It was in November that Harry felt the first change in Kathleen. She was as loving and as busy as ever, but she sang less around the house, and very often when he came home from work he would find her sitting by the fireplace, staring at the flames.

One evening he sat down opposite her and took her hands in his. "Is something troubling you, my dear? We're so happy. I don't want you to worry about a thing, yet I sense that you're concerned about something."

She raised her face to his, attempting a smile. "It's nothing, Harry. I'm sorry if I seem moody. Really, my thoughts are the best in the world. It's just that I want another baby. I expected that I would have one before this. But it is God's will . . ."

He pushed her short, soft hair behind her ear and whispered, "Perhaps we should try a bit harder."

She blushed and put her head on his shoulder. "I love you, Harry," she said, leaning against him in a position where she could still gaze at the now-dying embers of the fireplace.

The first week in December, a poised, confident Kathleen told Harry over the breakfast table that she had an appointment later that morning to see Dr. Sinclair. Looking at her serene expression, he felt his own elation. "Do you mean . . . you think there's a chance?"

She smiled, carefully buttering her toast. "No woman is positive at this stage, but I have my hopes, my dear. Certainly, it is wise that I see Dr. Sinclair."

That night as he came home, Harry saw the welcome smoke from his chimney and knew that there would be a fire in the fireplace as usual. He found Kathleen in her favourite chair, knitting, while Sahndra Mary was on a rug on the floor, playing with a set of blocks. He went over, kissed Kathleen, picked up Sahndra Mary and sat down, looking at his wife. He could not quite fathom her expression.

"Well, what news?"

Her pleasant, amused expression returned. "I like Dr. Sinclair very much, even if he's a Scot. Did you know he was at Ypres? Fifth Unit, so we wouldn't have run into him. But I believe he's a good man and I can't imagine anyone else looking after me."

"Then it's good news?"

She picked up a stitch she had dropped. "Well, not this time." She looked up, her eyes shining. "But Dr. Sinclair said there is no reason in the world why I should not have another healthy child. A brother for Sahndra Mary."

🐿 🐿 🐿

Harry was in his office the following afternoon when he received a telephone call from the nurse at Dr. Sinclair's office, asking if he would stop by on his way home from work. Fear engulfed him. All the stories he had heard, of doctors who would not break the news of serious illness to the patients themselves, but subtly confided in a husband, wife or family member, giving them the burden to withhold the truth or tell the patient as they chose, all came to him now, and he was sure that Kathleen was dying of some incurable disease. Could this be God's punishment for his sin?

He had to wait almost half an hour in the depressing reception room of Dr. Sinclair's office. It smelled of ether and stale tobacco. Finally the middle-aged nurse said, "Mr. Burman? Dr. Sinclair will see you now."

Dr. Alistair Sinclair was a big man, balding, clean-shaven, cheerful and forthright. He shook Harry's hand heartily, asked him to be seated and offered him a cigarette, which Harry accepted. "Well, your little wife tells me we were all in the big show together, almost neighbours at the front, you might say."

Harry had no desire to discuss the war, least of all in this hearty manner. His voice came out with his customary coldness. "What is wrong with my wife?"

Dr. Sinclair looked surprised, even offended at the abruptness of the question. "There's nothing wrong with her as far as I could ascertain." He leaned back in his chair, inhaling smoke from his cigarette. "She's a strong, healthy young woman."

Harry stared. "There's *nothing* wrong?"

"There's no reason why she can't have children, if that's what you mean."

"Then what did you want to talk to me about? I've been in agony all afternoon since your nurse called."

"I apologize." Dr. Sinclair leaned forward now, the grey eyes under the bushy eyebrows searching Harry's face. "Your little girl," he said gently. "Mrs. Burman showed me her picture—a beautiful child. She was adopted at birth?"

"Yes."

"You'd not been married a year, I understand. Rather early to adopt, wasn't it?"

Harry was silent, perplexed and uneasy.

"Did Mrs. Burman have any reason to doubt her ability to bear a child?"

Harry proceeded with caution. "Not at all. My wife and I both assumed we'd have a large family. We still expect to do so. It was simply that we were aware of the circumstances surrounding this child's birth, and we arranged to adopt her. Because the birth took place in Toronto, my wife and I have chosen to tell our family and friends that she is ours."

"Your wife," said the doctor slowly, "insists that it is yours. Yours, and hers."

"She seems to have talked herself into believing it's the truth. Makes it easier to convince everyone else." He stubbed out the cigarette the doctor had given him and lit one of his own.

"You've never observed any instances of any . . . mental disturbance in your wife?"

"Mental disturbance?" Harry's hand shook. "I don't understand. There's nothing the matter with her at all. She wants children very badly and she's made up her mind to accept Sahndra Mary as her own, and make everyone else believe it. Why should you be an exception?"

"I examined her. It was obvious she had never had a child. Yet she insisted on telling me the details of the baby's birth in Toronto," said Dr. Sinclair. "She's a nurse. She should know better than to try to fool a doctor."

Harry got to his feet and took his coat from the back of the chair. "I won't take any more of your time. I'm happy that you found my wife in good health."

CHAPTER FIFTEEN

Ships Passing

It was June 1923. Georgie Trevor stood in the front hall of Blenheim Oaks and tried on his officer's cap in front of the large, gilt-edged mirror. He had just been appointed second officer on the Canadian Pacific's latest vessel, the *Princess Beatrice*, which was due to leave for her afternoon run to Vancouver in an hour. He experimented with several angles, looking for an effect that pleased and flattered him, but finally, knowing that the captain would insist on his wearing it according to regulation with no deviation for "smartness" or individual needs, he allowed his mother to place it on his red head in the traditional manner.

"You look so dashing, darling," said Eleanor. It would be his first run on the *Princess Beatrice*, with his new stripes and rank. "I really must send Cousin Winston a snapshot of you and your ship. He'll be so proud."

Privately, Georgie thought that Winston would be much too busy to pay any attention to a snapshot of a distant cousin in the colonies, but he would not hurt his mother for anything in the world. He was as proud of her elegance as she was of his uniform, and she made him laugh with what he considered her charming pretentiousness.

Georgie was twenty-four, not at all handsome but undeniably likeable. The colour of his carrot-red hair had not softened as he matured. His freckles were so numerous that they seemed in places to form one continuous blotch, and his flecked hazel eyes with their orange lashes frequently squinted in the sun. He was six feet tall and thin, with rather large ears but a delightful grin, and an unexpectedly deep, pleasant voice. He was a bright, outgoing and popular young man.

Eleanor watched proudly as the chauffeur pulled up to take him to the dock. At forty-seven, she had no discernible grey in her glorious red hair, although her faithful maid Aggie knew about the little bottle of henna tucked away in the dressing-table drawer. She had kept her figure well, eating carefully and taking long walks around the grounds and through the winding streets in the neighbourhood she loved.

Not for a moment had she regretted marrying George Trevor and coming to Victoria. She still believed she had the best of all possible worlds, for here she was able to uphold the traditions of England amid the beauty of British Columbia, and she felt she had escaped the ravages of the war and the hardships that followed. She sanctified her husband for his glorious sacrifice for their country, and she crushed her loneliness as being unpatriotic.

Eleanor devoted herself to bestowing her favour on those who had served King and country well, and among them was Sir Adrian Jersey, who had come to Victoria in 1920 as an extremely distinguished British soldier. He had retired early from the 8th Division of the Northern Army because of a series of injuries, beginning with some nasty wounds suffered at Gallipoli—"a bloody stupid business"—that prevented him from meeting the Huns at close range in what he considered a "real war."

Major-General Jersey recovered well enough to return to his adopted home of India two years later, but his long absence from active service meant he was, as he told Eleanor, "left to stand at attention when General Dyer cocked up the nasty affair at Amritsar and gave Gandhi a better hand than he deserved." A few months later in Afghanistan, during the last chapter of the so-called Third Afghan War, he "merely stood around and watched the bastards run back to wherever they came from." One of the bastards, however, managed a final wild shot at the major-general, which lodged in his hip and put him out of commission for good. "It was," Sir Adrian would say with his fingers drawn up to the needlelike tip of his waxed moustache, "a ridiculous way to earn a knighthood."

When he came to Victoria, it was with his long-time companion, Edwina Brill, a very plain but devoted woman who barely spoke in his presence except to agree with him. Eleanor did wonder why exactly the city should be so blessed with yet another knighted man. Only Miss Brill knew that the real reason for their being in Victoria was Sir Adrian's estrangement from his wife, who had steadfastly refused to leave England. He said they could not return there as a couple "out of respect for Lady Jersey's feelings." Edwina managed to accept this explanation as gentlemanly, given the attention she enjoyed from him. Besides, he firmly avowed that when it came to Lady Jersey he "simply could not stand that woman."

Aggie had strict orders not to interrupt Eleanor's croquet games with Sir Neville and Lady Wallingford, Sir Adrian Jersey and Edwina Brill. They had just begun when Eleanor saw her hurrying across the lawn. "What is it, Aggie?" she said in her most cordial voice.

"Oh, ma'am, it's the *Princess Beatrice*. They're sayin' she hit another boat!"

"Who says?"

"The gentleman from the CPR office. He was on the telephone."

"Damn boats," fumed Sir Neville. "Captain's drunk, I suppose."

Lady Wallingford put her arm around Eleanor's shoulders. "The *Beatrice* is a fine ship. They'll know how to handle it, I'm sure." But Eleanor slipped from her arm and fled with Aggie across the lawn, leaving her mallet on the ground where she had dropped it.

⋘ ⋘ ⋘

Julia Godolphin sat on the deck of the *Islander III*, the small vessel of the Union Steamship Line that served the Gulf Islands, augmenting the CPR ships, which called less often and only at the larger islands. She sat on a bench right next to the railing and drew her legs up to let her coat fold over them and keep them warm. Her mother had been right: short dresses made for cold legs.

Despite her discomfort, however, she would not choose to be anywhere else, and this was *her* choice. At twenty-three, she seldom asserted herself, yet she knew she would soon see Arnason Island. The ship would dock there, perhaps for half an hour, as passengers destined for the Arnason Inne disembarked. She was returning from Vancouver, where she had attended the annual BC Music Festival to see one of her pupils perform. She was satisfied that he finished fourteenth out of fifty-eight competitors; his parents had been pleased and had given Julia much of the credit. Clarence and his family had stayed at a hotel, but Julia had spent three boring days at the home of the Elliotts, friends of Adelaide, who would never have consented to a young girl of Julia's age and upbringing staying at a hotel by herself.

It was assumed that she would return on one of the CPR boats, as Clarence and his parents had done, but a peculiarly powerful urge caused her to take the *Islander III*, which left the mainland from Horseshoe Bay, rather than the CPR docks in Vancouver, and would make mail calls at many of the smaller islands before reaching Victoria. One of those would be Arnason Island.

She had not forgotten Albert Aalgaard during the past four years. She had lived on without him, taking on more pupils, accompanying Lilas in her concerts, spending more time than ever with her parents and only rarely going out with people of her own age.

About once a month she had dinner with Kathleen and Harry Burman and little Sahndra Mary, and the odd time Kathleen would invite her to go shopping, but their friendship was not as close as it had been. The gap between them was widening, as often happened between a spinster and a young married woman with a child. Julia had begun to consider an unmarried life as her destiny.

In her large black purse she carried a postcard from Albert. It was almost two years old and featured a picture of a hotel in Nice, overlooking the Mediterranean. On the back was a short message that informed her he was going to be married to an English girl and would probably live in England. He sent his love and best wishes for her happiness.

Two months later there had been stories in both the *Times* and the *Colonist* about Albert's marriage to Joan Lapsley, a member of a prominent old English family. There was a picture of Albert and Joan. She appeared beautiful and self-possessed, a girl who was used to having her picture in the paper, thought Julia. They were both in riding clothes, the picture being taken at the Lapsley estate, and there was a horse between them. Albert, recalled Julia, had never liked horses.

Today, though, she would fulfill a fantasy she had nursed in silence for months; she would see where Albert had lived before he became a foreigner. And she would see her brother. They were still in the gulf, and the wind swept from the north down the open channel. Inside the small vessel children were laughing, and tourists chatting, but Julia preferred to be alone, feeling the wind.

Rising above and beyond Valdes and Galiano islands were the mountains of Vancouver Island. Ahead, between Mayne and Galiano, was Active Pass, the entrance to the islands that lay off the coast of Vancouver Island itself.

Julia saw what appeared to be a ribbon of smoke lying across Galiano and assumed it was the smoke from the funnel of the *Princess Beatrice*, headed from Victoria to Vancouver. That was the last thing she remembered before fatigue and the gentle rocking of the ship caused her to doze off.

Suddenly, she awoke as though she were in the middle of a war. There was the most enormous noise, then she was falling, and before she could orient herself she was in the cold water. Her wool clothing weighed her down as she struggled to the surface. She saw that her ship had collided with a larger one, and there was much shouting on the decks.

"Help!" she yelled.

A voice sounded clearly above the hubbub. "Hello! Are you all right? I'm throwing you a life ring!"

"Hurry! I'm sinking!" A large white ring fell close to her, and she grabbed it. A lifeboat descended from the side of a ship—not the *Islander*, she knew—and several arms pulled her aboard. She soon found herself on the ship itself, shivering in front of a young man with fiery red hair, his hat askew, holding a grey blanket. "Please, wrap yourself in this."

"I think," she replied tartly, "that I should remove the wet clothes I'm wearing first."

"Oh, oh. Right," he stammered. "Let me take you to my cabin."

"Are you the captain?" she asked, seeing the gold braid on his uniform. "What in the dickens happened?"

"I'm not the captain," he said with a gentle bow. "I'm George Trevor, the second officer. As for what happened, I can't explain it, except that the *Islander* appeared to have lost her steering as she came around Galiano into the pass. The tide is running fast now, and we couldn't avoid her."

Julia was soon ensconced alone in a small but tidy cabin, finally able to remove her wet clothes and lay them over two chairs to dry. She climbed into the bunk naked and slowly began to warm up, then was startled by a knock on the cabin door.

"Who is it?"

"The steward, ma'am. Just bringing some hot tea."

"Thank you. Please leave it at the door." Her mother would be scandalized if she let a man, even a servant, into the room while she was undressed. She wrapped herself in a blanket, opened the door a crack to assure herself that no one was nearby and found a tray with a pot of tea, a cup and saucer and two ham sandwiches.

Not more than ten minutes after she had finished her meal, another knock sounded. "Excuse me, Miss Godolphin. It's George—George Trevor. I need some things from the cabin."

"Oh," Julia said hesitantly. "Just a minute." She was sure that she looked a fright with her hair uncombed. She opened the cabin door and George entered, looking tidier and more official than he had on deck. "Do you have a moment?" Julia asked. "What's going on? Does my family know what's happened?"

"Yes, yes," he reassured her. "Everything's fine. We'll be in Victoria tomorrow night. Your parents will meet the *Beatrice* at the dock."

"Is everyone else all right?"

"A crew member on the *Islander* appears to have broken his arm, and there are some other bumps and scrapes. We're still trying to figure out how you were thrown off the deck into the water. Are you sure *you're* all right?"

"I'll be perfectly fine. If you could arrange for some help in drying my things, I'll be out of your way." She looked up into his eyes and said warmly, "Thank you, Mr. Trevor, for all your kindness."

"Oh, please, call me Georgie. Everyone does."

"Well, thank you, Georgie."

He retrieved a briefcase, smiled, bowed slightly and left the cabin.

Now there, thought Julia, is a man who would make some girl a fine husband.

🕊 🕊 🕊

Julia married Georgie Trevor in September, four months after the collision of the *Islander* and the *Beatrice*. Georgie had made up his mind immediately, practically from the moment he helped her onto the deck. It was all very simple to him. He had rescued and fallen in love with a beautiful girl, and they would live happily ever after.

His mother had some doubts at first. "The Godolphins," she said pensively, "are not one of Victoria's first families, dear."

"Now, Mum darling, we all know that the Trevors were here before anyone else, probably even the Indians, but Victoria has only been settled since 1847—not even a hundred years—and Mr. and Mrs. Godolphin have been here since 1898. That's twenty-seven years, for God's sake!"

"Don't swear, Georgie," Eleanor admonished. "Get me my *Burke's Peerage*."

That was better, he thought. She was coming round. She was always happiest when she was looking up families in *Burke's Peerage*.

They met again at teatime in the sunroom, and he could see by her face that she had changed her mind. "Well, really, you know, I didn't realize that the Godolphins went so far back. It's a very honourable name in Cornwall. We can't be sure that Lewis Godolphin is related to *the* Godolphins, but we shall tell everyone that he is, and no one will dispute it if *I* say so."

Georgie continued to play his hand well. "Adelaide Godolphin knows absolutely *everything* about European royalty. How many of your friends know that the third Duke of Schleswig-Holstein was illegitimate?"

Eleanor was impressed. "Well, now, why don't you bring Julia around tomorrow. No, not tomorrow. I promised Sir Adrian I'd go with him to the cricket match. How about tomorrow evening? I've asked the Wallingfords and Sir Adrian back here, but that's all right. Just bring Julia over and we can all get to know her."

Georgie sighed. "I'd hoped that you and she and I could have a quiet visit together." He didn't argue the point further. It was best to leave well enough alone. His mother had accepted Julia, and that was all that was necessary.

Adelaide Godolphin had mixed feelings. She was pleased that Julia was to be married; it had appeared that she might become an old maid. However, while she wanted the best for her family, she was wary of getting it. She was an anglophile and an admirer of royalty and the nobility, but she was also suspicious of the "upper class." She could not help feeling that perhaps Julia was exceeding her reach. The Trevors and their peers should remain on an exalted pedestal. One could read about them in the society columns, admire the sight of them from a distance, even gossip about them, but one should not marry them.

"I don't understand," Adelaide said to Lewis, "how Julia comes to attract the attention of these rich men! I don't know what they see in her."

"Addie, dear! Julia is a beautiful girl. She grows more beautiful every day."

Adelaide could see that her husband really believed this, and she assumed there was something in what he said. Julia *had* grown better looking as she matured. "Yes, she's a pretty girl. We must give her that."

He leaned over and touched her knee. "Let's be thankful she's done well, and that she's happy. That's the main thing."

"I hope so," said Adelaide. She would not express any more doubts to Lewis. Besides, what stories she would have to tell Miss Cooke and her other friends!

🐦 🐦 🐦

Julia had had a difficult time after the collision. When she returned home, she was in another world. Her mother believed she was in some sort of shock; perhaps it was true for a sheltered and introspective person like her. Her terror of the war was brought home to her personally in the sinking of the ship, and she would dream of the moment of the collision and her struggle in the water for years.

As with any serious maritime mishap, both the government and the shipping line held inquiries into what had happened, and Julia was called to testify. She told her brief story so frequently, both before and during the inquiries, that she felt as though she could recite it in her sleep. Finally, both juries came to almost the same conclusion: a mechanical failure had caused the *Islander* to lose control.

Georgie Trevor testified at the hearings too, so Julia saw him often at the courthouse. He finally took his courage in both hands and spoke with her. "Miss Godolphin," he said tentatively, "may I invite you to have tea with me after court today?"

Julia was taken aback. Why was this young officer, from a completely different social circle, asking her to tea? Her mother would certainly disapprove, but something within told her that she couldn't let this opportunity pass. "I would be honoured."

"Please, the honour is mine. I'll meet you at the entrance after the court adjourns, and we'll walk over to the Empress."

"The Empress? Oh, goodness!" She looked around, appalled at the thought that her mother would hear from one of her gossip-mongering friends.

"It's perfectly all right," said Georgie. "My mother has tea there most afternoons, and I'm sure that one of her friends will have an eye on us the whole time." Georgie proved to be correct: they ended up sharing tea with two of his mother's friends, and Julia enjoyed listening to them reminisce about the tea dances of their youth.

As their relationship continued, she was almost amused by Georgie's boyish enthusiasm for being with her, and she found that she liked him very much. She went dancing with him at the Empress, and on a cruise on a launch he wanted to buy. Despite his wealth and social position, she was less in awe of Georgie than she had been of Albert. His manner relaxed her and they became so inseparable that when he proposed to her she said "Yes" as though it was the only possible next step for their friendship.

Her doubts came that night at home. She was very fond of him, enjoyed his company and could say that she found him attractive and even that she loved him. But she was not in love with him in the magical sense that she had been in love with Albert. She worried that if he discovered this and repudiated her it would devastate her family. She spent a sleepless night, and determined that she would tell him the next evening.

They dined at the Poodle Dog, where Julia insisted on paying for her dinner. She wanted Georgie to know that, as a woman who earned her own living, she did not depend on him. But her halibut steak went almost uneaten. She had rehearsed what she needed to say so often that it was all she could think about. Georgie put it down to her concern over the wedding.

They drove home in Georgie's Model A. At her front door, instead of waiting for him to open the door for her, she put her hand on his arm. "I have to tell you something."

He knew, when he saw the intensity of her expression, that it was serious. He took her hand. "Tell me," he said gently, "but don't back down about marrying me. I can stand anything else."

"Georgie, I do love you very much. That's why you must know this. If I didn't love you I might just . . . keep it from you. But I have to."

"Go ahead, fire away."

"Well, you know I used to go out with Albert Aalgaard."

"Lucky man. If I'd known you then I'd have challenged him to a duel. Or something." Georgie grinned. How lovely she was, with her pale, earnest face.

Julia could not look at him. "Albert was much more . . . worldly than I was. And I . . . we . . ."

Georgie put his arm around her. "Are you trying to tell me that you were intimate with Albert?" he asked gently.

Julia looked up at him, amazed. She had never seen such an expression in anyone's eyes before—such understanding and, yes, sympathy and feeling for what it was costing her to reveal so much of herself. Her old shyness and self-consciousness returned. "No! I wanted to, but Albert . . . refused. But, Georgie, I was so much in love with him that I would have."

"You don't have to give me the details." Georgie kissed her ear. "I quite understand."

"But how could you?"

"My darling, I went to school with Albert. I've known him for years. If there was any woman that Albert Aalgaard desired and didn't get, it would have been a miracle."

Julia was embarrassed and began twisting her engagement ring around on her finger. Somehow his statement took the romance out of her memories of Albert. Had she been only one of many? She had never thought about it that way, but now that she did, it seemed logical.

"Do you still want me, Georgie?"

"Try me," he said and kissed her again, this time on the lips, and not for a short time.

≈ ≈ ≈

Although it was customary for the bride's parents to arrange and pay for the wedding, Eleanor would not hear of it. She had the house, the position and the money to give Julia the kind of wedding she wanted her son to have, and that was that. She was tactful enough not to make the Godolphins feel inferior yet overwhelming enough that no one would disagree with her. She did defer to Adelaide wherever possible, consulting her on the flowers, decorations and food, and leaving the dresses for the bride and her bridesmaids in her hands.

Julia's bridal dress, imported from Paris, was purchased from the specialty department at Spencer's. Adelaide told Lewis it was necessary to show the Trevors that the Godolphins were quite worthy of them. The dress was white satin, the skirt calf-length in front in the latest fashion, but floor-length in back, with a three-foot train. She would wear a simple lace veil with a Juliet cap. Adelaide was scandalized by the short skirt, but changed her mind after she saw photos in fashion magazines of British dukes' daughters married in identical dresses.

Lilas would be the bridesmaid and Kathleen Burman the matron of honour. Lilas was to wear pink and Kathleen held out for a pale green rather than blue, as green was an "Irish" colour better suited to her complexion.

Besides, Julia's going-away outfit was blue. Victor Trevor would be his younger brother's best man and the reception would be held at Blenheim Oaks. The mayor and his wife and prominent CPR officials were invited. The lieutenant-governor could not attend but sent a beautiful gift.

Lewis sent an invitation to Sveinn Arnason. He received a handwritten reply from Anna, saying that her father's business obligations in Vancouver prevented them from attending. She wished dear Julia every happiness, and sent a magnificent silver platter as a wedding gift. From the time of the gift's arrival, Julia began to brood.

On the Saturday evening exactly one week before the wedding, Julia excused herself from the dinner table, saying she did not feel well and wanted to lie down.

"What's the matter with you?" asked her mother sharply.

"I said I don't feel well," replied Julia and left the room.

Lewis looked worried. "Do you think we should call Dr. Muddsley?"

His wife shook her head, pinching her thin lips more closely together before she spoke. "She's not sick," she pronounced at last. "There's something on her mind. I know that girl. Something she's afraid to come out with."

"I thought all brides acted like that," said Lilas. "Wedding-night jitters, they call it." Her mother's look did not disturb her. "She's probably wondering if Georgie has freckles all over!"

"Lilas! Leave the table! That's a very unladylike thing to say. It's vulgar. You shouldn't be thinking things like that."

Lilas winked at her father, picked up her plate and went into the parlour. Her mother wasn't going to intimidate her.

Lewis sighed. Adelaide was clearing away the dishes without asking Lilas for assistance when she turned to see Julia in her dressing gown and slippers, standing in the doorway.

"I want my brother," said Julia. "I want him to come to my wedding."

For once, Adelaide felt the weaker. How could this happen to me, she was thinking; I don't deserve this now, not after all these years. "He can't come. He's sick, Julia. You know that."

"He's not sick! He's not!" Julia heard her own voice rising as though it were coming from somewhere else. "I want Stanley at my wedding! You took him from me. You sent him away. It's your fault, and if you don't let him come to my wedding, I will never forgive you!"

Adelaide was completely shaken, but she knew she could not unduly upset her daughter. "Julia," she said quietly, "your brother had to go away. It was impossible for him to stay here. You don't understand what he did."

"I don't care!" exclaimed Julia loudly, tears welling up in her eyes.

Lewis heard her and came into the kitchen. Julia threw herself into his arms, sobbing. "Daddy, bring Stanley home. I want him at my wedding. Don't let her keep him away anymore."

Adelaide told herself she was embarrassed by Julia's display of emotion. People in civilized houses should not act this way. A fleeting memory of her own behaviour toward Stanley on that terrible night crossed her mind and she closed her eyes, clenched her hands and kept her voice calm. "Lewis, get her a glass of wine. She's hysterical."

Lewis reluctantly detached himself from his daughter's arms, went to the cabinet and produced a bottle and three glasses. Julia leaned against the kitchen wall, her face buried in her hands, still sobbing.

"I never thought I would live to see the day when one of my daughters would speak to me like that," Adelaide declared, feeling that she was the wounded one.

"Daddy," Julia said again, "I want my brother at my wedding. You bring him home."

"It's impossible!" Adelaide's voice was getting louder.

"It's not impossible, Addie," Lewis said, gently but firmly. "Not anymore."

"Lewis! What are you saying? You can't mean it."

"I mean it." He turned to Julia, and to her surprise she saw tears in her father's eyes. "I want him too, Julia. I'll telephone Arnason Island tomorrow."

Later, Julia recalled how Lewis kissed her and wiped his eyes. She remembered hugging them both, how rigid her mother's body felt. Adelaide said no more; she knew that she had lost.

CHAPTER SIXTEEN

The Wedding

The wedding of Julia Godolphin and George Trevor III was set for noon on Saturday, the 15th day of September, 1923, at St. Andrew's Presbyterian Church in downtown Victoria.

At nine o'clock that morning, the doorbell rang at the Godolphin house. Adelaide supposed it was a messenger with a present, but when she opened the door, she was surprised to see a tall, thin man on the doorstep. He wore a grey suit and an overcoat and a felt hat of the same colour. His clothes did not appear to fit him very well, but they were clean and neat. He wore glasses, was clean-shaven and had an air of timidity. She did not recognize him. He took off his hat.

"Hello, Mother," he said.

She could not have reached into herself to touch her real feelings; she did not know how, and disapproved of the very idea of such emotions. She knew that he was coming, but she had not thought about how she would deal with the reality of his presence and had put the situation completely out of her mind. It was her duty to disapprove of him. Goodness knows what he might have done since they saw him last.

"Come in," she said and watched him curiously as he took off his overcoat and hat, placing them neatly on the rack in the hall. My goodness, thought Adelaide, he was a tall boy, not so very bad-looking behind the glasses and that stringy hair. "I'll call your father."

"Thank you," said Stanley. He looked around the room and then down at his mother and smiled gently. "Don't let me keep you from what you have to do. I'm sure you must be very busy."

"Yes, yes. I'll call your father," she said again, absently, and turned to the stairs.

Lewis came downstairs and was overcome with emotion. He embraced his son, and Stanley hugged him in return. He knew his father loved him, but even Lewis was not the most important person to him right now. He was here to honour his sister.

Then he saw Julia at the top of the stairs in her dressing gown, and he knew everything would be all right, at least for today.

🐦 🐦 🐦

Throughout the morning, Lilas was remarkably quiet. Not that she didn't know "Oh Promise Me" well enough to sing it without a rehearsal, but she was extremely conscientious about her public performances. When the bridal party went into the vestibule to sign the register, she would take her place in the balcony and, accompanied by the organist, sing her song.

Lilas was interested only in herself. While she was glad to see Stanley, who spent most of his time at the house with Lewis in his study, she found him dull and not good-looking enough to be interesting, and ignored him.

Kathleen never stopped talking. It occurred to Lilas that her tendency verged on peculiar, but she did not dwell on the subject for long.

Julia dressed in her own room with the help of her mother. "Thank you, Mama, for everything,"

Adelaide stiffened at this emotional display, then she reached up and touched Julia's cheek. "You're a good girl, Julia," she said, and Julia knew that for her mother it was the supreme compliment. They smiled at each other briefly.

Eleanor sent her Bentley with the chauffeur to bring the bridal party to the church so they could all arrive at once. It was right that the bride should have the Bentley while she and Georgie and Victor would go in the DeSoto.

Lewis and Stanley got into the front seat of the car with the chauffeur, Kathleen and Lilas perched on the two small pull-out seats and Adelaide and Julia sat facing them. Kathleen did all the talking, while Julia looked out the window and Lilas studied her face in the mirror of her compact, leaving her mother and sister to listen.

"Mrs. Godolphin, Sahndra Mary is the best child I have ever known and I'm sure you would find her so too. Remember I was a nurse so I know about babies, but she is exceptional. Harry and I have very great hopes and every reason to believe that it won't be too long before there will be a baby brother for Sahndra Mary. There now," she sat back. "I've told you my secret. But don't you dare tell anyone, will you?"

Adelaide shook her head.

The Bentley pulled up in front of St. Andrew's, and a young man in full naval uniform came down the steps to assist the bridal party. Julia scarcely had time to check her veil in the mirror when she was signalled and she could hear the organ beginning the "Wedding March." Her father gave her his arm. Kathleen and Lilas, clutching their bouquets, smiling, started ahead. It was happening. She was getting married, and in greater style than she had ever dreamed of. (What would it have been like if Albert had been the groom? No, don't think of that now, nor ever again.) She saw Georgie standing in front of the altar, looking at her and smiling. She smiled back, seeing the crowd that filled the church.

On the aisle to her left she caught a glimpse of Mr. and Mrs. Burman, and Harry holding his daughter on his lap. The little girl *was* incredibly beautiful, in her pink bonnet and coat, her dark, serious eyes taking in the sights around her.

Before she knew it, it was over, and "Oh Promise Me" rang out in Lilas's clear, steady soprano. Julia and Georgie came back up the aisle and stood on the steps of the church, while six naval officers formed an arch with their swords.

The reception at Blenheim Oaks was less clear to Julia than were the events at the church. There were simply too many people. They all seemed to be moving in waves of colour and fashion and conversation through the hallway and living room and into the garden and even the library, drinking champagne, talking, laughing.

She stood in the receiving line before the mantel in the large living room, with Georgie by her side, and Eleanor clinging to Georgie on the other side. There was Victor, never without a glass of champagne since the wedding party arrived at the reception. Lilas smiled at everyone, giving a very self-conscious performance of her own. Adelaide was ill at ease but doing her best to be gracious while disapproving of so many people congregated in one area. Lewis, more comfortable than he had been at the church, put his untasted glass of champagne down. Kathleen chatted to Reverend Allen about how beautiful Sahndra Mary was, while Harry sat with the little girl and fed her cucumber sandwiches. Edwina Brill, in an expensive purple satin gown that did nothing for her at all, leaned over and patted the hand of Sahndra Mary, who drew it away quickly; she was watching Sir Adrian Jersey with all her concentration.

The only words Julia could remember amid the hubhub were those of Sir Adrian. "I haven't felt so privileged since I stood in the old Queen's honour guard at her funeral back in 1901."

Stanley stood alone by the window, away from the others. He told Julia he did not want to join the receiving line; he was happy just to be present. She watched him at the exact moment of Sir Adrian's toast to the bride, which managed somehow to be gracious even though it was almost entirely about himself, and she saw Stanley lift his glass of champagne and smile at her over the crowd that separated them.

At last it was over. Julia flung her bouquet over the banister on the wide stairway, its railings decorated in white ribbon and lilies of the valley. Lilas just missed it; it was caught by Dulcie, one of Georgie's old girlfriends. Then she was upstairs alone with her mother, changing her clothes.

"Now be careful what you say and do, Julia, when you go anywhere fancy with your husband. Try not to bump into furniture, and remember your manners. I'm sure your husband will be very particular about things like that. And don't talk out of turn. Think before you speak."

Julia closed her eyes as she finished putting on her blue travelling suit, and the pale blue coat with its matching, dyed fox-fur collar. She must be patient and try to remember to accept Adelaide as she is, as Stanley had told her to do. In fact, she was proud of herself for having been deferential without feeling subservient in the weeks before the wedding, and she was surprised that her mother did not rattle her. She kissed her warmly. "Thank you. I will try to do all the things you told me."

As Julia opened the bedroom door, her mother said in a tight voice, "Julia, you . . . you know what to do, don't you?"

It took Julia a moment to realize what her mother was talking about, and she laughed inside. "Yes, Mother, I think so."

There were final goodbyes and masses of confetti, then Georgie and Julia were in the back seat of the Bentley, decorated with snow-white bows and rattling cans. The chauffeur drove them downtown to stay a night at the Empress before their departure for California.

≋ ≋ ≋

Julia's son, George David Trevor IV, was born in the Royal Jubilee Hospital on the first day of September 1924. The first Julia knew of it was when Georgie hovered over the edge of her narrow hospital bed. "It's a boy! Oh, my darling, how clever of you. Mother's absolutely beside herself, if you can imagine such a thing!"

She stirred hazily, wondering how other people knew she had had a baby when she couldn't remember a thing, except feeling sick as the anaesthetic wore off.

"Are you sure?"

"Am I sure? You angel—everybody in Victoria knows about it by now! He's got tons of red hair, so you can imagine Mother's joy, except I really think he's better looking than I am. We can only hope so, anyway." He leaned over and kissed her.

"I think Mrs. Trevor should rest now," said the nurse who was standing behind him.

Julia couldn't imagine why she should rest. "But I just woke up. Can't I see the baby too?"

The nurse left the room, and a few minutes later, Julia was holding her child in her arms, watching his tiny hands grasping at nothing, his mouth pursing in expectation of something. He was a miracle to her, particularly because she recalled so little about his arrival in the world.

Julia was grateful when, out of regard for the Prince of Wales, Eleanor suggested that they call him David instead of George. (The prince's official names were Edward Albert Christian George Andrew Patrick David, but he was called David by his family and friends.)

The first few weeks of marriage had been overwhelming to Julia. She had never been farther than Vancouver by herself, and to Seattle with her parents. She and Georgie had gone by train to California, visiting San Francisco, Los Angeles and Hollywood (sending postcards to Lilas, even catching a glimpse of Mary Pickford in person at a Hollywood theatre); then they spent a week in San Diego at the paradisical Hotel Del Coronado. She was comfortable with Georgie. He made her laugh, made her feel secure. She loved the way he would throw an arm around her and walk with her as though they were schoolmates.

In bed, their first experiences were gentle, not deeply passionate, and Julia worried about her adequacy. But as the months passed they began to relax. This is the way it is between married people, Julia thought, and they were content.

After they returned, they lived in the coach house at the back of the Trevor estate. Little David took his first steps across the Trevor lawn, and received his first slap on the hands for picking the heads off tulips. Georgie quickly rose to the position of chief officer on the *Princess Victoria*. Victor alternated his time between brief visits to his mother and longer visits to Vancouver and Seattle. He was in "importing," Eleanor said, and very successful. Julia's parents were welcome at Blenheim Oaks, and Eleanor was always most gracious to them when they visited the main house, although Adelaide was never really comfortable in her presence.

On rare occasions, and less and less often as she devoted herself to Georgie and David, Julia found herself thinking of Albert. She had received a card congratulating her on her marriage, but no word since. She wished him the best; after all, he had been important to her once.

CHAPTER SEVENTEEN

Confidences

Sir Adrian Jersey seemed like an original fixture at Victoria's Union Club from the day he first set foot in the place. Everyone soon greeted him as an old friend, even those who'd only exchanged pleasantries of the day with him. Sir Adrian was gregarious and curious and he quickly knew more about the club's denizens than most longstanding members, although his curiosity often appeared to his companions to be an excuse for him to launch into his own expansive stories.

Harry Burman was also a fixture at the Union Club but of exactly the opposite sort. For Harry, Union Club lunches were a duty of his employment; while his father enjoyed but did not relish his visits to the club, Harry always felt he'd rather be in church.

The Gordon Street building, completed in 1913, looked as though it had always been there, despite its spare, modern exterior. Sir Adrian, in his trademark gold paisley day cravat and burgundy vest, contributed to the effect. He knew that the Union Club had been founded in 1879 at a meeting above Benjamin Van Volkenburg's butcher shop, and although it was nearly a decade since the war had ended, he'd tell people so if he saw any occasion to utter the German name with a little menace and an arch of his left eyebrow.

Sir Adrian often ate with Dr. Alistair Sinclair; it was simply the club's unlikely busyness one Monday that obliged Harry to lunch with them at a table in the McGregor Lounge. His distaste for the idea was palpable when the two invited him to join them. Besides, Harry thought, what's the point—neither of the men did business that could matter much to the Bank of Victoria.

"Victoria is a peculiar place," Dr. Sinclair said to Sir Adrian, while Harry poked morosely at his salad. "There are days when attitudes seem to me more British than those in London itself."

"I think," expounded Sir Adrian, "that it's a tribute to the enduring power of the Empire. It's also true in India, that values such as ours are so powerful that their primacy is inevitable. When you've been in Westminster Abbey, when you've watched the House of Lords at work, you can't imagine why anyone would aspire to anything else."

Dr. Sinclair, being a good Scot, didn't entirely share Sir Adrian's views on the virtues of the Empire—he would more naturally diagnose the ills of any organization up for discussion—so he asked Harry what he thought.

"I respect Britain's civilizing influence, but there are days when this city's deliberate Britishness seems a tad affected." With that Harry moved on to his pork cutlet, which had just arrived at the table. He kept himself so occupied with his meal that he avoided any more questions and then rose to depart. "Thank you, gentlemen. I must leave to prepare for my one o'clock with the proprietor of Buckerfield's."

"Isn't that man the very definition of a banker," scoffed Sir Adrian as soon as Harry had departed. "Obsessed with punctuality, and grim as a prison warden. The only thing that makes me curious about him is that remarkably exotic little girl of his. I saw them at the Rogers Chocolates shop the other day, and she is a compelling child. I do so hate the phrase 'nigger in the woodpile,' but I believe he's somehow acquired a girl of exactly that sort."

Dr. Sinclair nodded, and his own distaste for Harry Burman got the better of his professionalism. "Clearly she's adopted, and I'm reasonably sure she's a half-breed. I don't think there's any doubt about her Indian blood, but she's not his wife's child. I shouldn't say this, and I trust your discretion, but I've considered the medical evidence. What confounds me more is the idea that Burman could be her father, but I can come up with no other likely explanation."

Sir Adrian put down his knife and fork and finished chewing before he spoke. "You've confirmed my feelings exactly, Doctor."

After Dr. Sinclair returned to his office, Sir Adrian went to the Billiard Room, where he expected to find Victor Trevor. He was not disappointed. Sir Adrian imagined he might exact some sort of redemption for the whipping he had taken from Victor at snooker the week before, although he knew it was unlikely, as Victor seemed to have an inordinate amount of time to play and become expert at the game.

Sir Adrian had known a few businessmen such as Victor, in ports from Dover to Hong Kong and Istanbul, and he had a pretty good idea what line of work he was in. Today he intended to test his theory and in so doing put Victor off his game. "Shocking business down in the San Juans last week," he remarked as Victor racked the balls.

Victor said nothing, so Sir Adrian pressed on. "It's a bit of a circus down there, what with so many interests trying to control the trade in liquor. The authorities seem more or less powerless to do anything about it."

Victor had to take the bait. "The Volstead Act was a ridiculous mistake. If the authorities want to take control of the situation, they'll repeal a foolish law that's only fostering the moral decay it purports to prevent. Prohibition is a failed policy."

"It's a particular shame when the violence affects us on this side of the border. I assume you saw the story in the Sunday *Colonist*?" Sir Adrian paused. "Nasty to have a good citizen of this coast found dead on an Orcas Island beach with two bullets in his back. Did you know Nels Aalgaard?"

Victor did not look at Sir Adrian for a moment, then eyed him very directly and in a cool voice said: "I was once introduced to his father-in-law. But that family has never spent much time in Victoria. My brother knew Albert at school, but he was much younger than I. As for Nels Aalgaard, no, I never met the man."

Sir Adrian believed that if Victor wasn't lying, he was at least deeply uncomfortable about this line of inquiry. Unfortunately, that didn't affect his billiards ability. Victor won so decisively that Sir Adrian immediately retired to the Reading Room.

🐦 🐦 🐦

The next afternoon, Sir Adrian was on the terrace at Blenheim Oaks, with Edwina Brill, Sir Neville Wallingford and Eleanor. Julia joined them, and Aggie served tea. Eleanor and Sir Neville had beaten Sir Adrian and Edwina soundly at bridge, and his pride was wounded. Gossip, however, might help to cure that ill. "What," he asked abruptly, in his typical rhetorical fashion, "can you tell me about the ancestry of that young Sahndra Burman?"

"Why . . ." Eleanor searched for words, wondering what had provoked Sir Adrian to raise the issue. She had once heard the whispers, but there were some things that were not fit for a distinguished person to discuss. "Why, I can't say as I've given it a moment's thought."

While Sir Adrian had needed some help from Dr. Sinclair in assessing the situation, he felt he had come close enough on his own that he wouldn't really be betraying a confidence. "I have it on quite good authority that Kathleen Burman is not the mother of that child. The girl is clearly of mixed blood. I can't help but wonder why they would adopt such a child, if not for some indiscretion on the part of Harry Burman?"

Eleanor was quite unsettled, exactly as Sir Adrian intended. Julia had once briefly considered the prospect that Sahndra was adopted, but it was not in her nature to worry about such things. Kathleen was her friend, and as such she had simply deferred to her many stories that suggested the child was hers. Only now did she confront what should long have been obvious: Elaine was the mother of Harry Burman's child. It was as clear to her as the placement of the last piece in a jigsaw puzzle.

"I must say," said Sir Adrian, filling the uncomfortable silence. "I can't imagine that such a man would have a rogue romance in him."

"Well," Sir Neville was concerned that his own penchant for indelicacy was being outmatched, "if there are going to be bastards and orphans in the world, then someone must deign to take care of them."

Julia became so lost in thought that she did not hear another word as Eleanor recovered her composure and the conversation moved on to other topics. It did not take her long to trace the story out in her mind—Elaine's trip to Toronto, her sudden departure. Harry and Elaine. No, that would not have been a choice Elaine had made. There was another word for it. She knew the word and its meaning, and it was not quite the same as *molest*, the subtleties of which she had also come to understand. How patient and good Kathleen must be to have made such sacrifices.

It was Eleanor who eventually brought Julia's attention back to the guests on the terrace. "Julia, dear. Did you hear what Sir Adrian just said? Nels Aalgaard has been murdered! Shot and washed up on a beach on Orcas Island! He thinks liquor smuggling must have been involved."

Julia shuddered as she tried to take a breath, excused herself and went inside. No wonder her mother had called three times yesterday. Now she couldn't bear to think of calling her back. She stood in the hallway as tears streamed down her cheeks.

The revelation about Sahndra had been disturbing, but it was the death of Albert's father that prompted her to weep, even though she had never met the man. Nels's life could not be reclaimed. Poor Anna, poor Sveinn. Her heart felt most deeply for people she did not really know, except through Albert.

☙ ☙ ☙

Kathleen Burman almost never went to Blenheim Oaks, despite Julia's regular invitations, but she welcomed Julia's company in her own Battery Street home, especially now that she was a mother too. She gave Julia gripewater for David's colic, and little pink pills to soothe her nerves, which Julia politely accepted and then discarded. Advice and enthusiasms and laments fairly spilled out of Kathleen whenever they met for lunch or tea. One day they stood in the kitchen, which was flooded with early spring light, as the kettle came to a boil. Both children were napping.

They talked briefly about Nels Aalgaard. "I don't quite understand why I was so upset, except that I really felt for Albert and his loss. I can't imagine being so far away from your family when such a thing happens." Julia knew, but did not say, that she was also upset by Sir Adrian's cavalier revelation about Sahndra.

Kathleen surprised Julia with her lack of empathy. "He crossed a line that should not be crossed. What he did was illegal. It's a trade run by criminals, and when you consort with criminals you can expect a violent fate." Julia thought she heard her mother in Kathleen's voice, but given that her friend did not know the Arnasons or the Aalgaards, she could be forgiven.

Kathleen quickly turned the conversation to her usual preoccupations. "I am so looking forward to seeing Sahndra Mary in St. Ann's," she enthused. The elegant Catholic academy stood between Beacon Hill Park and the Empress. "It seems a lovely school—the promise of firmness and rectitude but without the threatening sternness that so terrified me as an Irish child. It's such a shame you're not a Catholic. You wouldn't like to convert, would you, not with all that would entail for you at Blenheim Oaks. I so wish that when I have a boy to keep Sahndra company he would be able to have David with him at such a fine institution."

Julia smiled wistfully. She had always found Kathleen's nervous energy charming and her lack of pretension an example to be followed. But she worried also about her obsessiveness, particularly now that she felt she knew what Kathleen had gone through in Toronto, and what she'd put aside to live with Harry. "You have a child, Kathleen. You have a beautiful daughter, as beautiful and well mannered as any in Victoria. If you have no other children, still you have been rewarded with the love of a marvellous daughter. And you have been a wonderful mother to her. No child could be more blessed."

Julia expected a smile, but Kathleen's naïflike enthusiasm suddenly vanished; she looked quite unsettled, almost confused.

"What is it, Kathleen? Did I say something to upset you? You can tell me, and I won't take offence."

Kathleen burst into tears. "What is a life without your own children?" she sobbed. "What is a family? You don't understand. Why can't we have a child of our own, to repair what's been done?"

Julia went to her and held her. She'd touched a nerve in Kathleen in a way she had not intended, and was distressed by her own carelessness. She did not ask Kathleen for any explanation; she felt Kathleen understood somehow that she knew her secret. "A child is a child, a gift to us all, a blessing to be honoured," Julia said. "No one has honoured such a blessing better than you. You have a right to be proud of yourself, Kathleen, proud of the way you've made a family from what you've been given."

Kathleen squeezed Julia as hard as she could and slowly began to compose herself. They never spoke of the matter again.

That night at Blenheim Oaks, as Julia slipped into bed, Georgie noticed her distracted mood. "What's wrong, my love? Are you still upset by what happened to Albert's father?"

Julia paused and looked away, then turned to him and spoke with a firmness and directness she herself found surprising. "Georgie, you must never speak to anyone about any aspect of what I am about to tell you."

Georgie raised his head like a soldier, placed his hand on his heart and declared, "Upon my honour."

"When I was in school, there was a girl in my class, Elaine, who was a Nootka princess, a descendant of the great Chief Maquinna. She lived with the Burmans and worked as their maid. She did not take to that position well, but she dealt with her circumstances with dignity. After Harry and Kathleen were married, she went with them to Toronto for a year. When they returned the Burmans had a child, and Elaine was never seen or heard from again. I believe Sahndra is Harry and Elaine's child, and I believe that is one reason why Kathleen obsesses over having a baby."

Georgie gazed down and then up at Julia. There was a hint of a tear in her eye. "How could I not honour a confidence such as that? You are a good friend and a better wife, and I am very lucky to have you."

☙ ☙ ☙

It was only two months later that Kathleen in her turn unsettled Julia. Again, they were in Kathleen's kitchen, sitting at the little table that overlooked the garden. Sahndra was playing with David, tickling him on the living-room floor. David had the most delightful giggle.

"Harry met with Sveinn Arnason at the bank last week," Kathleen said casually. "Apparently, Albert is back on Arnason Island. And I understand that he has returned with a daughter who is both deaf and mute. Her name is Gudrun. Don't you think that's a lovely name? I believe it means 'God's secret.'"

Julia paused. She had never expected to see Albert again. Even when she learned of Nels Aalgaard's death, she did not think about what his son's return to British Columbia might mean to her. Now that she was denied those defences against the feelings that had once overwhelmed her, she was surprised by her own response. She did not think of the love she had harboured for Albert; she did not think of his daughter or the circumstances that had brought them both home.

Her first thought was that it would make it more difficult for her to visit Stanley. Her father seemed to have chosen peace at home over his wish to travel to Arnason Island, and Julia felt it was her duty to make the trip for him, as much as for herself and her brother. However, her discomfort at the idea of upsetting the polite détente that she had achieved with her mother kept the event perpetually in the future. Now there was a new impediment.

"Julia," asked Kathleen, "are you all right?"

"Well, I guess some fairy tales don't have happy endings. I wish him well, though. Arnason Island always seemed the right place for him. Perhaps he'll feel more strongly about it now that he's been away."

🐜 🐜 🐜

At the beginning of the summer in 1927, Eleanor invited Georgie, Julia, and David to join her in the main house. Victor no longer visited Blenheim Oaks. In the winter of 1925, his mother had refused to loan him money to pay income- and excise-tax bills levied by federal tax auditors. In the absence of her elder son, it was easier for Eleanor to let Georgie share the family home.

During that summer, Julia chose to do on paper what she felt she could not do in person. She wrote letters—first to Albert and then to Stanley. Not long after Nels's death, she had sent a sympathy card to Anna, Sveinn and Albert. Nevertheless, the idea that someone she still held dear had gone through such personal challenges without much more than a word from her did not sit right with Julia, and that was exactly how she began her letter.

"I can't imagine how difficult it would have been to receive such news of your father when you were so far away from home," she wrote to Albert. "To know he was gone, to know you could not hold your mother, to have in your mind all the doubts regarding the circumstances of his death, these are the tests by which we take our own measure. I know that you rose to them, just as you have risen to the test of caring for your daughter." Julia told him of her own life and happiness; she hoped that

Albert might provide a few details of his, unfiltered by the well-meaning exaggerations of third-hand sources such as her mother.

When Julia received Albert's reply, she visualized him with his fountain pen at a desk on his island, the moon on the ocean through a window just ajar. "Dear Julia," he began. "Why am I not surprised by your kindness? Thank you so much for thinking of me and the difficulties I have faced. You have no idea what a comfort your words are to me." He wrote about his life, about Anna's stoic resolve and Sveinn's anger that Nels had made a choice that could cause his family so much pain. Albert also said he was grateful for much that his father had shown him. "He taught me that there is a world of possibility in a single life, and that it's our responsibility to seize it. I'm grateful for that, just as I'm grateful to my mother for pointing out the virtues of the right choices."

Julia wanted to know more about his daughter and his time in Europe. Perhaps there will be another opportunity, she thought, but not now. She had her own life to cherish.

Her occasional correspondence with Stanley was more mundane. Julia had no wish to plumb the great tragedies of his life; she wanted to build a relationship with her brother, not to risk it. So she simply shared the details of the Godolphin family's life that might be overlooked by her father, and in turn she learned about oystercatchers and kingfishers, sharp-shinned hawks and cliff swallows. Through Stanley she also learned about Gudrun. He conjured a picture of a girl whose disability seemed only to magnify her radiance and joy, and whose love of nature's glorious cycles was matched only in the grandfather she had not known.

Stanley's descriptions of Arnason Island made Julia long to visit the place, yet as the years passed, it became harder and harder for her to make the trip. She was glad she found it in herself to reconnect with the Arnason Island threads from her past, but she was intensely devoted to her husband and son. Julia and Georgie were, in fact, so close that they

rarely basked in the social perks that accrued to Victoria's most prominent couples. It was as though they simply did not need the approval of
others.

Julia's domestic bliss was complete, but her relationship with Kathleen
eventually foundered. Kathleen behaved as though their emotional
exchange about Sahndra had never occurred, and Julia sometimes felt
their conversation tacitly demanded that she repudiate what she knew.
She found it increasingly difficult to humour Kathleen in this, and did
not have the heart to revisit the truth. While she enjoyed many happily
uneventful years at Blenheim Oaks, the dwindling end to her friendship
with Kathleen was one of her few regrets, along with her distance from
Stanley.

CHAPTER EIGHTEEN

The Vacation

At the beginning of summer in 1935, Harry Burman walked home from his office as usual, leaving precisely at five o'clock, just as he walked to work, rain or shine, arriving at the bank exactly five minutes early so he could be at his desk at nine o'clock on the dot. His father had retired on his sixty-fifth birthday in the winter, and Harry was now president of the bank. Although he was only thirty-five, young to become a bank president, no one questioned his promotion as he seemed years older. Someone once said Harry Burman was born middle-aged and probably would die middle-aged.

Even with the increased salary that had come with his promotion, Harry did not change his lifestyle. He owned an automobile but used it only on Sundays for family excursions, or an occasional evening out with his wife. They lived in the same house to which they had moved when they returned from Toronto. That their daughter went to St. Ann's Academy instead of the public school was not an extravagance; Kathleen Burman was a deeply religious woman and she could scarcely have sent the child anywhere but to a parochial school.

The winter of 1930–31 had been a difficult one everywhere. Effects of the American "slump" and the market crash of 1929 were being felt in Canada, and Great Britain's economy was not rising as political leaders had hoped; however, customers of the Bank of Victoria put their faith in the Burmans as good, safe managers and did not panic as many did.

It was a cold night for the end of June; the wind swept in from the east, a sign of impending bad weather. Harry was gloomier than usual, knowing what he had to face at dinner. It had happened again. Kathleen had called him at the office, her voice high and elated, telling him that she was almost certain that she was pregnant.

He had lost count of the number of times that she had announced her pregnancy. Initially, Harry found his heart aching for her grief when the doctor assured her it was not so, but over the last two years the pattern had changed. Kathleen had told Harry that perhaps it was a blessing she did not have "any more" children, as she expressed it, because of their grief over the "baby that died." She had become convinced that they had had a son who died at birth.

Harry knew that his wife was unbalanced, and that one day he might have to face the possibility she would become irretrievably insane. Yet in every other regard she was easy to live with. She was cheerful at all times, except when she discovered that another hoped-for pregnancy had not materialized. She was a kind and loving wife. If anything, she had grown prettier, with an air of wondering innocence about her. She kept the house spotless and served meals on time, and retained a quality of lightness and charm. She always deferred to Harry, was considerate to the older Burmans and was a marvellous mother.

No girl in Victoria was better dressed or behaved than Sahndra Mary. Kathleen made most of her clothes and ensured a proper education, insisting on good manners and friendliness both at home and elsewhere. For a few moments, Harry's personal cloud lifted as he thought of his daughter. Her presence was the happiest element in his life. He adored her, never tired of looking at her and listening to her confidences, and she repaid him with trust and affection.

Sahndra met him at the door, both hands behind her back. She looked at Harry with her magnificent grey-brown eyes. "Guess what I have here?"

Harry kissed her, took off his coat and hung it up. "I can't even begin to guess."

She shook her head, waited a moment, then produced her report card. "I passed into grade ten with my best marks yet."

Harry kissed her again, scrutinized the report card and produced a two-dollar bill. He had always given her a dollar when she passed into the next grade. "I think a girl going into grade ten deserves a larger prize."

Kathleen joined them, wearing a simple yellow flowered housedress and a white apron. Her eyes were sparkling and she made a small gesture, behind Sahndra's back, that suggested she did not wish her daughter to share in her "secret" as yet. He nodded. He was used to the routine, and some of his joy faded. Still, dinner was pleasant, topped off with an angel-food cake that Kathleen had made to celebrate Sahndra's success. While eating dinner and watching his daughter, Harry was able to relax, pushing away the thought of dealing with his wife's delusion.

Harry did not analyze his feelings for his daughter except to be aware of his love for her, and of the joy she brought into his life. He accepted Sahndra's beauty as her own, and tried not to think about the fact that she looked so much like Elaine.

On the few occasions when he did think about the source of her loveliness, he would look at her searchingly, trying to find some trace of himself or his parents. But there could be no doubt about the source of those startling eyes, the high, strong cheekbones, the long line of her dark eyebrows and the sweeping lashes. Her skin was lighter than Elaine's, her black hair was softer. She had exquisitely white, even teeth, which even the family dentist admired. Her mouth was smaller than Elaine's, and she rarely smiled. She did not look sad or aggrieved; rather she simply made almost everyone wonder what went on behind her beautiful, impassive features.

Kathleen had spent an hour that morning at the school with Sister Theresa, who had asked for a meeting to discuss Sahndra's progress and prospects for the fall. Her teachers felt that while Sahndra was an extremely bright child who earned her good marks, she never stretched herself or departed from what interested her.

"I'm not saying she is lazy," Sister Theresa observed. "It is just that she is capable of so much more. Perhaps learning is almost too easy for her. I really wish you could get her to try harder."

Kathleen nodded, eager to please the sisters in any way. "I can't understand why she should get a C in Home Economics. That was always one of my favourite subjects."

Sister Theresa watched Mrs. Burman as they talked. The Burmans were a source of interest to her and the other sisters at the school. She did not envy Sahndra. Sister Theresa knew that some of the girls disparaged her as a "dirty Indian" and she had had to speak severely to two students about this. She couldn't imagine that Sahndra had not heard such things. Perhaps that explained her peculiar aloofness at school. She was congenial with other students, but she had no close friends. However, instead of dealing with that uncomfortable matter, Sister Theresa found a subject that was a proxy for it.

"I'm afraid your daughter's beauty is going to be a burden to her," she told Kathleen. "People will either be jealous or try to take advantage, so as much as possible we must stress her education, and of course her behaviour, which I must say is excellent. You are to be congratulated, Mrs. Burman. I know you and your husband will continue to stress virtue as being all important as Sahndra grows into her teens."

"Oh, yes!" said Kathleen. "My husband and I are deeply religious, as you know, and Sahndra Mary is too."

Sister Theresa said nothing. She was not quite sure of the latter. It was too early to tell, and she tried to subdue the thought, but already she instinctively mistrusted the child, and was angry at herself for letting

Sahndra's beauty and mixed blood prejudice her. She would pray for herself when Mrs. Burman left. She also wished that she had not let the word *lazy* slip out. Perhaps Mrs. Burman hadn't noticed the insult, but Sister Theresa knew exactly what she had fallen prey to.

When Sahndra was in bed that night, Kathleen came over to Harry, curled herself up and laid her head on his shoulder. He touched her hair, a gesture of pity. She told him in her soft, light voice, still with the Irish lilt, how she was convinced that by next year they would have a brother for Sahndra.

By this time, Harry and Dr. Sinclair had become far too well acquainted. Harry hated the doctor's jovial war clichés, while Dr. Sinclair was in turn irritated by Harry's lack of humour. Nevertheless, they met once a year to discuss Kathleen's condition, always with the same result, what Dr. Sinclair called "hysterical pregnancy." The doctor noticed, and mentioned to Harry, that Kathleen's delusions were increasing.

This year, Dr. Sinclair made one constructive suggestion during their annual conference. "How about taking your wife and daughter on a trip somewhere? I should think a change of scene would be good for all of you."

Harry, whose modest home and unwillingness to spend money on vacations had left him rich at least in his bank account, for once agreed to such extravagance. A change would benefit Kathleen, and he wouldn't mind it himself as long as Sahndra came too. Kathleen was enthusiastic about the idea. Harry knew of the Arnason Inne, and one of his colleagues at the bank had recommended it highly for its excellent food and atmosphere.

☙ ☙ ☙

When Harry Burman wrote requesting reservations for the last two weeks in August for his wife, his daughter and himself, Albert Aalgaard felt only the slightest curiosity because of Harry's family's connection to Elaine. But when the Burmans got out of the station wagon and came up the broad stairs of the Inne, Albert saw immediately that the child was Elaine's. It was one of the few times in his life that he was caught off guard.

The fifteen-year-old girl, with her striking beauty and her long, slow, penetrating stare, was a disturbing personality, more conscious of herself than her mother had been. She was clearly aware of her sexuality, and Albert noticed his heartbeat. He turned away from her, embarrassed, went to Harry and shook his hand, welcoming him to the Inne. Harry introduced Kathleen. "I'm not sure you've seen her since you escorted Julia to our wedding."

"If I had, I'm sure I would remember," Albert said, giving her all of his attention.

"This is our daughter, Sahndra Mary," said Kathleen proudly. The girl did not smile. She gravely shook hands with Albert. He was aware of a strong grip, and he withdrew with as much haste as he could and still be polite, thankful that Anna was now also there to greet the new arrivals. But Harry saw Albert's reaction, and Albert saw that he had seen it.

At dinner, Anna said to her son, "Isn't that Sahndra Burman the most beautiful girl you've ever seen?"

Albert did not look up from his dinner. "I guess so."

Anna laughed. "There's no doubt that she's a very . . . I imagine she'll break a lot of hearts when she's grown up." Albert looked out the window toward the sea.

"Did you know that Mrs. Burman's going to have another child?" Anna inquired. "She's so excited. There will be quite a difference in their ages, but that doesn't matter. It would be so nice for the girl to have a baby brother or sister, and Mrs. Burman's such an effervescent woman. She seems a wonderful mother. Mr. Burman's rather dour, but I guess it's because he's a banker, poor thing,"

Albert was used to his mother chatting about her guests and usually he was interested, but today he was obsessed with the idea that Harry Burman must somehow have made love to Elaine, and he could not imagine how such a thing could have happened.

"What's the matter, darling?" His mother touched his hand. "You're scowling at your plate. Don't you like the lamb? I thought it was especially nice tonight."

"I'm not hungry," he said. "I think I'll go upstairs and see Gudrun before she goes to bed." He left the table and Anna shook her head, smiling, before departing for her father's room, to share accounts of the day's activities over a glass of port.

🐟 🐟 🐟

The Burmans were due to leave for Victoria on the noon boat on the last Saturday in August. To all appearances their vacation had been successful. Harry had picked up some colour in his normally pale features. He did not socialize with the other guests, who invariably played ping-pong, pool or cards in the evenings, all of which Harry shunned. Kathleen spent most of her days on the wide veranda of the Inne, knitting a baby sweater of delicate blue wool. She told other guests the new baby would most definitely be a boy. "To replace the one we lost," she occasionally said, to expressions of deep sympathy.

Sahndra Mary did not play with the other children staying at the Inne. She accompanied her father on his walks and held the wool for her mother when Kathleen wished to wind the skeins into a ball. She sat on logs on the beach and stared at the water, but she showed no interest in wading in the gentle waves that came into the cove.

Sometimes she watched the tennis players. Several of the male players noticed the serious girl and found her presence distracting but were not sure why. She also watched Stanley Godolphin as he went about his gardening and other chores.

Since he had returned from his sister's wedding, Stanley had not left Arnason Island. He was content with his life and his work at the Inne. In his spare time he was working on a book about the birds of the island; he had no literary ambitions but simply wished to record what he saw, and perhaps one day he would give it to Gudrun.

He loved Gudrun as he had never loved anyone in his life, and the purity of his feeling gave him self-respect. When he found himself attracted to older girls and young women who came to the Inne, he was repulsed by those feelings, and repressed them. Gudrun allowed him to love without kindling the shame he had come to associate with strong feelings.

As soon as Albert brought her to the island, he showed Stanley how to use sign language. Gudrun saw Stanley as one of the family, and Stanley became convinced that Gudrun was an act of fate meant to remind him of his lapse and at the same time reveal the virtue of pure affection.

Stanley had become a voracious reader of Russian novels, and he identified with characters who suffered through guilt-ridden introspection, through the conflict between religious ideals and natural human emotions. After he read Dostoevsky's *Crime and Punishment*, he felt that by his relationship with Gudrun he had been "cleansed."

But over the last two weeks, the old uneasiness had returned.

He had been aware of Sahndra Mary Burman's beauty the moment he saw her step off the *Islander* with her parents. He decided she was another challenge sent to tempt him, and he worked harder than ever on the grounds, searching for every possible job that would keep him busy. The problem was that the girl was watching him.

Stanley had never regarded himself as an object of interest to anyone but himself. There could be no doubt about it, though. She was seeking him out, watching him work as though everything he did fascinated her. Yet she never spoke to him.

On their final Saturday afternoon, Kathleen went to their room to begin packing for their return home, while Harry went on one of his long, lonely walks. His daughter had declined to accompany him. Instead, she went to the fields behind the Inne, where Stanley was clearing blackberry canes and underbrush.

Stanley saw her coming and pretended not to notice. She crossed the fields in a nimble, determined walk. She wore navy blue shorts and a plain blouse with short sleeves and an open neck. When she reached Stanley, she stopped moving and stood very still. As usual, she did not speak.

Stanley was crouching to pull at a tangle of bracken ferns. He pushed his hat back on his head and looked at her. It was not warm, but he was aware that he was sweating. He took off his glasses, wiped them with his handkerchief, and put them back on.

"You should go back to the Inne," he said. "Your parents might be looking for you."

She continued to stare at him, unmoving. "No, they won't."

Stanley's voice sharpened. "I'm busy. Why are you here?" He stooped and began pulling at a fern, feeling defeated when it did not budge from the rocky ground. She did not answer.

At last he sat back on his heels and gazed up at her. The sun went behind a cloud and it was very quiet. The tennis players had given up. "What do you want?" he heard himself ask.

"You don't like me to watch you, do you?"

"I don't care. I'm just too busy to talk to you."

"You watch me," said Sahndra. "You've watched me ever since I arrived."

He could not believe it. He stared at her wonderingly. How beautiful she was, and how threatening she seemed. He looked at the sky and stood. "It could rain," he said. "I'd better get back. I have to meet the boat at five."

Sahndra glanced at the little wristwatch her father had given her on her last birthday, the only jewellery she wore. "It's only a quarter past two." She went to the edge of the forest lining the field and stood with her back to a tree.

"Stanley," she said in a low, comforting voice. "You want to touch me. I know you do. I won't tell if you do."

She walked toward him until she was so close he could feel her breath. He was paralyzed. She leaned forward, and her breasts brushed against his chest as she slowly reached toward his lips with hers. When they met he stepped back, as though a spell had been broken.

"Why are you doing this to me?" he asked, as much to himself as much as to her.

She was perfectly calm. "Because I'm curious. I see men looking at me all the time like I'm a woman. Even Mr. Aalgaard looks at me. So does my father sometimes, although he doesn't know it."

"Those are your problems," Stanley said. "I have problems of my own. You have no idea."

Sahndra looked at him coolly and cocked her head. "Are those problems because of something you've done or something you haven't done?" The slightest smile touched her lips and lightened the heavy stare of her eyes.

"It is none of your business," Stanley said firmly. He stepped past her, turned and doffed his cap, then marched briskly back to the Inne without picking up his tools.

🙠 🙠 🙠

Stanley did not meet the five o'clock boat. He took off his glasses and put them in his pocket and told Mac, the high school student who worked at the Inne during the summer, that he had broken them while he was working in the fields and would be unable to drive. Then he went to his room, pulled out his packsack and stuffed it with some extra clothing, a blanket, a flashlight, cigarettes, tea, biscuits, two cans of tomato soup and his worn copy of *Crime and Punishment*.

He filled his flask with whisky and put it in the pocket of his jacket. Then from the back of his closet he retrieved his considerable savings, which he kept in an old coffee tin. Just before he left his room he went back to the bookcase, took down *The Possessed* and added it to his pack. On top of the Bible on his bedside table, he left a letter addressed to Anna.

From a linen cupboard in the hall, he pulled out one of the down-filled sleeping bags that were sometimes used by tourists who wished to camp out. Rolling it up, he tied it to the top of his pack and went out the back door.

Stanley took an old path through the woods down to the cove, avoiding the boardwalk for the guests. An old open motorboat, usually understood to be his, was tied to the float. He threw his pack in the front and placed an extra can of gas in the stern. The tide was in. The sound of the motor starting was sudden and sharp, yet no one took note of the noise and no one observed his departure. He made it into open water just as the *Islander* came into view. The cool wind enveloped him, and he reached for his flask.

He remembered the day, so long ago on the *Princess Maquinna*, the wind and rain stinging his face, when he saw Sa-Sin running down a rocky beach. This is how it ends, he thought; this is an adult's freedom, running from things you despise and cannot control in yourself. Stanley thought of that girl on the beach in his distant past, and the impassive figure just hours ago at the edge of the forest, and he was sure that somehow the moments were connected. Then he dismissed the idea: what a fool he was when he had anything other than a shovel in his hands.

He reached Vancouver Island near Yellow Point and worked his way north close to shore. The full moon rose at dusk, and the sky cleared. Stanley did not stop. He did not even think about the choice he had made. He just hoped he could leave everyone he had ever known behind him.

CHAPTER NINETEEN

A Bohemian Death

Gabrielle Riel—her real name was Polly Reilly, but she thought Gabrielle was more exotic—lived in Victoria on Johnson Street, not far from the harbour, in one of the less pleasant parts of town. She worked when she felt like it or needed to, usually in shops, millinery departments, or selling stockings or "notions." She had a very modest income left to her by her dead mother; her father had long ago disappeared. She was a small-time bootlegger (she knew every taxi driver in Victoria, or at least they all knew her) and also dealt in drugs when she could manage to find any. She bought opium in Chinatown and hung around the clubs when touring bands were in town, which allowed her to solicit marijuana and occasionally cocaine from the musicians. In all these ways, she sustained herself in her tiny apartment on the ground floor of a very old house.

She never bothered with prostitution because sex was, she said, her greatest pleasure, and she wanted it on her own terms only. There were some prominent names among those with whom she performed "for love," including a European prince whose family had sent him to British Columbia to study logging, an American senator who came to Victoria once every year for "the fishing" and, ultimately, Albert Aalgaard.

Gabrielle was not beautiful, but she had a gamin appeal. She was small and wiry, with large grey eyes and short, straight brown hair that she invariably streaked with peroxide. Her sense of humour was wonderful, she showed genuine interest in everything each man said to her, and she was an expert at making love. She was well read and had an amazing collection of phonograph records, from opera to the new musical operettas and popular songs. Her apartment was distinguished mainly by the unbelievable clutter, but there was soft lamplight, good music, always plenty to drink and most often something to smoke.

Every Monday, Albert took his own boat into Sidney, where he did all the shopping necessary for the Inne, and he often took the family car into Victoria for what Sidney could not provide. Anna tried to get him to have more of what they needed shipped to the island by steamer, but he resisted, and if his mother wondered at all about the motives for his excursions, she said nothing.

Albert Aalgaard had settled comfortably into his destiny at the Arnason Inne. He and his mother were an exemplary team, and Albert's sophisticated charm was key to the Inne's growing international reputation. He cultivated relationships with Vancouver entertainment promoters, and a young vaudevillean named Bob Hope was among the first of many celebrities who came to fish as a result. He was also a thrifty manager, and the Inne had finally begun to prosper financially.

On the second Monday night in October 1935, Albert finished his Victoria errands, parked down by the Crystal Garden and walked to Gabrielle's house. It was a long walk but he enjoyed it, and he preferred not to leave his car near her place.

Albert let himself in with the key she had given him. When he called, however, he received no answer. At first, he wasn't concerned. Gabrielle was unpredictable. She could be asleep, or on a foray into nearby Chinatown, or wherever her fancy took her. Albert enjoyed the total freedom with which Gabrielle moved, although he admitted her liberty was closer to anarchy.

The room was in darkness, and he reached for the light switch by the door. In the stark light, the room looked even more untidy than usual; clothes, boxes, and books were everywhere. Gabrielle was sprawled on the sofa, amid more books, more clothes and three mewing kittens. She did not move.

Albert went toward her, but even before he reached the sofa he felt that something was wrong. Gabrielle was dead. Then he saw the stocking tied tightly around her neck. He felt a great sadness as he looked down at his mistress. He touched her cheek, but it was already cold and he drew his hand away quickly. He looked around the room, not knowing what to do. For a moment he wondered if the murderer might still be there, but then he realized that she must have been dead for several hours. He stumbled over objects on the floor as he looked around the house, still fearful of what else he might find.

He should call the police, but Gabrielle's phone had long been disconnected. He wanted to put a cover over her, and started toward her but realized he should leave the place untouched until the police came. He shed a tear, blew her a kiss, turned out the light and locked the door behind him. He would find a public telephone and call the authorities.

But as he stood outside the house, he tried to think what he would say. He realized that he would have to explain his own position and what he was doing there and felt suddenly like a child who had committed an act of mischief. Then he remembered he was thirty-eight years old with a thirteen-year-old daughter; he was a man of influence, the owner and manager of the Arnason Inne. The Inne! Oh, God, thought Albert, what will they think of me at the police station?

Walking briskly away from the house, he put his feelings in order. Gabrielle was dead. She had been murdered. The police would have to know, then everyone would have to know, about their relationship. Albert was aware that Victoria loved its gossip. He thought of what his mother would think, what his grandfather might say. Walking toward the harbour, he told himself that his mother would understand, but the situation could certainly damage the business of the Inne.

Albert stood on Government Street, watching the *Princess Kathleen* in the harbour as the ship prepared for the midnight sailing for Vancouver. He wanted to talk to someone but could not think of a friend who could help him with a problem like this. He wandered back to the Empress Hotel to get a room for the night.

As he walked up the front steps he saw her coming out through the main doors. She stood straighter now, and the navy blue coat she wore made her look stronger. She had assurance. Albert sighed. He had loved her naïveté so much. Then, as she came toward him, and because he was Albert, he forgot everything else and decided he was in love with her.

He tried to compose himself. So much had happened since they had last seen each other, and he suddenly realized that the first order of business must be the disappearance of Stanley.

"Hello, Julia," he said. "I can't tell you how glad I am to see you again after all these years."

Julia knew it was Albert before she turned toward him; there was only one voice with that light, magnetic quality. He was still extremely handsome, slim in a grey suit and tie that were in the best of taste, but the fair hair was shorter than when she had known him, with streaks of grey just above his ears.

"Hello, Albert. You look wonderful."

"Julia, if that's true for me then it's doubly true for you. There's so much for us to talk about. Please, Julia, join me for a drink in the Bengal Lounge."

"Not a drink, Albert, but I'll have a cup of tea."

Julia was glad of this coincidence. It had been just over a month since Anna had phoned the Godolphins to let them know their son had left the Inne. They all agreed not to contact the police immediately; Stanley was an adult, entitled to leave the island as he pleased.

"We've had no news of Stanley," Albert said as they walked toward the lounge. "I do hope he will write to you or your father soon."

"I must tell you I'm deeply concerned," Julia told him. "I don't doubt that he's resourceful, but he'll always be my shy, gentle brother in plus-fours and a jacket that's a size too small for him."

"I understand your concern, but I have faith that he will be all right." Albert paused. "What brings you to the Empress tonight?"

"Georgie's captain of the *Princess Victoria*, and she's in Seattle on the Triangle Run tonight, but one of his old colleagues celebrated a wedding anniversary. He had a private party at the hotel, so I brought a present and his regrets."

They arrived at the lounge, and the host took them to a quiet table by a window at the back. Albert immediately lit a cigarette, and Julia saw the way his long, wonderful hands moved, but something was amiss: he had always been so sure of himself in her memory, and he was not sure now.

"Julia, I know Stanley's disappearance weighs heavily on you, but I need your advice on another matter. I've found myself in terrible trouble."

Julia wondered what could be more important than Stanley, yet she was also surprised to find herself feeling a wave of sympathy for Albert. Whatever he had become involved in, surely it could not be his fault.

Albert told her briefly about his relationship with Gabrielle Riel. "She was very sweet to me, and a lot of fun. I know she had other lovers—she insists the Prince of Luxembourg was among them—but I didn't mind. We had a good time together, though there was nothing more to it than that. But, Julia, when I went there tonight she was dead!"

"Dead? Are you sure?" She realized this was a foolish question and reminded herself to ask useful ones.

"Very dead. She'd been strangled. There was a stocking around her neck and she was cold."

"Did you call the police?"

"No. I came here to do that, and to get a room for the night. But I'm not sure what I should do. If I call the police, they may think I did it."

Julia was silent for a moment. "When they find her and investigate her death, they may still think you did it, especially if you didn't call them when you found her."

"It could have been anyone, Julia. She had a lot of lovers, and she trafficked in dope at times. There's no reason to believe it was me. No one saw me go in or leave."

"On this or any of your other visits?"

Albert hadn't considered that. "Julia, I can't be connected with this thing. Think how it would affect business at the Inne. What kind of knowledge would this be for my mother, and for a daughter to have about her father?"

"Albert," she said, and her voice was a bit cold, "you *did* have a relationship with her. Suppose she hadn't been murdered. It wouldn't change the fact that you were her lover."

Albert realized Julia was right, of course. His mother and grandfather knew he had affairs with women, but he told himself they considered it natural. Now he was less comfortable with his rationalization.

Julia added something else for him to ponder. "When you were in her apartment tonight, did you touch anything? Might the police find your fingerprints?"

Then he remembered the light switch and felt physically ill. They were silent. He knew she was waiting for him to make his own decision without further persuasion. "Will you go with me to the police?" he asked.

"Albert, I can't!"

Julia said that for him to involve her was unfair. Albert argued that the social force of their combined presence would help to deflect attention from him. The police would not regard Mr. Albert Aalgaard of the Arnason Inne as a common criminal; if he had a dalliance with the deceased, it was something the rich and powerful did, and was accepted as a fact of life. The rich were treated differently. If Mr. Aalgaard was also a good friend of the Trevor family, then he deserved even more consideration, and undoubtedly the whole matter would be politely hushed up.

In the end, Julia agreed to deliver Albert to the police station on Wharf Street but not to stay any longer than required. Albert booked a room before they left. When the two arrived at the station, they caused no little stir, and when Sergeant Collins discovered they wanted to report a murder, he could scarcely believe what was happening. He immediately called his superior.

As she waited, Julia thought about how their relationship had changed, and how she had reacted to his predicament. Did other women exonerate Albert so quickly for whatever wrongs he had committed? He still had the charm that had caused her to swoon, yet the strength that she had worked so hard to acquire over the years did not desert her in his presence. Yes, she once loved him; perhaps she still loved him in some way. But now she knew how to manage mixed emotions, and tonight she was the confident one. When she thought of Georgie and David, she knew that she could not be more content.

The murder of Gabrielle Riel was the talk of Victoria. Had the victim been simply a prostitute or drug addict, murdered by a client, it would have been much less interesting. But she had indeed told her landlady that among her "patrons" was the Prince of Luxembourg and a Member of Parliament.

Julia's name was not mentioned but Albert's was. He was not implicated in the murder, but the newspaper stated politely, "Mr. Albert Aalgaard of the Gulf Islands' prestigious Arnason Inne had been acquainted with the deceased, and is assisting the police in their investigation."

A few weeks later, the police picked up a merchant seaman who had been in port that night, and he admitted to having visited Gabrielle. He was held on suspicion of murder, and the excitement over the story brightened again. Eventually, however, the police could find no evidence to charge him with any crime, and finally it was declared that Miss Reilly had been murdered by "person or persons unknown" and the case was closed, except to the gossips.

CHAPTER TWENTY

Old Flames

On the weekend following the chance meeting on the steps of the Empress, Julia and David travelled to Arnason Island. Julia wanted to find out more about what had happened to her brother, and she had a few other questions for Albert. David was almost eleven, a curious boy quite happy to be going away for the weekend with his mother. Julia brought David, she told herself, to give him an opportunity to see the Gulf Islands, but she knew that his presence would show Albert that she was a happily married woman.

Albert himself greeted them at the dock. The weather was mild, and he insisted that the boy and Gudrun come out on his boat for an hour. David was so enthusiastic that Julia could not refuse. Besides, it gave her an opportunity to be alone with Anna.

The Inne was not busy. Anna made tea and took Julia to her office. She was impressed with the younger woman's beauty, recalling how her son had once gone out with her. Julia wore a soft green sweater over a pleated, green silk skirt, tiny green shell earrings and a matching necklace and bracelet. Such good taste, thought Anna. She found herself wondering what might have been different if Albert had married Julia. That dear little boy—he might have been her grandson. But she feared her own son might be getting involved with Julia again. That would compound one scandal with another.

"Thank you for helping my son in this trouble over the Riel girl," she said. "I just hope your involvement won't cause you any problems."

Like wrecking my marriage, thought Julia, even though Georgie had been his usual remarkably understanding self. "Mrs. Aalgaard, as you know, we've still had no word from Stanley. I'm here to try to get a better sense of why he left."

Anna got up at once and went to her desk, which she unlocked with one of the keys she wore on a long gold chain around her neck. She took out the note that Stanley had left her. "Your poor dear brother was obviously very upset, but I haven't an idea in the world why. Perhaps this will mean more to you."

Julia took the note. "Dear Anna," she read. "It is with regret that I must leave you. You and Sveinn and Albert have been so good to me that I can never thank you enough. You gave me a whole world that I would have missed if I had not come to Arnason Island. However, what I have felt and done, and what I fear I might do, is not worthy of your world. Your family offered me a refuge, but now I must seek another one, in order to be at peace with myself. I know God, if there is one, will bless you and your family, especially Gudrun. Sincerely, Stanley Godolphin."

The two women looked at each other. It was then that Julia first thought of Gudrun. She struggled with the idea; she did not wish to imagine her brother taking advantage of another girl's innocence, but she could not dismiss the possibility. "I don't know how to say this. I fear he might have . . ."

"Might have what, dear?" Anna asked. "That's what I don't understand. What did he do? Nothing has been stolen."

"There was no complaint from anyone?"

"Complaint? Who would complain about Stanley? He was so quiet. He just did his work and kept to himself."

Anna obviously did not know why Stanley had been sent away. What was she going to say? Anna was watching her carefully for an explanation, Julia thought.

Anna was also going over her own thoughts. "You know, dear," Anna said, "I remember Papa telling me that your brother had once got into some trouble over a girl. He never considered it serious."

"Mrs. Aalgaard," said Julia, "I know of no delicate way to say this. My brother was accused of molesting a six-year-old girl. My parents sent him away to keep him from being arrested." She stood up on account of her nervousness.

Anna stood also and put her arms around her. "Please, dear Julia. What's past is past."

"I don't wish to alarm you," Julia said, "but I fear it could have happened again."

Anna drew back then, as she considered the possibility. She thought it all out swiftly. "Gudrun? I am sure, Julia, it was not Gudrun."

Julia looked at Anna with a tear in her eye, and Anna spoke again. "No, my dear, I will never believe he harmed Gudrun. Because . . . do you know why I believe this?" She touched Julia's shoulder. "I trust your brother more than you do." She paused. "I admit that I didn't understand the extent of Stanley's problem, but no matter how he felt about Gudrun, your dear brother would never have harmed her. I *know* that."

For a moment the two women held hands tightly. Julia began to recover from her fear. "If this didn't involve Gudrun, then who? There must have been someone."

"We may never know," said Anna. "I expect it may yet turn out to be something much simpler and more innocent. We can only hope that Stanley is all right. And rest assured, he can come back here any time. We'll always welcome him."

Anna went over to the window, pulled back the curtains with one hand and looked out on the sea. Julia believed her assurances about Stanley and

Gudrun, but there was a moment when something in Anna's expression suggested she had an inkling of what might have happened. "I hope Albert is back," Anna said impatiently. "The sun is getting low, and the children will be cold."

🐦 🐦 🐦

That night they all dined together: Anna, Albert, Julia, Gudrun, David and Sveinn. Sveinn was eighty-five and suffered from arthritis, but his mind was sharp. He had a brandy after dinner and insisted on Julia having one too. He talked to David as though he were an adult and David responded as one, but he also made faces at Gudrun when he ate a pickled herring. Gudrun laughed, and Julia was at once proud of David's maturity and relieved that he was still a child.

Later, Julia and Albert sat on the veranda. A few clouds framed the waning late October moon. It was a windless night but cool. Julia wore a fox-fur coat. Albert settled his checkered deerstalker hat at a rakish angle and pulled up his coat collar. "Are you warm enough?"

She nodded. Here she was at last, sitting alone in the moonlight just above the beach on Arnason Island, with Albert Aalgaard giving her his full attention. Yet what she wanted was information about Stanley, and she believed Albert could supply it.

"Dinner was wonderful," she said, not looking at him but watching the moon's reflection on the water. "And I adore your daughter. Wasn't it delightful how she and David got along?"

Albert was quietly watching Julia, not the moon, but came to life at the mention of the children. "David's a wonderful boy. I love to see Gudrun react to others her age. She doesn't see that many that she can connect with."

"Tell me about Gudrun. You must have had a difficult time with her in Europe."

Albert bowed his head. "Just before I finished my management studies in Geneva, I met a lovely girl on the Riviera, or thought I did. Joan and I were engaged too quickly, and from the day I first stepped into her parents' house I knew I was in trouble. Her father I could charm, her mother hated me. The Lapsleys. I do not need to hear their names again. They were, as you probably know, a very wealthy family. I think they thought their daughter would become the Queen of England and when they saw the likes of me they practically married us in secret." He paused. "I'm sorry. You asked about Gudrun, but the story really begins with the Lapsleys. I'm burdening you with my troubles again."

"No, Albert, it's all right." Julia smiled warmly. "Please continue."

"In any event, we were married and I'm convinced it was only because Joan told her parents she was pregnant. She was probably already beginning to have her doubts. I think she liked horses better than children.

"Then Gudrun was born. It was a difficult labour and Joan seemed to resent her even before we learned she was deaf. That news tipped her over the edge. I've never seen such vitriol. She wanted to give the child away, as though that could be the end of it. I felt so defeated that I went to Paris and found a girl to help me care for Gudrun."

He laughed. "I fell in with some expats, mainly Americans, artistic types. Remarkably, I had some modest success as a painter. I did portraits of Indians, and landscapes of the West Coast, but I think they succeeded more because they were exotic than because they were any good. The attention, however, *was* very flattering. I could afford to stay, so I revelled in it, and just enjoyed Parisian life for a few years. It may sound odd, but I needed to reclaim my self-respect. I felt I'd found it by the time Father died and I had to come home."

Julia had once put Albert on a pedestal, then a week ago she thought he was a fool. Now she was beginning to simply like the man. "Has Arnason Island been a good place for Gudrun?"

"In many ways it has. It's both social and pleasantly insular, and I think nature offers great respite for a girl who can't always be an equal in human relationships. But I'm afraid we may have to send her away to a residential school in Vancouver soon, so she can learn with other children who have the same problems."

"Must you? She seems so happy here. Wouldn't it be wrong to send her away?"

Albert shook his head as though he didn't know the answer. "I ask the same question, but I also know she needs more help than we can give her."

Julia thought of Stanley, who once needed more help than his family could give him. "Albert, I need to ask you about my brother."

"I'm so sorry," said Albert. "You must think I'm a man with nothing but my own problems."

"No, no. I do want to know about Europe, and about Gudrun and your plans for her. It's just that when you mentioned a problem—well, that's what my brother has too. I talked with your mother this afternoon while you were out with the children and I think she knows something that she won't tell me."

"Mother knows lots of secrets. She'd never say anything that might hurt someone."

"Albert, Stanley got into serious trouble involving a girl."

"Didn't we all?" said Albert, smiling.

"No, Albert, you don't understand. He was accused of molesting a girl. And she was just six."

Albert stood up and went to the railing. "I'm sorry, Julia. It must be terrible to have something like that happen to your family." He was looking at the water, fishing for something else to say when he turned back and she saw his apprehension.

"I did think about Gudrun," Julia said as casually as she could. "But I trust Stanley, and your mother trusts him even more. What Stanley did so long ago I believe he did in ignorance. Also, I can't imagine that if Stanley had abused Gudrun she wouldn't have communicated that to you by now, at least through her behaviour."

"Forgive me, Julia," he said simply. "You're right, as always. I just never thought about Stanley this way. He was just—well, he was just Stanley."

"Albert," she said firmly, "your mother thought about it, and it didn't take her very long before I saw a look in her eyes that I interpret as knowledge."

"I don't understand. What could my mother know about it?"

"Stanley left suddenly. What happened on that day, Albert? What can you remember?" Even in the moonlight, Julia could see that Albert was unsettled again. "All right, Albert. Now you must tell me."

"Are you still friendly with Harry Burman and his family?"

"I was friends with Kathleen, but we've grown apart."

"You know their daughter then."

"Of course."

"The Burmans were here the last two weeks in August. They left on the Sunday, the day after your brother disappeared. I feel sure I can speak for my mother, Julia. She believes that something happened between your brother and Sahndra Burman."

Julia was shocked, more at the way Albert looked than at what he said. "If something happened between Stanley and Sahndra Burman, wouldn't someone have known? Or would she have been too ashamed to tell her parents?"

Albert thought that if Stanley had been involved in any kind of incident with Sahndra, it was not as Julia imagined it. "She's a very beautiful girl," he said, and he tried to make his voice sound cool. "One cannot blame your brother."

"Albert, please!"

He looked out at the water. "God forgive me, Julia, but I would swear that girl was responsible. I believe that she may have seduced your brother. I have *never*," Albert said firmly, "seen a girl of that age so sure of her sexual power."

Julia was silent. She understood now that Albert had been attracted to the Burmans' daughter. Yet while she expected life to be complicated, especially Albert's life, this was a layer of entanglement she was not prepared for.

Julia and David left the next day. Anna promised that if she heard from Stanley, she would contact Julia immediately, and Julia contented herself with that assurance.

CHAPTER TWENTY-ONE

Life and Blood

Lewis Godolphin received a letter at Macauley's on November 30 of 1935, postmarked Zeballos, addressed to him in his son's writing. He did not wait for lunch, but immediately went to the little office at the back of the store, sat down and opened it.

"My dear father," he read. "As you see by the postmark, I am no longer at the Inne. I left because I fear I can no longer trust myself to live with such gracious people. The crime that I committed so many years ago has always haunted me, and what is worse, I have lived a lie ever since. I told myself such a thing could never happen again, because now I am informed. I have avoided temptation and I have resisted it, but at the end of the summer I was overwhelmed by it. I felt I could no longer stay with the people who have loved and trusted me. I don't deserve them, and in another sense, they do not deserve me. I left because I am incapable of facing my weakness.

"In hard work and nature, I can find peace. I don't think I'll find much temptation in Zeballos, Gold River, Winter Cove or Yuquot. There is work here in Zeballos right now, as there have been some gold discoveries in the area, and I've found a comfortable place to live.

"I will try to write about what I see—the birds, the country. I want to be worthy of living here. Maybe some day, someone will accept what I have written and I can make you proud of me, at least.

"Father, I have a feeling that I will not see you again. I know I could never face Mother. I am happy that we had the one wonderful meeting at Julia's wedding, and I hope that you do not think of me with bitterness. I have the utmost love and respect for you, and one of my greatest sadnesses is that I have disappointed you and not been the son you deserve.

"As for Mother, you can tell her, if you wish, that I am sorry for what I did in the past to disgrace our family. That is indeed the truth.

"Remember me to Lilas. I never really knew her, except as a bright thing in my early life—a little like Tinker Bell, I always thought. Please tell Julia I love her very much, and that I am well. I trust her, as she has always shown me love and sympathy, and perhaps one day I will see her again, but I do not think I will write to her now.

"Please know that I am well and, within my limitations, happy. I would prefer that you did not tell anyone where I am, or attempt to see me.

"I love you, Father.

"Your son, Stanley Godolphin."

🙢 🙢 🙢

On December 1 of that year, Lewis Godolphin passed away in his sleep. He was sixty-two.

Adelaide Godolphin sat on the edge of the bed on which her husband lay. She always woke up at five-thirty in the morning and she always would. She sensed at once that something was wrong with Lewis, and soon knew that he was dead. She sat now, not looking at him, letting the tears run down her pale cheeks. There was no one to see how she felt, so it was all right. There would be time enough for her to put on a "proper face," as she called it. For the moment, she could indulge her grief by herself.

They would all say what a fine man Lewis had been. He hadn't an enemy in the world, but no one knew better than she about Lewis Godolphin. He was good. A really good man. For some reason that Adelaide did not understand, God made all too few of them.

She was aware of her own faults—her short temper, her impatience at the mistakes of others, her intolerance. And yes, she probably did place too much importance on "what people would say." But she had wanted so badly to have a good, decent family, and to know that she and her family were loved and respected as they deserved.

In the early years, it seemed as if they had succeeded. She and Lewis had worked hard, stood side by side for the kind of life they wanted. Then came that fateful day when their world, or at least a large portion of it, collapsed. Their son's actions seemed to have nothing to do with the way they lived; what better father could a boy have than Lewis? She could not understand it at all, and she never would. It was as if the boy had "bad blood." Both sides of the family, as far as she knew, were decent people. Her father had apparently sowed some wild oats, but every young man was expected to do that. Except Lewis.

Lewis. She would miss him so.

She went over to her dressing table. On the top was a small wicker basket with a red velvet ribbon winding through it. She opened the lid and drew out a white cambric handkerchief with white tatting along the edge. She saved it for only the best occasions. She wiped away her tears and prepared herself to go downstairs and call the doctor.

Dr. Muddsley attributed Lewis's death to "natural causes"; his heart had simply stopped while he slept.

Lewis Godolphin was buried in Ross Bay Cemetery on a cold clear day. The waves lashed up close to the shore, the whitecaps breaking on the rocks below the bank; the mourners could hear them while Lewis's coffin was being lowered into the grave. Earlier, there had been a small memorial ceremony at the funeral parlour, Adelaide having refused a church service.

The pallbearers consisted of two of the men from Macauley's store, plus Georgie Trevor and Albert Aalgaard.

Adelaide was against having Albert as one of her husband's pallbearers. She had never approved of him when he was a boy, and now that she suspected Julia might be having an affair with him, she had even more reason to disapprove. But Sveinn Arnason had insisted. Too old to come to his friend's funeral himself, he insisted that his grandson take his place as a token of respect.

Julia watched her father's coffin and then looked out across the Strait of Juan de Fuca toward the Olympic Mountains, thinking of how dear he was and hoping he had been happy.

Lilas was the most demonstrative in her grief. Always considered her Daddy's "little soubrette," she was inconsolable. Adelaide, her face lined and strained but controlled, held her youngest child as she wept. Julia, watching her, felt very old.

Afterward, they went back to the Godolphin home, where tea and sandwiches, cookies and cakes were served. Lilas pulled herself together and became the good hostess. Julia was increasingly annoyed that her sister always seemed to be playing a part. Eleanor pleaded a headache and had Georgie drive her home. Albert also left, saying that he had to get to Sidney in time to catch the *Islander* at five o'clock. Julia and Miss Cooke, Lewis's fellow workers and a few old family friends stayed on.

Harry and Kathleen were there, while Sahndra visited her grandparents, who sent their regrets. Kathleen and Julia barely spoke. The gulf between them had become unbridgeable. If Julia's increasing awkwardness at Kathleen's baby fantasies weren't enough, now there was the matter of Sahndra and Stanley.

Julia wanted this day to honour her father. Instead, as she watched Harry and Kathleen, she obsessed over Sahndra. Had Sahndra done something to drive her brother from Arnason Island, or did her brother do something for which she, as his sister, should now feel ashamed? If he did do something, why should she feel responsible? Julia wondered if there was some of her mother's sense of shame in her. What of our character and destiny comes from blood, and what comes from our lives? At least she found herself grateful on both counts that she was Lewis Godolphin's daughter.

Georgie soon returned to the Godolphin home, and Julia sat with him in her mother's parlour, her head on his shoulder. Could she explain to him all the complex emotions she was feeling? No, she thought, this time she could not. Stanley's difficulties on Arnason Island and her reaquaintance with Albert were matters she would have to work through on her own.

སྐ སྐ སྐ

On the afternoon after Lewis's death, Mr. Macauley had come to the house. He was a small man, sixty-five himself, who had hoped to turn over the business entirely to Lewis when he retired at the end of the year. He and Adelaide sat in the parlour with the blinds drawn, talking in hushed voices of Lewis and of the small pension that Adelaide would receive.

Upstairs, Julia tried to comfort Lilas. Adelaide made tea for Mr. Macauley, who had brought a paper bag that contained a few of Lewis's personal belongings. He offered them almost reverently to Adelaide, who put them aside. When he had gone, Adelaide opened the bag. She found a bank shaped like a frog that Lilas had given her father one Christmas and in which he had kept a few foreign coins that occasionally turned up at the shop. There were two fresh handkerchiefs, a comb, a bag of lemon drops, a picture taken in 1912 of Adelaide and the children and the last letter from Stanley.

Adelaide frowned as she picked up the envelope. Lewis had said nothing of receiving a letter. She noticed the postmark from Zeballos and the date, took the letter out of the envelope, then put on her glasses.

She read the letter through carefully, her lips moving as she mouthed some of the sentences to herself. When she came to the part where Stanley stated that he had again been overwhelmed by temptation, she put down the letter, her hands shaking. This is the thanks that Lewis got for his patience with Stanley, she thought. This is what he lived with his last day. This may have been what killed him.

At the reference to herself, she tossed her head, sniffing with distaste; for Stanley to say he was sorry did little good as far as she was concerned. When she read the statement about trusting Julia, she felt angry and cheated. Julia! The old resentment against her elder daughter returned. What right had he to trust Julia? And how dare she respond with "love and sympathy"? That just showed how little Julia knew about decent conduct.

The only comfort she took was in the knowledge that they would probably never hear from him again. "Up there" on the west coast was a good place for him. No one was likely to recognize him or talk about him. No one they knew, anyway, and a good thing too.

Adelaide looked toward the staircase. The girls must never see this letter. She got up and went to the kitchen where there was still a low fire burning in the stove, tossed the letter and its envelope into the fire and watched them burn.

CHAPTER TWENTY-TWO

The Asylum

Harry Burman came home from work, his emotions, as always, in conflict. He was eager to see his daughter. Her beauty, which grew more obvious each day, the interest she showed in his stories of the bank (not usually very exciting, but Sahndra was a good listener), her own stories of school—these made up his reason for living. But even the happiness that his daughter brought him was overshadowed by the ever-increasing signs of his wife's madness.

For the last year and a half, Kathleen had had none of the hallucinations of pregnancy that he dreaded. He hated to see her childlike happiness destroyed when it finally came to her, her heartbroken crying as she struggled with the fact that she was not pregnant. But even though there had been a long stretch of time since her last delusion of childbearing, Harry had no cause for hope, as he could see her tenuous hold on reality diminishing month by month. She talked incessantly about the babies she had borne and lost, about children as though they were in the backyard playing. He never knew, when he came home, what might await him.

Tonight he let himself in, hoping to see Sahndra greet him, then recalling that Thursday afternoon was her Girl Guide meeting and she would not arrive home until sometime after he did. She had recently become more sociable, Harry noted, and he encouraged her. She had been a silent and undemonstrative child, but perhaps she was beginning to "come out of herself," as his mother put it.

Kathleen sat in the rocking chair she had bought a few years ago for living room. She was often there when he came home, rocking, sometimes singing, sometimes with tears streaming down her cheeks. Today, he sighed with relief as he heard her singing. Then he saw what she held in her arms and he stopped in the hall, wondering about his own sanity.

Kathleen, her pretty face radiant, was holding a baby wrapped in a blue blanket. She was singing "Rock-a-Bye Baby" to the infant, who stared up at her, apparently content.

The enormity of what she must have done welled up in him. A bank president's wife arrested for kidnapping? How was he to deal with this? It was not fair and he didn't deserve it, but then came that other feeling, of guilt and the fear that perhaps he did deserve it, that it was his punishment, not hers.

"Oh darling, I didn't hear you come in." Kathleen had risen, holding the baby firmly. "Little Harry has been so cross this afternoon. He must be teething. I don't care if the book says three months is too young—I just know it's teeth. This is the first time he's been quiet. Really, I never had any trouble like this with Sahndra. She was always such a good baby. I guess it's true that boys are harder to raise than girls. Take off your coat and hat, Harry, and I'll put little Harry in his crib and make you a drink. Would you like that?"

He could not move. He had no idea of what to do. Then he heard Sahndra opening the front door behind him. She wore her Girl Guide uniform, which barely reached her knees, her long legs clad in ribbed black stockings. She stood beside her father in the hall and took in the situation at a glance. "It's the Hollander baby," she said to him under her breath. "They've got so many kids, they'll never miss it."

He stared, shocked at the coldness in her words. She put her school-books on the hall chair and went to Kathleen.

"Let me hold the baby, Mother," she said, and her voice had the bright impersonal tone of a nurse or a social worker.

"Thank you, dear. Now just watch his back. That's it. I declare, Sahndra, you're a born mother." She placed the baby tenderly in Sahndra's arms, bent over and kissed his cheek.

Over her mother's head, Sahndra made an expression of disgust that her father could see. But she held the baby expertly, and as she went into the hall she cooed to the child, "That's a good little boy. Go to sleep."

Kathleen helped Harry off with his coat and hat, chattering happily about her day. Harry heard the back door shut, and knew Sahndra had taken the baby home. Kathleen accepted Sahndra's handling of the baby without question. "Now he's safe in his little crib. How nice and quiet he is at last." She poured Harry a drink and finished preparing an excellent dinner. As usual, the three of them sat in the cheerful dining room.

Sahndra spoke to her father when Kathleen was in the kitchen. "I took the baby back. Nobody noticed. She must have taken him out of his buggy on their porch. I told you they've got so many they never missed it. But, Dad, we have to do something about her, right away." He looked at her and was aware of the level gaze. "Next time I might not be here, or it could be someone else's baby. We don't want a kidnapping charge. You know how people are ever since the Lindbergh thing. We have to protect ourselves. Besides, it's the kindest thing we can do for her. You know she's crazy. Everybody does. The kids at school, the nuns, all the neighbours."

Harry's face went ashen. How could his own daughter talk like that? He waved a hand at her to be silent, and in a moment Kathleen pushed open the swinging door with her body and came in with a cake with three candles on it.

"Surprise!" she laughed. "I'll bet neither of you remembered that it's little Harry's three-month birthday. No, I can see by your faces you didn't."

She put the gaily decorated cake in front of Sahndra. In blue icing it said "Happy Birthday, Harry Jr." and the tiny blue candles flickered over the inscription. "Sahndra dear, you get to blow out the candles. Your brother's not quite ready yet. Make a wish for him, dear, something really nice, and then blow."

When Kathleen went back to the kitchen after dinner, Sahndra spoke again. "Dad, you've got to take action. What are you going to do when she goes upstairs tonight and discovers there's no little brother?" Harry winced. "I can keep her busy while you call Dr. Sinclair. Maybe she'll forget about the baby tonight, but we don't know. Anyway, something else is bound to happen again soon."

"I'll call," he said. He watched her as she walked away from him, through the dining room and into the kitchen, with her lithe, graceful stride.

The telephone was in the hall on a small table, a high-backed chair beside it. He sat down and called Dr. Sinclair, keeping his voice as low as possible.

Dr. Sinclair's wife answered. They were still at dinner, but she knew that Harry Burman was not an alarmist. If he had to speak to her husband immediately, he probably had a good reason, and she knew what it might be. Dr. Sinclair had seen it coming, but he was reluctant to have Kathleen committed to an insane asylum. She was so gentle and vulnerable, even in her madness. If she had to be sent away, he hoped that her husband would see fit to provide her with the best care.

"There's nothing we can do tonight," he told Harry. "I'll come by first thing tomorrow on my way to the office."

"What about tonight? What if she becomes upset or irrational?"

"Give her a sleeping pill. You must have some left from the last prescription."

The rest of the evening was uneasy. Kathleen dutifully asked Harry about his day at the office. Once or twice she looked up at the ceiling, as though listening for a baby. At ten o'clock, Harry suggested that they go to bed, and she agreed. Harry was torn between the hope that there would be no upset until morning and the fear that if she behaved normally, Dr. Sinclair would not be able to commit her.

After they'd prepared for bed, Sahndra arrived at their bedroom door. She wore a long pink nightgown and held out a glass of milk. "Little Harry's just fine," she said calmly. "Here, I brought you some milk. It will be good for you, Mother."

Sahndra left, and Kathleen drank the milk obediently, as though she were the child. "Harry, we're the luckiest people in the world to have such a beautiful daughter, and for her to be such a good girl."

He looked at her and felt an emotion he could never express. If he had ever allowed himself to cry, there would have been tears for his wife, this good-natured, gentle person. Somehow, the greatest happiness in her life had come to her from the child that his own terrible conduct had produced. Sahndra had made Kathleen happy, and he was grateful.

🐟 🐟 🐟

Dr. Sinclair arrived at eight-thirty. Kathleen was still asleep. Harry opened the door for him, and they shook hands automatically. The doctor saw Sahndra at the kitchen table.

"Would you like a cup of tea?" she asked.

"No, thanks, my dear. We'd better get on with this business." The doctor suggested that he and Harry go into the living room. Sahndra looked at the clock, made a face, then picked up her satchel of books. "So long, Dad," she said. "Good luck." She gave him her little wave and left.

Dr. Sinclair told Harry about the Rosemoore Rest Home near Sooke. It was an old house, with a magnificent view of the ocean. There were two doctors in residence, and others on call. He had recommended it before and would find out right away if they could accommodate Kathleen. "I warn you," he told Harry. "It's expensive."

"I have no choice," said Harry glumly. "As long as she's happy and well cared for, what else can I do?"

"I agree. You could send her to Essondale on the mainland, but that's a harsh place for a gentle woman like Kathleen. It's better for a man in your position to have his wife in Rosemoore than in a public asylum."

Just then they heard Kathleen calling. Her light voice was high-pitched and excited. "Harry! Harry!" She came hurrying down the stairs in her nightgown and stopped on the last step, surprised to see Dr. Sinclair. Then a smile lit up her face; she came into the room, extending her left hand to the doctor and keeping her right hand on her body. "What a wonderful time you chose to call," she said gaily to the doctor. "I've such happy news." She turned back to her husband. "Oh, Harry darling, this baby's alive—I can feel it moving. He's so active! Not like the others at all. Here," she took Harry's hand and placed it on her belly, "can't you feel it? That's your son kicking, Harry dear. Now let Dr. Sinclair have a turn!"

Dr. Sinclair put his hand on the indicated spot. He nodded.

"Did you feel him?"

"Well, I certainly felt something," he said kindly.

Kathleen caught herself. "Really, I should get dressed before I come downstairs." And without another word she turned and went back upstairs.

Dr. Sinclair turned to Harry. "Well, this provides an excellent pretext for suggesting she enter Rosemoore. It's a rest home where she can get the attention she needs so that she won't have any trouble delivering the baby."

"Is that ethical?" asked Harry?

Dr. Sinclair shot Harry a cool glance. "I'll be the judge of that."

When he got to his office, Dr. Sinclair confirmed that Rosemoore had space, and then called Harry at his office to suggest he bring Kathleen by for an exam at noon.

After the exam, Dr. Sinclair talked to Kathleen about entering the home. He said that as she had suffered problems with her "previous pregnancies," it might be an idea for her to be in a private home where she could get the most complete medical attention from the start. He praised the beauty of Rosemoore, the gardens and the pleasant care, and Kathleen brightened. She was unnervingly receptive. Her only worry was how her husband and daughter would manage, but Dr. Sinclair, assuming his smoothest manner, the very manner that Harry so disliked, assured her that Sahndra was most capable, and this would give her an added opportunity to learn responsibility, a good thing for any young girl these days. They could both visit her frequently, and perhaps it would not be long before she came home.

"With my baby!" Kathleen exclaimed.

"Yes, yes," said the doctor.

Harry picked her up at one o'clock and they drove to Sooke. Kathleen clapped her hands when she saw Rosemoore, and Harry was happy to see how beautiful it was: a large, lovely Tudor-style home, with a circular driveway, stretches of green lawn and manicured gardens. The view of the water was magnificent. The strong wind off the strait bore the scent of the ocean and the arbutus trees were bent toward the east, beaten by that wind. Today Harry found the sound of the wind in the leaves somehow comforting.

The staff were courteous and friendly, and Kathleen was delighted with everything. Her room looked out on the lawn that sloped down toward the sea. Harry was thankful that she had not noticed the bars that extended halfway up the windows. When he went to sign the commitment papers, he left her with a nurse who, by good luck, was also from Ireland, and the last thing he heard was Kathleen telling the woman about the baby she would soon have.

As he drove home, he thought about how he would miss Kathleen. Even with all the embarrassment and worry that her condition had caused him, he would miss her. He believed that his love for her was purer and more satisfying than most men felt for their wives. A few large drops of rain spattered suddenly against his windshield and he thought he did not deserve her. Then he thought of Elaine and how she had aroused in him such a different passion. He tried to conjure up her face, but all he could see was Sahndra's.

☙ ☙ ☙

Harry and Sahndra sat opposite each other at the dinner table that night. Sahndra had made fried chicken, with peas and mashed potatoes, and it was actually a passable dinner for a young girl whose strong point was not Home Economics. "C-plus, maybe," she said. "Tomorrow I'll try for a B." Harry smiled wanly, but she could tell he was not amused.

Sahndra watched him across the table. "I guess you're going to miss Mother," she said coolly as she stirred sugar into her tea.

"Yes," he said shortly.

Then she put down her teaspoon and gave him her long, level glance. "She isn't my mother, is she?"

They took stock of each other in silence. "What," asked Harry at last, "makes you think that?"

"Everyone says so."

"Who is everyone?"

"The kids at school. Lots of people."

"They're only schoolchildren. What do they know? You shouldn't listen to them."

"I can look in the mirror."

He stared at her. "What does that mean?"

"I've been told, and I've overheard, that I'm half Indian, and when I look in the mirror . . . Well, it seems that way, doesn't it?"

Harry said nothing. He folded his linen napkin neatly into a square and placed it on the table. Then he said, "Excuse me" and got up. He went into the living room and sat down in his chair. It was too much. After all he had been through today, to have to listen to this from his child.

Sahndra was not about to give up. She tossed her napkin onto the table and followed, throwing herself into the chair opposite him, her long legs stretched before her. She put one foot on the footstool, then crossed the other over at the ankle. Harry watched her, terrified.

"She is not my mother," said Sahndra firmly.

Harry realized that, in this situation, he was no match for her. "No, you're right. She isn't your mother." Sahndra sat up straight in her chair, taking her legs off the footstool and tucking them under her. Before she could speak, he looked at her pleadingly. "But no mother could ever have been better. No mother would have loved you more than Kathleen has. I hope you know that."

She nodded. "I know. And I loved her."

He saw that the words did not come easily to her. Just as well, perhaps. "You shouldn't talk about her as though she were dead. She could get better, you know," he said drily.

Sahndra resumed her inquiry. "All right. So Kathleen wasn't—isn't— my mother. Then who is?"

He was silent.

"She was an Indian, wasn't she?"

He got up then, went to the cupboard where they kept the liquor and poured himself a brandy, aware that his hand shook and that his daughter was watching him.

He sat down again opposite her, feeling the brandy warming his blood, trying to get hold of himself, to remember that he was a mature man, a bank president and the father of this girl who was upsetting him so. He put his day with Kathleen out of his mind and tried to deal only with the matter at hand. "Your mother was a Moachat princess."

He had at last succeeded in making an impression. Yet, as he said this, he hoped Sahndra would not use such a ridiculous expression to describe herself. He took a cigarette from the silver case the bank had given him.

"Tell me how you met her."

Harry smoked nervously. "Her father, the chief, knew your grandfather. My father handled a lot of his business matters—property and investments. He and my father trusted each other. When your mother was about sixteen, my father wanted her to have a better education than she would have up on the reserve and the chief agreed. She boarded with my parents, helped out your grandmother at home and went to school here in Victoria."

Harry heard his own voice, droning away, explaining something that had happened in another life. He was perfectly objective, but he knew that he was getting closer to the end of a road that led off a cliff.

Sahndra had relaxed, but her great eyes watched and waited. "So you met her right in your own house? It's really a very romantic story," she said with a fifteen-year-old's condescension.

Harry had reached the edge now; he did not know how to continue.

"All right, Dad, you couldn't have been married to her. You and she had an affair, and she had me, and then you married Kathleen. Right?"

He put a hand over his eyes. He nodded.

"Okay, so what happened to her?"

Harry realized there was no turning back. "Kathleen and I agreed that we should adopt her baby. That was you. She was very fond of Kathleen, and Kathleen, well, you know what she's like."

"Sure, she's an absolute saint."

Harry found Sahndra's coolness was more disturbing than anything else. He wondered if she felt anything or was simply deciding which parts of the story she could use to her own advantage.

"Well," he said. "That's all I have to tell you. We adopted you. And your mother—Kathleen and I—are very happy that we did."

He felt somewhat relieved now. It was better for their relationship if they were going to have to live without Kathleen, but Sahndra wasn't finished with her inquiry.

"Somehow I can't see you being involved with an Indian, even a princess."

Harry made a gesture with his hand, hoping to imply that what had happened had happened and they would have to make the best of it. Surely she would be satisfied now.

"Is my mother still alive?"

"I don't know. I never heard from her after she left us. It's better this way."

Then she asked, quietly, "Are you sure you're my father?"

He was totally unprepared for the question. "I have no reason to doubt it," he replied tightly, when he was able to speak.

"Well, you never know. I don't look like you or Grandpa or Grandma."

"You look like your mother," he said firmly. He looked up at the clock on the mantel. "Don't you have homework to do before you go to bed?"

She brought her legs down to the floor then and stood up. She leaned over his chair and kissed the top of his head. "Thanks, Dad," she said and went upstairs to her room.

Harry sat very still for a long time, finishing his brandy in sips and eventually pouring himself a second, something he never did. This girl, his daughter, Sahndra, had upset him more than even his experience during the day had done.

CHAPTER TWENTY-THREE

The Year of Three Kings

On January 20, 1936, King George V died. On January 28, his funeral was broadcast by the BBC throughout the world, the first time this had been possible. Although this historic event would be rebroadcast, the original began at two o'clock in the morning, Pacific Standard Time, and only the original would do for Adelaide and Lilas.

Adelaide set the alarm on her bedside clock for one-thirty and placed it on the night table. When she awakened, she sat up sharply, then remembered what was happening, put on her navy blue flannel dressing gown and blue hand-knit slippers and went into Lilas's room to wake her. Lilas put on her pink chenille robe and matching slippers, and the two ladies sat down in the living room, pulling their chairs as close to the radio as possible and putting their heads down near the speaker. They kept the volume low, as though they might wake somone.

First the Canadian announcer's voice said reverently, "We take you now to London," then considerable static and interference until there came the cool, precise voice of Stuart Hibberd saying, "This is the overseas service of the British Broadcasting Corporation," from St. George's Chapel at Windsor. The women listened, Lilas with tears in her eyes that soon spilled down her cheeks as she thought of her own father's death. They would see in the local papers the famous photo of "The Four Princes," which showed George V's four sons standing guard, one at each corner of his coffin. As Adelaide listened, she could picture the four sons marching behind their father's coffin: Edward, the oldest, looking so worn (she already had an idea of what his extra secret sorrow was); Albert, the poor dear duke of York, the most like his father; Henry, the Duke of Gloucester, the least interesting brother; and George, Duke of Kent, a nice-looking young man. She beat time with her small hand as the band played the "Dead March."

When it was over Adelaide put the kettle on and they had tea, still huddled by the radio that was playing appropriate organ music, and talked about the good old King and Queen Mary, whom Adelaide had never quite trusted, and about the young princes, and how there was going to be trouble when Edward became King. Lilas, like every young woman in the Empire, defended him. He was the first young, romantic king that England had known for several hundred years, but her mother knew better. "You mark my words," she said, "it's not going to be smooth sailing with that young man on the throne." Adelaide already knew, though most Canadians did not, a great deal about that distracting American woman, Wallis Simpson. She shook her head.

With virtue being cast aside by time and fashion, there was trouble brewing. And Adelaide knew about Adolf Hitler too.

🕊 🕊 🕊

Julia first heard from Stanley the day after King George's funeral. He did not know about his father's death, but he was concerned because he had not received his usual Christmas letter. She phoned Arnason Island right away, and then went to visit her mother. Julia wakened her from an afternoon nap, a practice that Adelaide almost never indulged in. She saw her mother peer down the stairs, and then she came down in her dressing gown. "I'm sorry to disturb you," Julia said, "but I wanted to let you know right away that I received a letter from Stanley. He's well, and he's living in a town called Zeballos, west of Campbell River."

"I understand they've discovered gold there," Adelaide said coolly. "There's a fool's errand."

Adelaide offered Julia a cup of tea, and they did not mention Stanley again.

Julia wrote and destroyed six letters to Stanley before she felt ready to send him the news that she knew would break his heart.

Six months after Lewis Godolphin's death, Adelaide sold the house on Humboldt Street. It was much too big for her to keep up, with only Lilas at home, and had too many memories. She didn't do it for the money; the Depression had been keenly felt in British Columbia, and many people were forced to sell their houses or even let them go for taxes. The home was purchased by an Italian family, who proposed to turn it into a rooming house, as was happening to many such old homes.

She and Lilas took a ground-floor, two-bedroom apartment on Fort Street. It was a modern place, with white exterior, in what became known as Art Deco style. At first Adelaide was horrified, as the interior of the apartment consisted of all-white walls. "Just like a hospital," she said. "What will my friends think?" But Lilas convinced her that houses with oak panelling and corbelled ceilings had become unfashionable and less appreciated than bright new apartments.

Adelaide, somewhat to the surprise of her friends, quickly adapted to the changes. They had forgotten that she was a pioneer, that she had lived in several places, each time starting life over again. True, she had come to think of the Humboldt Street house as her final home, but when Lewis died, she knew that it was not.

The new living room was large enough for the old chesterfield, the Oriental rug, her wicker rocker, and Lewis's stuffed pheasants, which fitted nicely on the top shelves of the built-in bookcase. The one problem was the piano. However, Julia came to the rescue: she fitted out the coach house at Blenheim Oaks as a music studio for Lilas.

So Adelaide and Lilas settled into their apartment. On the radio, they listened to Jack Benny, Fibber McGee and Molly, and Aimee Semple MacPherson and the Foursquare Church. Miss Cooke and her widowed sister-in-law, Mrs. Cooke, came every Friday night for tea and cake and gossip, in which Adelaide considered herself a great authority. She had made friends with two reporters at the *Times*; she would visit their offices and write letters to the editor, and became recognized as something of a local character. Occasionally, she'd invite them to visit, as it crossed her mind that perhaps one of them might want to marry Lilas, but nothing ever came of that.

Lilas was now thirty-three and a Victoria celebrity. She sang with the symphony, in the summer band concerts in the park, on local radio programs, at weddings and at funerals. She starred every year in the glee club's annual operetta. She had played the roles of Mademoiselle Modiste, Naughty Marietta and Rose Marie, and her most recent triumph was in *The Merry Widow*, although there were many who felt she was a shade young to take on such a demanding role.

But why had she not married? At one time, she had gone out with Walter Chilcoate, now assistant conductor of the Victoria Junior Symphony but then a struggling musician. But the vibrant Lilas had said Walter had no "joie de vivre." Adelaide was relieved, as she did not want a musician for a son-in-law. Lilas sometimes dated a young man who worked in the music department of the Victoria library, but that seemed to be all either of them expected from their relationship. Julia thought that Lilas was looking for a man who answered the description of her operetta heroes, and such men were not easy to find.

᠅ ᠅ ᠅

On December 11, 1936, the bell at St. Ann's school tolled, and the girls were all requested to assemble in the main hall. Such a summons meant something very special indeed, and while the little ones were puzzled and nervous, the juniors and seniors knew exactly what was happening.

Sister Mary-Rose had decided to bring the whole school together to listen to the speech of King Edward VIII. She already knew that he would probably announce his abdication, but she still had hopes that he would make a noble gesture, renouncing any claims to a selfish, private life and sacrificing himself to the demands of the British Crown.

The speech was broadcast at eleven o'clock and only a few diehards (such as Adelaide and Lilas) had heard the original at three in the morning. The girls lined up in the main hall of the school, a plain, colourless room dominated by a large crucifix on the front wall, at the back of the small stage. There were about fifty girls in all, as well as eight nuns and four lay teachers.

Sister Mary-Rose made her entrance from the wings, her black robes sweeping around her. She was deeply upset, but she felt that at such an important moment in history, her girls should know first-hand what was to become of the British Empire.

"Girls," she said, raising her chin and looking her noblest, "this is a very important occasion. You are about to hear the voice of a King of England." She stooped and turned on the radio. There was much static, and then the emotionless, wonderful voice, "This is the overseas service of the British Broadcasting Corporation." Then the King was introduced and in a pinched, tired voice, so vulnerable in its timbre, said, "At long last, I am able to say a few words for myself . . ."

Sister Mary-Rose dabbed at her eyes with her white handkerchief. It was the end of a way of life. When the King of England would abdicate to marry a twice-divorced American woman, why, anything could happen. How were the nuns to instruct their young charges in virtue and decency when the King believed love was more important than duty? Of course, he was an Anglican and not a Catholic. She would mention that in the speech she would make to the girls after the broadcast was over. Had the

King been a Catholic, he would never have done such a thing, Henry VIII being a cruel aberration.

The little girls were bored, the older ones were interested and some were moved to tears. Sister Mary-Rose looked at Sahndra Burman, at the beautiful, expressionless face, and wondered what the girl's thoughts were. She was listening, at least.

Sahndra was thinking that if King Edward had only met her first, there would have been no need for Mrs. Simpson. She might have been Queen of England. It showed how necessary it was to be in the right place at the right time.

CHAPTER TWENTY-FOUR

The Answer

One Saturday in the summer of 1938, Harry Burman took his car out of the garage. It was a custom he observed every Sunday, driving the road to Sooke to spend the day with Kathleen, sometimes with Sahndra. But this was a Saturday, and Harry did not drive west but instead headed north toward the Malahat Drive.

Like most of his fellow Victorians, he almost never explored the world north of Victoria. There was no need. There were a few daring souls who tackled the highway for a Sunday drive, and Harry had a few times been as far as Nanaimo, to confer with the branch manager of the bank in that city. Today, however, his journey was a personal one.

His life was falling away from him. His wife was in an asylum, his daughter would soon be an adult and his mother, Doris, had passed away in March. She had been sick only a short while, but the heart condition she had always contended with finally proved fatal, and her weight, which had increased with the years, had not helped. Harry had mourned his mother sincerely. She had not been particularly likeable but she was not a bad woman, and she was his mother. They had got along better than many mothers and sons. She had been kind to Kathleen, and attempted to be a responsible grandmother to Sahndra. If she had any doubts about Sahndra's parentage, she never revealed them.

Sahndra had graduated from St. Ann's in June. Harry offered to pay her tuition if she wanted to go to college, but she did not wish to continue with her education. What she did want was a job as a teller in her father's bank.

The neighbours became used to the sight of Harry Burman and his beautiful daughter leaving the house every morning at eight-thirty precisely, silent, solemn, walking to the bank, then returning home at five-thirty. The pair elicited sympathy, the young girl, working with her father and preparing meals for him. They had a woman in once a week to do the heavy cleaning. They preferred to keep to themselves. And every Sunday they would drive to Rosemoore to visit his poor wife. It was really a very sad story.

Matthew Burman was another burden. He would come for Sunday dinner, and talk as though he were still running the bank. It was not overbearing; it was just a constant stream of advice on loan defaults and the virtues of bonds, nothing that Harry did not know as well as the route he took to work. The senior Burman didn't talk about Indians anymore. The spark that that had once given him had been extinguished and he filled up his time with chat about the prime rate and the money supply and the evils of the Social Credit crusade against bankers that had flourished during the Depression. "It's a political party founded on a lie," he would say. "It's politicians trying to buy votes with money that doesn't belong to them. It's a good thing they'll only fall for it in Alberta."

Harry worried about his father, knowing he could not live on his own much longer. Yet he feared the thought of two bankers living alone together, the younger becoming ever more like the elder.

Sahndra was still sleeping when Harry left. He went to her room, stood at the foot of her bed and watched her. How beautiful she was. She was almost the age Elaine had been when he first saw her. Harry knew that what he was doing was the only course he could follow. He had to find Elaine. He must know the answer to the question that was obsessing him more each day: was he Sahndra's father?

He wrote a note to Sahndra and left it on the hall table by the telephone, explaining that he had to go to Nanaimo on unexpected business and would be gone all day; he would make up the plausible story she would demand before he returned.

Harry did not expect a happy ending to his quest. He drove fast, even on the perilous road over the Malahat Summit, and his knuckles were white from the tension of holding the steering wheel. He did not stop for lunch, but continued through rolling farmland until he reached the Cowichan Indian Reserve. Years ago, when Matthew Burman was still making trips up the coast to see Chief Maquinna, he learned that Elaine had married a Cowichan man and lived with him near Duncan.

As Harry approached the reserve, a few drops of rain began to fall. The houses were plain but tidy, and there were wooden planks for sidewalks. A few children stared at his car as he passed. My God, how can she live here? he thought. She could have had a life in Victoria. He parked his car and asked one of the children if they knew where he might find Elaine, but the child shook his head. A woman came out to the porch of one of the houses and called to them. Slowly they left the road, now splattered by a shower.

Harry approached the woman and took off his hat; his father had told him to show Indians the same courtesies that one showed to whites. He tried to ignore the two dogs that were hovering close to his trouser legs.

"Good afternoon," he said politely. "I am looking for a woman named Elaine. She's married, about forty years old. You might also know her as Sa-Sin." He felt foolish as he said this.

The woman smiled, cocked her head and nodded.

"Do you know where I can find her?" he asked.

The woman nodded again, but this time extended her arm toward the road along which he had driven. She said something he was unable to understand. One of the silent children, a young girl, came forward. "You want Mrs. Jack. She works at the big store on the highway."

The woman looked at the child and back at Harry, and smiled and nodded again.

The Valley Store was two miles from the reserve. It was an unpainted wooden building, with a sloping roof, a covered porch and a gasoline pump on one side. The store sold candy and cigarettes, ice cream and soft drinks, and native crafts, mainly Cowichan sweaters and cedar baskets. Harry parked his car and walked toward the entrance, his chest tight.

An Indian man came around from the back of the building and went to the side by the gas pump where he was working on an old car. He saw Harry, smiled and waved. Not a bad-looking chap for an Indian, thought Harry, and then hesitated for a moment as it occurred to him that the man might be Elaine's husband. He walked up the steps and opened the door into the store.

She was waiting on two elderly American tourists, giving them directions, showing them a map. He was startled to realize how very much Sahndra looked like her mother, not only in her face but in her long-limbed grace and the way she held her head. He turned away quickly to examine some postcards.

When the couple had gone, he looked up. Elaine was staring at him, and he saw again the hostility that he had known so long ago. She had gained a little weight but had kept her figure well. There were some grey streaks in the black hair, which was tied in a bun low on her neck. She wore a brown cardigan over a white shirt, a brown skirt and earrings and a necklace made of shell. She had never worn jewellery when he knew her.

He had to speak first. He knew her well enough that she might not speak at all.

"Hello, Elaine. You're looking well."

"What do you want?"

"I . . . I wanted to see you again. I've thought about you a great deal."

She did not answer, but put the road map she had shown the last visitors away in a drawer, tidying up the counter carefully.

"Is there somewhere we could sit and talk for a few minutes?"

She gestured toward one of the two tables at the side of the room. "I can serve you tea if you wish. We're not busy right now."

Harry went to the table by the window. He saw her lips part slightly as she watched him take out his handkerchief and dust off the chair before he sat down. She brought the tea, and when he had taken his first sip, she asked, "Will there be anything else?"

He looked at her in astonishment. She was standing by his table, with her familiar stare. "Elaine, for God's sake, sit down!"

She showed such a look of revulsion that he winced. He had never understood her hatred. "That man outside," she said quietly, "is my husband."

Her anger somehow calmed him. She was making something out of nothing, he thought. "Call him in, by all means," and his coldness now matched hers. "I'd like to meet him." She looked outside for a moment, then slowly pulled the chair opposite his away from the table and sat down.

He sipped his tea, trying not to look at her. Outside, he could hear the voice of her husband. A driver stopped for gasoline but did not come in.

"How is Kathleen?" she asked softly, as though she had decided to call a truce.

"Not well," Harry replied. He didn't want to discuss Kathleen, but perhaps talking about her would start their communication. Besides, finding out from her what he wanted to know would not be easy. "She's in a private hospital for nervous disorders. She's been there for four years. There's no improvement."

"I'm sorry." Her head dropped for a moment. "Were there . . . are there any children?"

There was a touch of irony in his voice that he could not hide. "Only yours."

"I'm sorry for Kathleen," she said. "She was very good to me."

"Don't you want to know about your daughter?"

"No. She's your child, not mine."

"Well, she's very beautiful. She looks exactly like you." He watched her carefully, but her face was thoughtful and impassive, as though she were still thinking about Kathleen.

She got up and walked away from him. "Will there be anything else?"

"I haven't finished yet," he said, pouring more tea into his cup, stirring the sugar carefully with his spoon.

"I have."

He must get her back somehow, get her in a more receptive mood before he touched on the question that was uppermost in his mind. "You and your husband—are you happy?"

She still did not look at him. "Yes," she said without expression.

"You have other children?"

"One. A girl."

"Ah, good," he said as pleasantly as he was able. "I would like to see her."

"You can't. Klea ran away from her residential school and went over to Nootka to live with my father. She discovered that she's a princess and she intends to restore the power of Maquinna." She looked out the window then, and a faint smile touched her lips. "Perhaps she will," she said gently. "She is a very strong person."

Harry got up and went over to the window, where she stood with her back to him. He wanted so much to touch her, to say, "Why can't we be friends now? You can come to visit your daughter, our daughter." But he could not say it.

"Elaine," he said, and he made his voice as gentle and persuasive as he could. "Elaine—will you tell me the truth about Sahndra?"

She turned, her hostile stare once more in place. "Sahndra?"

"Sahndra Mary. But she prefers just Sahndra."

"It's a pretty name. Kathleen told me she would name her that before she was born."

"I told you she was beautiful, like you. Now I must know the truth. Am I her father?"

Elaine was surprised by the question. The dark brow rose, and she took a sharp breath. "Why do you ask that?"

She was moving away from him now. He must be careful. "Because I want to know. I must know. Is there any chance that she isn't my child?"

"Why should you doubt it?"

"Because there is something about her, something I cannot fathom. It's the only part of her that isn't like you, and it isn't like my family either. Also, I know that she was born . . . shall we say prematurely? Or was she?"

She tried to walk away from him, but he stopped her.

Then she raised her chin, and he saw the defiance. "I will tell you nothing. You don't deserve to know anything. What difference does it make anyway?" She went to the door and held it open for him. "It is time for you to leave."

Harry reached for his wallet. "What do I owe you for the tea?"

She gave him an ironic smile, and once again she was the girl he remembered. "It's my treat."

CHAPTER TWENTY-FIVE

The Tryst

David Trevor turned fifteen on the day Germany invaded Poland. England declared war two days later. David knew the war was coming; everyone did. His Grandmother Adelaide had kept him well versed on world affairs for years, and had warned him that Hitler would not stop until he had everything he wanted, just as the kaiser had attempted to do. The heads of European countries, royalty and statesmen alike, were as familiar to him as movie stars, and even more exciting.

His only disappointment was in being too young to participate. But Grandmother Adelaide assured him that the war would continue for many years, and that quite likely his time would come. She foresaw only the long, hard struggle.

David was a sponge for much of what the many women in his life tried to teach him, but he also learned well how to manipulate them: his two doting grandmothers, a lovely, lonely mother and his Aunt Lilas, who was always good for some extra pocket money as long as he pretended to be interested in classical music.

With his Grandma Eleanor, he showed great pride in being descended from the Churchills and kept his shining red hair brushed the way she wanted—the way, she assured him, that Cousin Winston would favour in a young cousin. By the spring of 1940, Cousin Winston was running Britain and was a household word once again. David could never find out just how exactly Cousin Winston was related. The distance between them seemed to have increased over the years and his school friends called him a liar for assuming any relationship whatsoever.

That didn't bother him. As he became a teenager, the only real sadness in his life was his father. David loved his father, and wanted to be exactly like him. When he was small, his father had built a gymnasium for him in the basement. They played ball: soccer and baseball when the sun shone and basketball when it rained. He remembered taking the Princess boats to Vancouver and Seattle, and because his father was an officer he got to go to the ship's forbidden places. Once, Georgie had even let David steer the ship for a while. David wondered what the passengers would think if they knew an eight-year-old boy was in command of the ship.

When David was thirteen, his father had been showing him how to use a golf club; he had told Grandma Eleanor that they must turn the east lawn into a putting green. Suddenly, his body went rigid, his face whitened and he fell on the grass. The look of fear on his father's face terrified David. He remembered his grandmother's remarkable self-possession, and his mother's suppressed panic, and the ambulance that took his father away.

When his father returned home, he had difficulty walking and using his right arm, and as the months passed he did not get any stronger. He spent most of his days in his chair, looking out at the lawn, his face very set. The war depressed him deeply because there was no possibility of his taking part in it. He could only sit and listen to the radio and read the newspapers.

In June of 1940, when the fall of France hung over them all, and for the first time in any of their lives it was possible that England might be in peril, Georgie complained of chest pains. Julia went to get his medicine and call the doctor. When she returned, he was dead.

David heard her cry out, and when he came to her side he saw a grief he had somehow not expected from her. "Oh, David," she sobbed when she saw him. "Your father's dead. Oh, Georgie, Georgie." She seemed to slide down on to the floor in front of the chair, took the dead hands in hers and began to kiss them.

His Grandma Eleanor was in the library, playing bridge with Sir Adrian Jersey and Miss Brill and a new friend, Dr. Birnbaum.

Miss Brill at once put her arms around Eleanor, while Dr. Birnbaum bent over the body in the chair, nodding professionally. Sir Adrian, who nodded back, then fetched the brandy.

Grandma Eleanor came over to him, holding her glass. She seemed remarkably composed as she placed her hand on his shoulder. "David, you are the man of the house now. You must look after your mother and me. You are the only George Trevor left to us." He put his arms around her and felt the touch of her hand on his hair.

Dr. Birnbaum telephoned the family's doctor, Dr. Redding. Julia still clung to her husband's hand. Eleanor went over to the chair, put her arm around Julia and shed a tear. "Now, Julia," she said, "he's gone. We knew this would happen one day. He hasn't been . . . he wasn't happy for a long time. Now he is with God."

She bent over and kissed her son's white face, touched once again the red hair that made her so proud and took Julia's hands away from his.

Julia rose, gave a strange, shuddering sigh and nodded. She walked out of the room, and as she passed David, she touched his hair too.

"Let her go," said Dr. Birnbaum. "She'll be all right now. I'll get Redding to prescribe a sedative. As soon as he comes, we'd better discuss the arrangements."

Eleanor nodded without emotion. "The funeral must be very beautiful and dignified, as befits a Trevor and a Churchill."

The day after the attack on Pearl Harbor in December 1941, Sveinn Arnason slipped away quietly in his room at the Arnason Inne. He was ninety-one. He had been bedridden for some time, but he remained sharp, and even in the hours before his death there was a bit of mischief in him. The sun was streaming through his windows when Anna greeted him with his breakfast and the words, "Papa, this is truly a glorious day."

"Is it then?" Sveinn said, and as though the words had caught in his throat, he succumbed to a coughing fit. When he collected himself, he looked up at Anna with a wink and a smile. "I'll do my best not to spoil it for you."

Two weeks after he died, a raucous wake was held at the Inne, and a special sailing of the *Islander* brought the many mourners who wished to attend. The next day, Anna, Albert and Gudrun scattered Sveinn's ashes in the placid water within view of the Inne, where Nels once set his crab traps, and where his own ashes had been scattered seventeen long years before.

≈ ≈ ≈

At eighteen, David joined the Royal Canadian Navy. His Grandmother Adelaide had been right, as she so often was; in fact, the war was getting worse. To David it was oddly thrilling. He would go to war after all; he would live out his father's ambition, and honour his Churchill blood. He was sorry his mother did not see it the same way, but he could tell that his Grandma Eleanor was very proud of him.

His Grandmother Adelaide was also pleased with him. She got out her maps on his last visit and he promised to report regularly, although he reminded Adelaide that he could not reveal details of the military campaigns.

He trained close to home at the HMCS *Naden* naval base in Esquimalt, but his first deployment was out of Halifax. The night before he began his trip across Canada there was one last thing he had to take care of—he had a girl.

Madge Loring was just out of school and already working for a firm that sold war bonds. David did not want his mother and grandmother to know about their relationship because Madge was not exactly a member of Victoria society; her father worked in the shipyards. The two had fumbled their way through sex at her home when her parents were out, and they had vowed to be married as soon as he returned. Now, he was about to say goodbye to her, and had persuaded her to meet him at the Empress Hotel. Madge said the Empress "made her nervous," but David insisted.

He entered the crowded lobby in his sailor's uniform; there were many such men in the lobby that day. It was tea time. The string trio was playing vigorously, including some contemporary songs suitable to the occasion, such as "Lili Marlene," and their current concession to the times, "Roll Out the Barrel." He was looking about for Madge when his eyes stopped travelling: he had found something worth looking at. Two young women were having tea at a table close to the trio, but only one seized his attention.

She wore a pink corduroy velvet suit with a matching turban. Long gold earrings dangled from her ears, and as she had her elbows on the table and had clasped her lovely hands in front of her, he saw heavy gold charm bracelets. Her black hair poured out under the turban, over her shoulders.

She looked up. She had noticed him too.

He had never seen such eyes. They were framed by magnificent cheekbones, with thin dark eyebrows and long, sweeping lashes. She looked foreign, he thought, but he could not quite place her origin. Perhaps she was Turkish. He stood very still and stared. Madge was forgotten. David had known Sahndra Burman as a precocious and enigmatic child, but now that he saw her as a woman, he did not recognize her.

At the tea table, Lucy Worth saw that her friend's eyes were straying, not for the first time, and she saw the young sailor staring back. "A sailor, really! Isn't that beneath you, darling? And he looks awfully young."

Sahndra was silent, as though weighing the potential value of David Trevor. "Maybe. Maybe not. I think there is a hint of mischief lurking beneath the innocent exterior. And you know how I feel about that."

"You're quite incorrigible," said Lucy.

Sahndra opened her gold cigarette case, extracted another cigarette and snapped the case shut without offering one to Lucy. She carefully blew smoke rings, to the fascination of David.

"What would the major say?"

"I have no idea and I couldn't care less."

"But you're engaged to him, aren't you?"

Sahndra nodded. "What has that to do with this?" She indicated David with her cigarette.

Any answer that Lucy might have made would not have been suitable at the tea table.

David felt a tug at his sleeve. "Darling, where were you? I've been waiting for so long." Madge was standing beside him, frowning. He wished she weren't so possessive.

"Let's get out of here," he said and abruptly led the way out of the lobby. He could not understand why he felt so angry, and why the sight of Madge did not please him as it usually did. By tomorrow he would be away from all this anyway. He would go to war, and that was what really counted.

☙ ☙ ☙

The end to the war had been in sight for a long time. Now it came in two distinct parts: V-E Day in March and V-J Day in August.

David came home in September. He was now twenty-one years old and for Eleanor, everything centred on her grandson's return. It was as though, despite her flamboyance, the core of her being came to life only for the men in her family. When George II had not returned from the first war, she had concentrated all her energies on George III—Georgie. But even before his death she had given up on him; once he became an invalid, Eleanor had turned to George IV—David. Never once did she doubt that David would return from the war. David would come back to take care of them all; he would be the returning war hero that George II had not been, that George III could not have been.

She had planned the dinner party for months. She would serve David's favourite, roast chicken, and there would be champagne for everyone. His Grandmother Adelaide and Aunt Lilas would be there, as well as Sir Adrian and Edwina, and quite possibly several members of the provincial legislature, although recently Eleanor had fewer connections with government figures. There was a "new lot," as she called them, and they weren't the right lot.

Julia alone met David at the Naden base in Esquimalt. She threw her arms around him and searched his face for reassurance that her only child had come home. He was thin, but he looked well enough, his handsome face tanned by the winds, his brown eyes lighting at the sight of her. But when she looked into those eyes, she recognized that something had changed.

David thought he would be glad to be home, but once he arrived at Blenheim Oaks, he found all the greetings quite discomfiting. As each woman—Adelaide, Lilas, Edwina Brill—arrived there were the requisite hugs and kisses, but they felt like moments in a dream in which something was about to go terribly wrong.

Sir Adrian pumped his hand. "We got the bastards finally! Good show, my boy—damn good show! I want to hear all about it. We'll have a long chin wag over a brandy and soda." David nodded politely, though he actually dreaded the prospect.

Once everyone had a drink, Sir Adrian offered a toast: "To the conquering hero—welcome home!" The others raised their glasses and echoed the words.

"Wait, my boy!" Sir Adrian continued. "We've got to welcome you in style!" He raised his glass again. "To the Trevor family—pioneers of

British Columbia. To the men of the sea—heroes all—and to the beautiful women who wait for them."

Julia felt sudden hot tears in her eyes. Sir Adrian had stood in the same spot twenty-two years before and proposed the toast at her wedding. Her mother and Lilas were in almost the same position as they had been then.

She looked at her sister, remembering with difficulty the candy-box prettiness of the young girl in her pink organdy dress and hat. Lilas was still wearing pink, still had her masses of curls, which were still blond but with touches of gray. If she didn't wear too much makeup, thought Julia, she simply wouldn't be herself. Standing beside Lilas was Adelaide, wearing a plain, navy blue silk dress. She was nodding and smiling now at her grandson.

Georgie, thought Julia. Poor Georgie. She took a drink hurriedly, barely tasting it. And then she found she was thinking of Stanley and the tears fell again.

Instantly David was beside her, holding her free hand. "Don't worry, Mother! I'm home. The war's over and we're all going to have a wonderful time!"

"Hear, hear!" avowed Sir Adrian, pouring himself another drink.

Dinner was almost as awkward as the greetings. David's military service in both the Atlantic and the Pacific had been two years of boredom aboard a merchant cruiser on choppy grey seas. He had no exciting stories for Sir Adrian and Grandmother Adelaide. The experiences that had changed him were not those that sailors discussed in front of their grandmothers. David finished his dinner hurriedly. "I'm really sorry," he explained, "but I can't stay. The CO's having a farewell party tonight on board ship."

There was a moment when the only sound was of cutlery on china. "Of course," Sir Adrian said finally. "The boy's right. Duty comes first. That's what makes a good man."

"Mother, would you mind terribly if I took your car tonight?"

"No, darling," said Julia. "But be careful."

"We must see about getting you your own car next week. I've been thinking about it," said Eleanor.

He kissed his female relatives once again, and shook hands with Edwina and Sir Adrian. Then he retrieved his coat and hat from the hall, ignoring his grandmother's suggestion that he take an umbrella, and left.

It had been a long time since he had felt the wheel of a car in his hands. How wonderful that was, although he skidded on the wet curves of Rockland Avenue and cursed the brakes on his mother's car. He'd make sure to get a decent one out of his grandmother.

Some of the men were bringing their wives to the party, others were taking sisters or girlfriends. Madge had written to David more than a year ago, to tell him she was getting married. He had been relieved, really. He hadn't been faithful, and her betrothal freed him of guilt during a remarkable dalliance with a prostitute in Hong Kong. Now he walked up the slippery gangway to the deck of the *Prince Robert* alone. The last time, he thought gratefully. No more ships for me—ever.

There were about seventy-five people in the mess, and the bar was clearly being well patronized. David went first to where his hosts, the CO and his wife, were standing, shaking hands with other officers and their guests. Then he went to the bar, ordered a double Scotch and began to circulate, searching for familiar faces. He finished his first drink as fast as possible and got a second.

Above the continuous sound of voices and the clinking of glasses, he heard another sound. It was a small sound, as though someone had shaken a handful of little bells, and he saw that it came from silver charm bracelets worn by a woman. She was leaning against the wall not far away, holding a drink in her hands, her bracelets jingling every time she raised her glass. There were three young sailors trying to impress her. She was silent, except for her bracelets, looking beyond them as though searching for someone else.

The woman was tall, and her long, thick black hair hung down over a black silk blouse. Her shoes, below a short skirt, were of some black, glittering material that reminded him of anthracite, with incredibly high, thin heels and a narrow black strap. On her left ankle she wore another silver charm bracelet. Wide silver hoops dangled from her ears.

She couldn't possibly be from Victoria, he decided. He looked at those cheekbones and the dark eyes, and then remembered the girl he had seen in the Empress Hotel. There could not be more than one person with beauty like this.

"How about that?" Charlie Pleasance, one of his shipmates, was beside him. "Ever see a dish like that?"

David shook his head. "Who is she? Do you know?"

"Sahndra Howarth. You know Major Howarth from Duncan? She was his wife."

David took another drink, disappointed at the news. "I might have known she'd be married."

"I said she *was* his wife. They divorced a couple of months ago. The major got the divorce, and I hear he had plenty of grounds."

Excitement stirred in David. Would there be a chance? Would such a woman be interested in him? In the few opportunities offered him in his twenty-one years, he had been successful, but this woman was beyond any he had met so far. It was certainly worth a try.

She was looking at him now. Then she began to move her body in long, languorous steps, away from the admiring males around her and straight toward David. He tried to maintain his composure when she approached him as though they were old friends.

"You're bored," she told him flatly. Her voice was low; it would have been impossible to imagine her possessing a high one. "Are you alone?"

He nodded.

"Good. Let's get out of here." She steered him through the crowd. Charlie Pleasance whistled, watching them leave.

"I should say goodbye to Mrs. Drake and the commander," said David.

"Not necessary. You probably won't see them again anyway."

True, he thought, and now he reached to take her arm, but she drew it away and took his hand instead. "You have a car?" she inquired.

Before he could form a plan of his own, they were driving to her apartment, in one of the new buildings on Gorge Road. When they entered and she switched on the light, he was surprised to see an Oriental rug and some fine paintings, and a wonderful teak bookcase filled with apparently well-read books.

"It's not what you expected," she said.

"No, but I had no idea what to expect. I've had trouble enough trying to figure out where you're from, let alone what your life might be like." The Scotch had loosened him up.

She did not smile. "Actually you've known me for years, and I'm from here in a way you have not yet imagined. I'm Indian."

He looked at her with some confusion.

She was standing by the fireplace, lighting two cigarettes. She handed him one. "My mother was a Moachat. Or as you might call them, a Nootka."

David couldn't quite believe it. "You don't look like any Indians I've ever met."

"I suspect that you haven't met many Indians." She stood still. Slowly she unbuttoned the black blouse. When it slid off her shoulders, she removed her bra, coolly and casually, and he saw her dark nipples, her elegant breasts. She turned slightly away, untied her purple silk sash and let it go, then unfastened the side of her black silk skirt and let it fall. She was wearing black stockings, with purple garters.

He stood and stared, transfixed by what he saw—the long, lean body bronzed by the lamplight, the subtle undulations of her spine. And then he went to her. He could not believe it. Nothing could equal the feel of her silken body, nothing in his short experience compared to this.

He awoke at three o'clock, his head pounding, and wondered if he should return home. He had already offended his family by abandoning them after dinner. He wrote a gracious note with his phone number and left it on the kitchen table. Sahndra stirred but let him slip out without a word.

It was raining hard, but David drove quickly, as though they'd be waiting for him at the door. The black-limbed trees on Rockland Avenue knitted together above him like the fingers of clasping hands. He felt as though he was in a tunnel, and he stepped on the gas. The spot where he lost control of the car was not far from Blenheim Oaks. An old tree didn't give any quarter, and the neighbours were drawn by the sound of the car horn blaring in the night. The conquering hero was dead.

CHAPTER TWENTY-SIX

The Maquinna Line

On July 1, the Dominion Day holiday, a little more than nine months after David's death, Julia came down the stairs after her morning visit with Eleanor. Although the day was beautiful, clear and sunny with just the lightest breeze, she could not prevail upon Eleanor to leave her bed. Eleanor would read the *Tatler* and that was all. She would no longer even write to her old friends in England. It was as though the light had gone out, and despite Julia's efforts, nothing she brought to the older woman could return her to her former animation. She had even lost interest in local gossip, although Julia did her best to glean what she could, mostly from her mother and Lilas, about what was happening. Eleanor's concentration seemed slight at best, and her attention mostly forced, but she was grateful to Julia for trying.

Through the glass panes in the front door, Julia saw a taxi pull into the drive. The driver got out, went around to open the back door of the car and Sahndra Burman emerged. There was someone else in the back, someone Julia could not see, to whom Sahndra was still talking. Then she turned toward the house, carrying something in her arms, something bundled in an elaborate white shawl.

"Oh my God," Julia said aloud. "I'm dreaming. It can't be real."

She descended the rest of the stairs, crossed the hall and opened the door before Sahndra could ring the bell.

🙢 🙢 🙢

Julia had last seen Sahndra in February. Sahndra had called and invited her for tea at the Empress. "It was the place where I first knew how important David would become to me," she said on the phone. That was enough of an enticement, and they arranged to meet the same afternoon.

As she stood in her bathroom preparing to go out, Julia found herself shaking. Sahndra had once been a fixture in her life as a disturbingly well-mannered child; now she loomed as a strangely powerful woman who might have been the lover of both her brother and her son. Sahndra must know Julia's family secrets, and she felt helpless and alone.

Yet when Julia entered the Empress lobby, Sahndra stood up and greeted her as though they'd always been close. Remarkably, in that moment, Julia did feel close to her. How could this woman give her comfort?

Then she noticed that Sahndra was pregnant. Julia couldn't bear to ask the question that instantly burned in her mind. Could fate be this convoluted? Then she relaxed as they talked about family. Sahndra said that her grandfather had moved in with Harry, and her father was devoting himself to raising money for the church. Kathleen remained a happy madwoman. "She treats Rosemoore as though she's on a long vacation but will soon be going home to a son she doesn't have. I don't know how she remains so happy. Perhaps it's because she's perpetually anticipating a wonderful event."

Sahndra smiled and touched her belly. "Which, ironically, is exactly why I'm here." She intended to make this as easy as possible for Julia, and there was no one to dispute what she said. "David and I were . . . very close. We connected very briefly but deeply just before he entered the service. After I met him I felt there was no one else for me. This is his child."

"All right," Julia nodded. She couldn't find any other words, just as she couldn't choose among the fear and joy and doubt she felt in that moment.

"Julia, I can't raise him," Sahndra continued, "so I'm coming to you. After he's born, will you take him? You're a much better mother than I could ever be."

Julia was stunned. Her David had been just a boy when he joined the navy. Sahndra was four years older, and that four-year difference seemed unbridgeable. And how could she be sure that this was David's child? Yet she could not utter the question she needed to ask. "How do you know it's a boy?"

"I know it's David's." Sahndra knew what Julia was thinking. "He was conceived on the night he died. If I knew differently, I'd have . . . done something by now. I wouldn't have any baby but David's. As for whether it's a boy, I simply know that it is." Sahndra paused. "Every now and again, despite ourselves, things are made right somehow. I think this is one of those times and I hope that you might feel the same."

Julia began to weep. "Tell me what you can, Sahndra, about my son's last few hours." Sahndra took her hand and said that when she had seen David at the Empress, she felt he was her destiny. And when their eyes met again in the mess of the *Prince Robert*, she knew she was in love in a way that would never occur for her again. "I'm so sorry I didn't stop him when he left my apartment that night. So much might be different today if I had."

Julia took a moment to compose herself. "I'm having some trouble taking this in, but I believe you when you say the child is David's. And so I think that I must agree to your request."

"Oh, thank you!" Sahndra said gratefully. "I'll make sure all the proper papers are drawn up, and I'll bring him to you after he's born. Thank you so much."

Julia simply couldn't think of another thing to say. She wondered how Eleanor might react and decided to say nothing to her. She thought of

Harry Burman, and how this woman who sat before her brought real joy into his life. She thought of Matthew, and his fascination with Indian culture on the coast. "Your grandfather," she said, dabbing away her tears with a handkerchief. "I remember hearing that he was going to write a book about the history of the island. About the history of natives on the coast."

"Ah, yes. He never finished it. I doubt he ever will. He once told me that he wouldn't know how to complete it, that the ending was simply beyond his comprehension."

They finished their tea and parted. Julia walked down the front steps of the Empress as though she were in a dream. And until Sahndra arrived on her doorstep, she would treat the event as though it were just that.

☙ ☙ ☙

Julia had never imagined Sahndra becoming more beautiful, but there was no doubt about it: as she walked up the steps at Blenheim Oaks, there was a radiance about her that was startling, as though she had stepped out of a Hollywood movie.

She wore a white sharkskin suit and white pumps, with a white silk turban on her loose black hair; golden hoops dangled from her ears. She was smiling, actually smiling, and her dark eyes sparkled. "Here," said Sahndra, and her voice lacked its old, matter-of-fact flatness. "Here's the baby."

Julia was aware of a faint squirming within the lacy shawl. "Won't you come in?"

The golden hoops swung. "I'm sorry, Julia, but I can't stay. I know this sounds a bit ridiculous, but it's how it must be. This child must be yours alone, your family's alone. I won't see him again. He's three weeks old today, and he's very good, or at least that's what they tell me. Anyway, my lawyer is sending you the papers. If you have any questions, please call him. His number will be in the letter.".

"Papers? But Sahndra . . ."

"He's yours, Julia. I told you that I don't want him. I'm neither interested nor capable. I know you can look after him. I know how dearly your family's personal losses have cost you and I know that you will treasure this opportunity. Eleanor needs this great-grandchild, and you need him too."

Julia paused. How could Sahndra know about Eleanor's needs? But before she could say a thing, Sahndra was thrusting the bundle into her arms.

Julia gazed down at the child. The hair that crowned his head was a dark copper colour, and the luminous cheeks bore the promise of freckles. She felt foolish as she took him, as though she were being drawn into some childhood mischief. What, she thought, will my mother say? She looked at Sahndra. "You . . . you *can* come and see him whenever you want."

The beautiful smile, so rare on Sahndra's face, flashed more widely. "I'm going away."

"Away?"

"I think it's time I left Victoria, don't you?"

"Where are you going?"

"India."

Julia was silent. She moved a corner of the shawl away from the baby's face and it made a small noise.

"I've always wanted to see the world," said Sahndra, "and now I'm going to."

"Are you going alone?"

"No." The dark eyes were teasing, as though ready to reveal some wonderful secret.

Julia knew somehow that the situation was about to become even weirder. "Is it anyone I know?"

Sahndra paused. She knew how to create an effect. "Sir Adrian Jersey." She noted Julia's stunned expression and then continued. "I really must go, Julia. Sir Adrian's waiting in the car. We're sailing tonight. He wants to see India again and he wants me to see it with him. I can't imagine having a better guide."

"But," Julia heard herself say, "Sir Adrian must be nearly eighty . . ."

Julia followed Sahndra to the car, and Sir Adrian looked out rather sheepishly. "I'd rather have all Victoria talking about me after I'm gone, dear Julia," he said. "Please give my warmest regards to Eleanor. Tell her I'm sorry I've seen so little of her these past few months, but they really have been a whirlwind."

Sahndra smiled again as she stepped into the car, almost regal in her white suit, as though she were already in India, heading for the palace of a rajah. "I have always," she said, "except for David, had a preference for older men."

And then she was gone. It was only after the taxi sped down the drive that Julia remembered that she had not asked Sir Adrian about Edwina Brill.

The being in the white shawl stirred as Julia went inside. She looked down at him. He's David's, she thought. This is David's son, my grandson, my mother's and Eleanor's great-grandson. Then the child almost smiled, and there was something about it—the way the corners of the mouth rose—that reminded her of Albert Aalgaard's smile. "Oh God," she said aloud as she sat down in a chair in the foyer. "How will we possibly cope?"

From upstairs, she heard Eleanor's querulous voice. "Julia, who is that down there? I don't want any visitors."

The sound of Eleanor's voice cleared the fog. All the confusion, doubts, shadows, insecurities vanished and at last, there was only Julia and the bundle in her arms. As she stood up, she was aware that she was perfectly capable of controlling the situation. She was a grandmother; David had left something of himself after all. She finally had it in her power to take her place in the Trevor house, and to give Eleanor a gift that was worthy of her starchy generosity.

She mounted the stairs, carrying the baby.

Eleanor's elaborately furnished bedroom was dim, lit by one bedside lamp. The dark velvet drapes were drawn across the windows, keeping out the sunshine. Eleanor was sitting up in bed, pale and dishevelled, wearing a pink bed jacket and propped up by four pink satin cushions, surrounded by copies of the *Tatler*. Her hair had had no attention for weeks, so the henna was shot through with grey. She wore no makeup. She looked very old.

She stared at Julia as she entered with the bundle. Though she had neglected her body, her mind was still alert, and she sat up straighter.

"Eleanor," said Julia, and she scarcely recognized her own voice with its determined tone, "this is David's son. Your great-grandson."

Eleanor lay back against the pillows as though she had decided she was dreaming, but her watery eyes became greener as she warmed to the possibility. The old spark of interest reappeared and her tongue flicked suddenly over her cracked lips.

Julia walked to the bed and sat on the edge. She removed the gorgeous lace shawl from the baby's face and carefully placed the child in Eleanor's arms.

Eleanor sat up very straight, holding the baby as though she were a professional nurse. When she spoke, her voice was as crisp as it had been twenty years ago. "Julia, can you assure me that the child's mother comes from a good family?"

"Yes," Julia replied. "The very best. But"—she thought quickly—"I gave my word not to reveal who she is."

"David was such a charmer," Eleanor said, and her heart warmed to the idea that her grandson had achieved at least some fulfilment with a person of stature. She looked at the child and imagined that the woman must have been very beautiful. "Oh, heavens. Look at that hair."

Julia looked too, but at Eleanor, not at the baby. She was at last alive again. She was Eleanor as Julia had first known her.

"The hair!" cried Eleanor, fussing over the baby, shifting him around in her arms to see him in more detail, while he grunted and blinked. "Oh, this one's a real Churchill, a true descendant of the Marlboroughs. Why, the darling! He's absolutely at home here. Julia, look at how content he is!"

He was indeed content. He stirred happily in Eleanor's arms and blinked his eyes again. Nothing could change Eleanor's delight. He was her reason to live. All she had lost had been returned to her in the form of this child.

"Oh, Julia, I'm the happiest woman in the world!" The baby nestled in Eleanor's arms, and they both saw the black pupils, the deep brown irises, the thick whites. "I would like," said Eleanor, "to call him Winston. Not only is it a family name—on my side—but I think it's rather a patriotic thing to do right now." She paused and looked at Julia. "The mother didn't express any preference as to a name, did she?"

Julia hadn't thought about a name, but she was positive that Sahndra hadn't either. She shook her head.

Eleanor smiled. "You know, Julia, I'm sure the mother was Spanish. Do you notice how dark his eyes are? Very unusual, with the dark red hair, but he could grow up to be quite distinguished."

Julia wasn't sure about Winston. She was always conscious of the difference between whimsy and pretension. "Don't you want to call him George? George Winston, perhaps?"

Eleanor looked out the window. "We haven't had much luck with the name George. I think it's time for a change, and I know you wouldn't want another David. Julia, last night I suddenly thought about your father. He was a very nice man, as I remember, a true gentleman. I think we should call the baby Lewis Winston. That sounds very nice, quite aristocratic. I like it."

Julia could not speak, but Eleanor was satisfied with her reaction. "Then it's settled." She leaned back again onto her pillows, cradling the baby in her arms. The child began to squirm, then let out a loud wail. "My goodness, how long has it been since he's been fed? He's probably hungry.

Here, Julia, take him. I have to get up—there's so much to do. Aggie!" she called for her maid. "My hair! My clothes! We have to make arrangements for his christening."

Aggie came bustling in. "Yes, ma'am?"

"Aggie, this is Lewis Winston Trevor, my great-grandson. Please prepare the nursery." Aggie stood at the foot of the bed, open-mouthed. "Don't just stand there—the nursery!"

Aggie turned and left, still open-mouthed, and Eleanor swept back the covers, spilling the magazines to the floor as she got up. "Julia, take the baby to the kitchen to be fed. I'll call you when I'm ready."

Julia went downstairs with the child in her arms. Aggie found one of David's old baby bottles in the back of the pantry and warmed some milk.

Once young Lewis had had his milk, Julia settled in the parlour, the now-quiet baby in her lap. Yes, there was much to do to bring this newest member of the Trevor family into the world. She thought of Sahndra in India, and then she imagined her grandson Lewis's future as a great traveller. There is no time like the present to begin an adventure, she thought. Julia had always wanted to visit the Orient. They would take trips to England and France, New York and San Francisco. Eleanor would certainly go with them to London.

Perhaps they would go to Arnason Island, just because. She wondered about Albert and Anna and dear little Gudrun. She would be a young adult now. Gudrun, "god's secret," what a beautiful name. The *Princess Maquinna* still travelled the historic route up the west coast of Vancouver Island. Yes, she would take that storied CPR ship to see her brother in Zeballos. That would be the right thing to do for Lewis Winston Trevor, the latest child in the Maquinna line.

Afterword

How exactly did the Los Angeles-based voice of the world's most famous cartoon ghost come to write a ripping yarn about the history of Vancouver Island? And how did it come to be published nine years after her death? Like *The Maquinna Line* itself, it's a complicated story, and a good one. It begins with the fact that Norma Macmillan knew a thing or two about possibility.

Norma was the daughter of a prominent Vancouver doctor, a York House girl for whom success was supposedly a given. Yet it was the impoverished actors of the city's nascent post-war theatre scene who taught her about the power of imagination. There was also that unlikely relationship with an orphan wunderkind from Mozart, Saskatchewan.

Family lore has it that Thor Arngrim, a young actor who met Norma in 1949 at a Vancouver Little Theatre audition, viewed her as a rich hobbyist, a dilettante. Macmillan in turn saw Thor—who had left his adoptive small-town Icelandic family for Vancouver not long after he dropped out of school in grade eight—as a farm boy with unearned pretensions regarding his budding genius as a theatre producer.

But in 1951, as Totem Theatre found itself becoming Vancouver's first year-round professional theatre company, Macmillan, thirty, and Arngrim, twenty-two, found themselves working together at a seminal period in the city's performing arts history. Vancouver's largely amateur theatre companies produced only intermittently. As Arngrim and his producing partner, Stuart Baker, brought Totem Theatre from its beginnings as a summer stock company in West Vancouver's Ambleside Park to a downtown venue across the street from the main bus station, Macmillan was there, keeping "the Gold Dust Twins" as close as possible to the straight and narrow. "She could type," Arngrim once recalled with a wink. And keep the books, and act, and also write.

Yes, Norma Macmillan could write. Historical records give us a spotty accounting of the development of original British Columbia theatre, but Macmillan certainly figures in it. In 1954 Totem Theatre produced her play about a BC family, *A Crowded Affair*, at Victoria's old Pantages Theatre (now the McPherson Playhouse) and at Vancouver's Georgia Auditorium. Was that the first original BC play written by a woman for a professional Canadian theatre company? Quite probably. There were other women before her who marked firsts in BC theatre—playwrights Constance Lindsay Skinner and Gwen Pharis are two—but neither could say she was the first woman to have a play set in BC produced by a professional company in the province.

Who knows what Macmillan, Arngrim and Baker might have accomplished through Totem Theatre if the company hadn't struggled with the lack of a suitable permanent venue? But Totem Theatre had become a dream without a home, and Macmillan and Arngrim, having exhausted their professional and perhaps even their personal options in Vancouver, found themselves standing alone together on the lot of a West Georgia car dealership. Arngrim proposed. Macmillan accepted. And they moved to Toronto.

CBC Radio dramas became their lifeblood, but there were stage roles as well, and in 1956 Thor found himself on Broadway in the original New York production of *Tamburlaine the Great*, which directing titan Tyrone Guthrie brought to the city from the three-year-old Stratford Festival, where Guthrie was a driving force. Soon Thor, Norma and their young son, Stefan, were living in New York.

Macmillan did voice work and advertisements. Arngrim's acting career continued—he had a part on the *Phil Silvers Show*—and he also produced theatre at New Jersey's famed Grist Mill Playhouse, where Macmillan's play *Free as a Bird* was staged with Tony winner Edie Adams in the cast. In 1962,

Norma played both Caroline Kennedy and John F. Kennedy Jr. in the live recording *The First Family*, a satire of Kennedy family life that became the fastest-selling record in history. (The mark of seven million copies sold in seven weeks stood for decades.) In 1963, she became the voice of Casper the Friendly Ghost on ABC's *The New Casper Cartoon Show*.

In 1964, Arngrim performed opposite Albert Finney in the Tony-winning production of *Luther*, which was produced by the legendary David Merrick. At the time, Macmillan was the star of a hot TV commercial—for All-Temperature All laundry detergent. During *Luther*'s curtain calls, a member of the audience almost invariably shouted the ad's signature line, "Mrs. Thor Arngrim wants to know . . ." and then variations on "So when're you going to tell her, huh?"

Arngrim would get used to living in the shadow of his family, although he did achieve some personal prominence the following year as the inventor of the Fashionstick, a cane wrapped in stylish fabric, often to match a woman's outfit, that sold for $185 at Saks Fifth Avenue. (In an interview with the *Los Angeles Times*, Arngrim said of the year's hottest fashion accessory, "They're of absolutely no use whatsoever.")

In 1965, Macmillan, Arngrim, Stefan and three-year-old Alison moved to Hollywood, setting themselves up first at the legendary Chateau Marmont hotel, where actors famous and not-so-famous slipped easily in and out of their lives. Macmillan thrived. In addition to Casper, she became the voice of Gumby, Sweet Polly Purebred in the show *Underdog* and Davey in *Davey and Goliath*. She was one of those Kraft mayonnaise ladies, and she was Alice in an odd 1966 animated film called *Alice of Wonderland in Paris*.

Arngrim worked as a manager with such figures as Liberace, Rene Simard, Debbie Reynolds, Susan Anton and *Slap Shot* star Michael Ontkean, whose Vancouver parents were involved with Totem. He also managed the acting careers of his children. Stefan starred as young Barry Lockridge in Irwin Allen's TV science fiction drama *Land of the Giants* and opposite Kirk Douglas in *The Way West*. Alison played the hated grocer's daughter Nellie Oleson on *Little House on the Prairie*.

With her husband and children so successful and her time paying family bills behind her, Macmillan returned to writing. One of her projects was a script called the *Santa Margarita Rock 'n' Roll Murders*, about renegade seniors whose acts of terror sought to prevent their sleepy retirement community from being disrupted by the concerts at a new amphitheatre.

However, it was the idea of creating a Canadian *Forsyte Saga* that really possessed her. She'd pack up her typewriter and head north to ride the *MV Uchuck III*, which traced the northern reaches of the elegant *Princess Maquinna's* old CPR route up the west coast of Vancouver Island. She'd come back invigorated by her time in a faraway cabin, a kerosene lamp on one side, a glass of scotch on the other, and the old Olivetti before her.

What she created—a saga that touches on issues of class, culture and race as families try to find happiness and grace in a rapidly changing province—is unique among BC novels. *The Forsyte Saga*, which became a BBC miniseries in the late 1960s, was one inspiration. At the time of her writing, the popular rage was for the miniseries *Roots* and then Australia's *The Thorn Birds* (which was brought to television in 1983 by another Vancouver cultural pioneer, director Daryl Duke). There were also Canada's own Jalna books, which Ontario's Mazo de la Roche began writing in the 1920s, prompting an RKO movie in the 1930s and a CBC miniseries in the 1970s.

After Macmillan finished her book, a couple of multi-generational BC sagas were published: David Corcoran's 1986 *The West Coasters* and David Cruise and Alison Griffiths's 2003 *Vancouver*. Nothing, however, matches *The Maquinna Line* in all its peculiar aspects. It was written during Canada's literary coming of age, but by a woman steeped in another country's rich entertainment tradition. It is an artifact, and yet it remains surprisingly contemporary. The book respects BC history, but it is not afraid to enliven it.

In 1993, Thor and Norma returned permanently to Vancouver to retire and spend more time with old friends. Unlike Los Angeles, the city's West End offered quiet, car-free comfort *and* universal health care. As Alison Arngrim recalls, "My mother didn't want to walk out of a theatre and get shot."

Of course, retirement didn't really suit Thor and Norma. Macmillan volunteered with community radio and continued to act, appearing with Katharine Hepburn in *Mrs. Delafield Wants to Marry*. Arngrim continued to produce theatre, including Aaron Bushkowsky's *Strangers Among Us*, a 1993 play about Alzheimer's disease that won two Jessie Richardson Theatre Awards. He also championed the Performing Arts Lodge, which opened in 2006 and provides affordable housing for retired arts professionals. Thor and Norma found that Vancouver hadn't forgotten them: both have their names on Granville Street's Star Walk, where the city's entertainment pioneers are remembered.

One of Thor Arngrim's great regrets was that he didn't get to grow truly old with his beloved Norma. She died of a heart attack in 2001 at the age of seventy-nine. A few years later, he pulled an old box out of his closet. "I think this might be publishable," he told a friend. TV personality David Frost, he said, had thought highly of it when he was looking for film properties to develop. "He said it was very cinematic." Thor asked the friend to help him get the manuscript in electronic form and submit it to a publisher.

I was that friend. Barbara-Anne Eddy, who achieved her own peculiar fame as a five-time *Jeopardy* champion known as "the Shakespeare lady," put the manuscript in electronic form, and TouchWood Editions is the publisher Thor and I found together. In the course of creating the book you have before you, with the most able and gracious assistance of Marlyn Horsdal, Ruth Linka, Emily Shorthouse and the TouchWood team, we discovered that Norma's novel, despite being of the proportions of a James Michener doorstopper, was still in some small aspects not quite complete. However, this shorter, tighter book remains Norma Macmillan's. Her

Vancouver Island is real and her characters are true. When that's the case, latent details tend to take care of themselves.

Norma Macmillan and Thor Arngrim had fascinating careers during a remarkable period in the development of Canadian culture. They were there as BC began telling its own stories. Now, in a new century, they offer this book as their final production.

A few days before Thor died, on December 16, 2009, a copy of *The Maquinna Line* cover by his bedside, he told me, "I'm happy." And after an actor's generous pause he added, "I don't know why."

Thor Arngrim and Norma Macmillan both had enough reasons to be happy. They helped make imagination real onstage in Vancouver and Victoria more than half a century ago.

They had two very talented children. Today, Stefan Arngrim acts extensively in film and TV in Vancouver, while Alison Arngrim continues as an actress and comedian in Los Angeles. Both of them write: Stefan for stage and screen, Alison as the author of comic memoirs.

Yes, Thor Arngrim and Norma Macmillan received and offered enough gifts to be truly happy, and this book is certainly among them.

— Charles Campbell, Vancouver, January 2010

Charles Campbell once wanted to write fiction but got sidetracked by journalism. He edited *The Georgia Straight* for a decade, worked at *The Vancouver Sun* as entertainment editor and an editorial board member for five years and is a contributing editor to The Tyee website. He studied creative writing at the University of British Columbia, was a Southam Fellow at Toronto's Massey College, and has taught in the writing and publishing programs at the University of Victoria and Simon Fraser University.

Norma Macmillan had a wide-ranging career in the arts, including the production of her plays, *Crowded Affair* and *Free as a Bird*, in the 1950s and 1960s by BC's groundbreaking Totem Theatre and New Jersey's famed Grist Mill Playhouse. But she is best known as the actress who was the voice of television's Gumby and Casper the Friendly Ghost. Born in Vancouver in 1921, she worked in the city's theatre industry, where she met her husband, Thor Arngrim, in 1949. Together the two moved to the States in 1956. After living much of her adult life in Hollywood, Norma returned to Vancouver in 1993 and continued to be active. She hosted a show for seniors on Co-op radio and played a role in *Mrs. Delafield Wants to Marry* with Katharine Hepburn. Both she and Thor are honoured on Vancouver's Starwalk, and their two children have enjoyed highly successful acting careers since childhood. Their daughter, Alison, played the extremely evil Nellie on *Little House on the Prairie*, and their son, Stefan, starred as Barry Lockridge in *Land of Giants*.

The Maquinna Line began when the family lived at Sunset Boulevard's legendary Chateau Marmont. Television's David Frost once considered the manuscript a promising film property. Norma continued to work on the book after she and her husband returned to Vancouver, but it languished in the back of a closet after she died in 2001, at the age of seventy-nine. Thor and veteran Vancouver writer Charles Campbell revived it, and it is a tribute to an old-fashioned storytelling tradition that respects history but isn't afraid to enliven it.